THE *Lighthouse* LIBRARY

DONALD F. AVERILL

The Lighthouse Library
Copyright © 2022 by Donald F. Averill

All rights reserved. No part of this publication may be reproduced,
distributed, or transmitted in any form or by any means, including
photocopying, recording, or other electronic or mechanical
methods, without the prior written permission of the author, except
in the case of brief quotations embodied in critical reviews and
certain other non-commercial uses permitted by copyright law.

ISBN
978-1-957378-35-0 (Paperback)
978-1-957378-34-3 (eBook)

Other books by the Author include:

Glacier Fires and Ornaments of Value

Missing Notes, Hidden Talents, and Other Stories

Wolves' Hollow Murders

Detour in Oregon

An Iceberg's Gift

The Lighthouse Fire

The Niffits

The Kidnapping of Megan Isaacs

A Professor's Affair

The Antarctic Deception

The Kuiper Belt Deception

The Bitterroot Diamonds

The Bitterroot Fire

Acknowledgments

v

Thanks to my group of readers: Bob Griswold, Kaethe Flack-Mentrum, Jill Nicklos, Barbara Schroeder, and Efren Sifuentes for their assistance with the preparation of the manuscript. Cover painting by Mary Stebbins

Chapter 1

Summer Vacation

It was August 12, 1952, a Tuesday, a little over a month since my birthday. I'm big for a ten-year-old, just over five feet tall, and weigh eighty-four pounds. I guess I'm a little skinny. Having been born during the Second World War, and having always been promoted, I'm ready for the fifth grade. Nearly everyone I meet thinks I'm at least eleven and some people even think I'm twelve, but I'm ten. I guess being thought of as older is better than younger. I mention it because it happens a lot. Sometimes it's a problem when my mom takes my sister and me somewhere and kids under twelve get in free. People in charge think we're lying about my age, so they ask me my birthdate. Being bigger than other boys my age seems normal to me because my dad, Leland, is a little over six-feet tall, and my mom is five-nine and nice looking. Dad always calls her Beautiful instead of her real name, Sandra.

Its pretty neat having my birthday on the Fourth of July. Fireworks after dark are always fun, the explosions high in the sky echoing over the entire city of Boston, as if bombs were dropping on the city from airplanes out of sight high above. I always pretend people are celebrating my birthday instead of Independence Day. I guess I pretend a lot, mostly about the old west. I collect the Lone Ranger comics, each one is only a dime.

I'm Rocky Lee Linfield. I have a sister, Susan Diane. She's five, going on six in September, on the twelfth. In a way, she's lucky because he first grade class will undoubtedly give her a party. It kind of goes along with starting school in the fall. I guess Suzy is of average size for a girl her age. I think she's kinda cute. She wears her light reddish-brown hair in pigtails most of the time, but sometimes in a ponytail. Freckles on her cheeks and nose show up after she's been in the sun for a while, but most of the time I don't notice them. Dad once told me that people living next to a garbage dump don't smell it.

Mom has red hair and some freckles, too. My hair is a little darker than Suzy's, a bit of brown mixed with the red, and cut short, but not as short as a crewcut; if I use some Brylcreem, I can part it. I like it short, especially during the summer.

Suz follows me everywhere, like a little dog in love with its owner, curious to see everything that's going on. I've never had a dog, but if I did get a dog, I'd name it Suzy, even if it was a male. Like today, I asked granma if I could visit the lighthouse, and before granma could say yes or no, Suzy said, "I wanna go, too." Suzy was pulling on granma's apron and looking like she was going to cry if granma said no.

Granma thought a minute and said, "Okay, Susan, but you have to do what Rocky tells you. Hold onto his hand whenever you're walking near cars, okay? And when you see Mr. Waicukauski, tell him hello for me."

"Okay, granma," Suzy put her hands on top of her head, spun around, and smiled. "Thank you."

Granma likes Mr. Waicukauski, the lighthouse keeper. His first name is Wayne. She has him over for dinner occasionally, but not recently, at least not in the last couple of weeks. Later, I discovered she had seen Wayne on the 4th of July. They watched fireworks down at the pier. No one worries about fires down at the water.

"Rocky, you and Suzy need to be back home by four o'clock. Keep an eye on the time, okay? There's a big clock at the lighthouse."

I answered, "Okay," and stuck out my hand for Suzy to grab. We had to walk about ten minutes along the lighthouse road to get there. Granma's house was next to Mrs. Nesbitt's gray house with white trim. The next house toward town was across the road, but I don't know who lives there. Granma said there weren't many cars on the road, but the ones passing by the lighthouse were usually going too fast, especially on the weekend, or Friday night after work.

Mom had dropped us off in Crafton, Maine at granma's on Saturday when she didn't have to work at the parachute factory. She took one day off during each week, when someone subbed for her. Ever since Dad was reported missing, Mom has worked six days a week, five days at the factory and one day at the Sweet Tooth Bakery. You'd think we would always be eating sweet rolls and stuff like my favorite, maple bar doughnuts, but Mom doesn't bring those things home, except once in a while. She says too much sugar is not good for us. Suzy and I have lived in the city all our lives, except for the summers, when granma has us for six weeks after the fourth of July, but before school starts.

I guess I should explain about my dad. He's an F-86 fighter pilot and got shot down over Korea in February of 1951. I miss him a lot. We all do. We don't know if he's a prisoner. I hope he is.

"Let's go, Suzy." We had to walk to the road outside the white picket fence and make a left turn. She walked beside me along the shoulder of the gravel road. I had to tell her to quit kicking the gravel. I was afraid I would get a little stone in one of my shoes, then I'd have to sit down, take off a shoe, and remove the sharp-edged boulder. I walked close to the road and watched for cars. We heard a ring-ring sound from behind us and looked around to see a lady on a bicycle riding toward downtown Crafton. As she passed by, she waved and smiled. She had blonde hair; it looked like a yellow helmet, and she wore a blue dress with a white collar. Suzy and I waved back. I wondered where she was going. Suzy grinned and said, "She's nice."

There was a cool breeze blowing from the ocean but we weren't cold. The sun was out and seagulls were flying all over the place. Those birds could sure be noisy. I think they were looking for fish at the harbor and bits of food left by picnickers at the park that bordered on the water close to the lighthouse. Granma said seagulls flew around the pier all the time, looking for something to eat. Visitors and fishermen would toss food to the birds, even though they weren't supposed to. The birds pooped on the pier and sometimes on the people.

Suzy and I arrived at the little white fence surrounding the lighthouse tower and the adjoining buildings, but we didn't see Mr. Waicukauski. According to granma, he was usually sitting on the porch of his house reading or whittling. She seemed to know a lot about Mr. W. There wasn't a gate to go through, just an open spot in the fence. It looked like when the builders made the fence, they just left one section out. We walked on stepping stones to the porch and could see through the screen door into the house.

Suzy looked at me and said, "Should I knock?"

"Go ahead. He's probably in the kitchen or the bathroom. If he doesn't answer the door, we can wait for him."

Suzy knocked, but very softly. I said, "Harder, Suz." She did what I said and pounded on the door with her little fist. It surprised me a little, but it got results.

"Who's there?" We heard a man's voice from inside the house, some footsteps, and then a large man appeared at the door. He had on work pants and a black T-shirt. I could see a screwdriver and a flat pencil sticking out of his pants front pocket.

I asked, "Are you Mr. Waicukauski?"

"That's right. Who are you people?"

"I'm Rocky Linfield. This is my sister, Suzy. Our granma, Mrs. Makler, said it would be all right to come see the lighthouse."

"Oh, your grandma is Marty Makler?"

"Uh-huh. She said to say hello for her. Can you show us the lighthouse?"

"Well, do you have a dollar?" He raised his eyebrows.

I didn't know there was a charge so I said, "We have to buy a ticket?"

"Just a joke, young man. Let me close the door and we'll go to the tower." Mr. W pulled the door closed. I blinked when the screen door slammed behind him as he stepped off the porch onto the gravel pathway leading to the tower.

Mr. W walked slowly so we could keep up with him. He was pretty tall. I thought he would have a big stomach, but he was thin. Most of the men I had seen that were granma's age had big bellies hanging over their belts and their shirt-tails out, but not Mr. W, he was neat. He wore glasses and had short gray hair, and no hearing aid. I think he had been in the army or the navy; by the way he walked, I knew he was in charge.

The top of the tower was high above us. I asked Mr. W, "How high is the tower, sir?"

"Well, I never measured it, but they tell me its ninety-two feet, four inches above the ground at the very top of the lightning rod."

Suzy had her head thrown back, looking up at the tower, and when Mr. W stopped to unlock the door, she walked into his legs and fell down.

"Are you all right, Susan?" Mr. W reached down and helped her up. "You didn't skin your knees or anything?"

Suzy grabbed Mr. W's pants leg and said, "I'm okay." She brushed off her dress where she had sat on the ground. I couldn't see any scratches on her legs.

The big wooden door creaked as it swung open. Suzy stepped behind me, a little afraid of the dungeon-like interior, which she could barely make out. I noticed a funny smell and it was kind of dark inside the tower. The inside of the tower wasn't what I expected. It had eight walls. The tower seemed bigger on the inside than it seemed from the outside. The outside of the tower was rounded like an ice cream cone, but upside down. Mr. W turned on a light; no, there were several lights on the walls, every ten feet or so above the walkway, all the way to the top. But what interested me most was the stairs. A railing on the steps went round and round up to a small door that was open at the top. The steps had books on them. Mr. W was using the stairs as bookshelves.

I had to ask, "Why are the books on the steps, Mr. Waicukauski?"

"I had too many books for the shelves in the house, but there was a lot of space on the steps in the lighthouse so I put them in alphabetical order. The first step starts with A and near the top is Z. They're all non-fiction."

I asked, "Can I go up to the top?"

"Sure. You can't fall. The railing will keep you safe. You might get scared, so don't look down. I think Susan better stay here with me. I wouldn't want her to fall on those metal steps."

I said okay and started climbing. I stopped at the letter C and checked if there were any comic books, but then I remembered Mr. Waicukauski said all the books were non-fiction. The Lone Ranger was my favorite. Someday I'd like to go to New Mexico, or Utah maybe—even Arizona.

The steps for the letters K, Q, W, X, Y, and Z were empty. I had counted forty steps when I reached the top. There were three steps for the letter S. I could feel the wind blowing through the hole at the level over my head. There was a small ladder up to the hole. The door was open but I could see it could be locked from the top of the ladder. I climbed up onto the platform. There was a giant lightbulb in the center with mirrors around it. It was scary, especially when I looked down to the ground. Everything looked little, even the buildings. I grabbed onto the railing really tight; the wind was blowing hard. I took a deep breath and looked out over the ocean. I could see some ships that looked like toys far out where the water met the sky. I'm glad Suzy didn't come up here with me. She would really be scared and I would have to take her down, maybe even have to carry her.

I backed down the ladder and started down the bookshelves to the ground.

Suzy yelled at me, "Don't fall, Rocky," when I was about halfway down.

I waved to her and said, "Don't worry I'm holding on to the railing."

Mr. W yelled at me, too. "Rocky, when you get to the window, please open it for me."

The window was at the letter H. I stopped, turned a latch and shoved the window open. Warm air from inside the lighthouse went rushing out. I got goose bumps when the air tried to push me toward the opening. I noticed a book with fancy writing on it. It said Heraldry. I decided to ask Mr. W what it is about, I didn't want to open the book, I wanted to get back on the ground. The rushing air made it a little bit scary.

"Thank you for opening the window, Rocky. It smells musty in here if I don't get some fresh air in the tower."

"You're welcome. What is Heraldry?"

"You saw that written on one of the books, did you? Heraldry is all about the fancy designs the Knights had on their shields and clothing."

"So the book has stories about the knights? Like King Arthur?"

"No stories, Rocky. It's real history. All the books I have are non-fiction. Fiction is imaginative stories, like Goldilocks and the Three Bears; that isn't a true story, it is make-believe. You are a very observant young man. Did you notice that some of the letters have no books?"

"Uh-huh. K, Q, W, X, Y, and Z are empty; Did someone borrow those books?"

"Nope. I don't have any books for those letters. I'll make you and Susan a deal. For every book you can find that belongs on those shelves, I'll give you a quarter, and for any other books, I'll give you fifteen cents. But, remember, the books have to be non-fiction. If I already have a book, I'll give you a dime."

"Okay, Mr. Waicukauski." I looked at the big clock beside the door. "We have to go. Granma said we have to be back by four o'clock. Thanks for letting us in the lighthouse."

"You're welcome, Rocky. Be careful on your way home. Tell your grandmother hi for me."

"We'll tell her, bye." Suzy and I waved to Mr. W and he waved back as we walked away from the lighthouse. We didn't see any cars, trucks, or the lady on the bicycle on the way home, but we heard some boats in the harbor. As we walked, I tried to think of books for the letters K, Q, W, X, Y, and Z. I could only think of a couple: knights and zebras.

Suzy and I got home just before four o'clock. Granma was sitting on the sofa reading a book when we opened the screen door and went into the living room. I asked, "Whatcha readin', granma?"

"Oh, it's a love story from the Reader's Digest. It's wonderful—it makes me cry sometimes."

Suzy moved next to granma, looked at the book, and said, "Is it friction?"

Granma marked her place with a playing card, put the book down, and smiled, "Yes, Suzy, it's *fiction*—nor."

Suzy scrunched up her face and looked at granma, "Nor?"

Granma replied, "It's a make believe story, dear. It's fiction, not friction—oh, never mind." Granma got up from the sofa and started into the kitchen. "Do you want a cookie and some milk? Come into the kitchen, I've got some peanut butter cookies that I made while you were gone. They're still warm. How was your trip to the lighthouse? Was it fun?"

Suzy answered, "Rocky had fun, I just watched. But we saw a pretty lady on a bicycle. She waved to us." Suzy smiled and said, "She rang a bell on her bicycle."

I suddenly remembered what Mr. W had said. "Mr. Waicukauski said to tell you hello, granma. He gave us a job."

Chapter 2

At Work

Granma was reaching into the cupboard to get some glasses. She suddenly stopped moving and turned around. She looked surprised; her eyes were wide open and her mouth was too. "Mr. Waicukauski gave you a job? You can't work, you're children."

"I'm the man of the family, granma. I can work—besides, it's not really work. We're going to find books for Mr. W's library; nonfiction ones. He doesn't want fiction books, I think there are too many—he'd run out of shelves."

Granma's serious face faded away into a smile. "Oh, I see. Well, that's okay then. Where are you going to find books?" granma had us come in the kitchen and sit at the table where we usually ate lunch. She poured us some milk in orange juice glasses and gave us each a cookie on a white paper napkin.

I wasn't ready for granma's question. I thought for a minute and said, "Suzy and I can ask people if they have any old books they don't want anymore. People put stuff in their attic or maybe in a closet." I suddenly remembered seeing a sign about a garage sale. "We can buy some books at garage sales, too, if we can get them for a dime."

Suzy had been sitting quietly, listening to granma and me. She put down her half-eaten cookie, drank some milk, took a breath, and said, "Who would want to buy a garage?"

Granma smiled, and before I could say anything, she said, "Suzy, a garage sale is when a person has some things they no longer need. They sell those items from their garage, but they don't sell the garage."

Suzy said, "Oh, I get it," and took another bite of cookie. I almost laughed because Suzy had a milk-moustache, but she wiped it off with the back of her hand.

I told granma what Mr. W was going to pay us for the books and she said, "That means if you get them free, you'll make more money than if you have to buy them, right?"

"Yes. Granma, do you have a pencil and a piece of paper? I need to write down the letters of the books that will earn us the most money."

Granma said, "Tell me the letters and I'll write them down for you. I'll make a copy so if you ever lose your list, we'll have a backup."

I said, "That's a good idea," and gave granma a hug. I ate another cookie and finished my milk. While I was chewing on the cookie I got another idea. "Do you have any neighbors that have books they don't want?"

"I'm not sure, Rocky, but you can ask Mrs. Nesbitt next door. She reads lots of books. Sometimes she borrows books from the lighthouse."

There were two houses next door, a yellow one on the left, and a green one on the right, a little farther away, with granma's white house in the middle. "Which house is Mrs. Nesbitt's," I asked.

"The green one with white trim. I think she's home. She'd like some visitors. Her son hasn't been home for several weeks."

"Is he a salesman?"

"No. He's a Lieutenant in the Navy. Carla said he works on codes, or something like that."

"Come on, Suz, let's go see if Mrs. Nesbitt has any books." When granma said *codes* I was wondering if her son was a secret agent. I had to ask Mrs. Nesbitt about that.

I pushed on the table, slid my chair back, and helped Suzy get down from her chair. As soon as she hit the floor, she ran to the front door, looking back at me. "Which way, Rocky?"

I pointed to the right and she ran across the grass and pebbles to Mrs. Nesbitt's front porch. Suzy stood there, waiting for me to catch up. When I was almost at the porch, Suzy rang the doorbell.

I heard a voice from inside the house say, "I'll be right there, hold your horses."

Suzy laughed. "She said hold your horses. That's funny, isn't it?"

The door opened slowly to reveal an old lady, kind of bent over, holding a dish rag. I think she was older than granma. She wore an apron over a white dress that had little blue flowers arranged in bunches around a larger yellow flower that looked like a sunflower. She had black hair, with some gray streaks, in a bun and light brown stockings with black shoes. Her glasses were hanging from a string around her neck.

"Can I help you," she asked, smiling.

Suzy just stood there, not knowing what to say so I stepped up to the screen door and said, "We were wondering if you have any books to give away; non-fiction ones for the library, for Mr. Waicukauski."

Suzy nodded and said, "Non-fiction— no r."

"Well, maybe I do. Do you want any special titles or subjects?"

I remembered the list granma had copied and pulled it from my pocket. "Yes, ma'am. Were looking for titles that start with these letters, especially." I held out the list and Mrs. Nesbitt unlatched the screen door and took my list with her kind of boney fingers. She squinted at the letters for a bit, gave the list back to me, and turned around.

"Wait right here, kids, I'll take a look. I have lots of books."

Suzy stuck her nose against the screen and looked into Mrs. Nesbitt's house. "It smells funny," she said, "—like granma's-—and fried chicken."

I stepped closer and took a whiff. Suzy was right, Mrs. Nesbitt's house smelled like the stuff granma rubs on her fingers and elbows. Granma told us it helps with the pain of arthritis. Granma's knuckles were swollen. They looked like they hurt, but she still knitted stuff. She made red, green, and white mittens last year for Suzy and me at Christmas. I couldn't smell any chicken.

Mrs. Nesbitt returned to the door with some books. "I found three books for you, each one starts with a different letter: Q, W, and Z."

Suzy took one of the books. It said Queensland on it. I was handed the other books: *Walruses* and *Zebras*. Mrs. Nesbitt said her husband used to read about all kinds of animals.

Suzy said, "Where is your husband?"

"Well, dear, he's in heaven."

Suzy then said, "Do you think he knows my granpa? He's in heaven, too."

Mrs. Nesbitt smiled and replied, "I'll bet they are good friends. Your grandpa was a good man, just like my George. What's that on your nose, dear?"

I looked at Suzy's nose and the tip of it had a black mark on it. I knew what it was and said, "She pressed her nose against your screen and got dirt on it, I guess."

Suzy nodded and we both said, "Thank you for the books."

We took the books home and I wrote down the titles of the books on another slip of paper and kept it with granma's note of the letters that we needed. I put a line under each letter we had a book for. I wanted to keep track of the number of books we found for Mr. W. So far, we had earned seventy-five cents. Suzy and I planned to use the money to buy Mom and granma something for their birthdays. I remembered they were about the same time of year. I forgot to ask Mrs. Nesbitt if her son was a secret agent. Next time I see her, I'll ask.

Granma asked us to wash our hands before dinner. She said we didn't know where those books had been. I knew what she meant. I didn't say anything, Suzy and I washed our hands. We had spaghetti and meatballs, celery and carrots from the garden, and milk for dinner. Granma drank coffee with a little cream. I watched her pour the cream and put it back on the table. She picked up her spoon and started stirring and then she reached for a lump of sugar. That lump made a little plop when she dropped it in the coffee. She looked at me and smiled.

After dinner, granma turned on her TV and we watched the Jack Benny Show. Mr. Benny tried to play the violin, but he'd stop and talk and then play it again. It didn't sound very good. I liked the colored man with the funny voice. Suzy fell asleep before the show was over. Granma couldn't carry her to bed, so she woke Suzy up. Granma had to hold onto Suzy to keep her from falling over, she was kind of dizzy; maybe from the meatballs. Suzy went to bed without brushing her teeth, but I brushed mine.

In the morning the sky was gray, and the wind was blowing, but not very hard. It was a good wind for flying kites, but Suzy and I were excited about taking the books to Mr. Waicukauski. At nine o'clock we were ready to walk to the lighthouse. It was cool outside. Suzy wore a yellow sweater and I had a tan jacket. Granma said she didn't think it would rain this morning; maybe in the afternoon. We were to be back home for lunch.

When we started walking, granma yelled at us, "Come back kids. I'll give you a wagon to carry the books." We hadn't gone very far, maybe twenty yards. I heard the back door slam and then granma came walking around the corner of the house pulling a little, red, American-Flyer wagon. Suzy put the book about Walruses in the wagon and I put the other two books in it. I said, "Thanks granma." She said, "You be careful," and went back in the house. We took turns pulling the wagon, but I pulled it most of the way, being a lot bigger and stronger.

We were about halfway to the lighthouse when the lady on the bicycle rode by again. She rang the bell and waved as she passed us.

"That's the same lady, isn't it, Rocky? She has a pink dress today."

"Uh-huh."

Suzy always noticed stuff like colors of dresses. I was looking at the reflectors on the back fender of the bike. There was a small yellow one above a bigger red one. We watched the lady as she went down the road and stopped next to a man who was walking in the same direction as we were. They talked for a moment, and then she gave the man something, but we were too far away to tell what it was.

The lady rode away and the man continued walking slowly. As he walked, he seemed to be looking at whatever she had given him. A big blue and white truck went by. We could feel the air pushing at us and then we couldn't see the man any more. I watched the truck, there was a sailing ship painted on the back doors. We could hear the brakes, the truck slowed down, but it didn't stop, and then it speeded up and continued to drive away.

Suzy said, "Look, Rocky! Something fell off that truck." She pointed ahead of us, across the road.

Since I was taller than Suzy, I could see what it was by the road. It was the man. The truck must have hit him or he had tripped and fallen beside the road. I let go of the wagon and ran across the road to the man. His leg was bent funny and his face was all cut up. He needed a doctor. "Suzy," I yelled, "run over to that little yellow house and tell them to call a doctor. The truck hit the man, I think he needs an ambulance." Suzy hadn't seen the man up close, she was running after me. She stopped when I yelled, turned and ran down a dirt road about half-a-block to the yellow house.

The man said, almost in a whisper, "Take book to Elena."

I didn't know what he meant. I didn't see a book at first. I looked around and there it was, a thick black book laying in the dirt. I got the book and took it over to the man. I held it so he could see it and said, "Do you mean this book?"

The man squinted his eyes and said, "Da." He tried to turn over, but wasn't strong enough and lay back on the ground. I told him, "A doctor will be here soon. You'll be all right."

The man sighed and lay his head in the dirt and gravel. I couldn't see his chest move or hear him breathing anymore and his eyes looked up into the sky. I had never seen a dead person before, but I thought the man had died. I stood straight up and looked at the book. It had some regular letters mixed with some others but it also had the words *English Dictionary* written on the front.

I could see Suzy coming from the little house with a lady in a black dress wearing a red and white apron. I yelled, "Don't come over here, Suzy. The man is hurt real bad." I knew Suzy would have bad dreams if she saw all the blood and the broken man in the dirt. The lady kept coming and knelt beside the man. She put her finger tips on the man's neck and waited a few seconds, and then she took off her apron and covered the man's head. She looked at me and asked, "What is your name, young man?"

"Rocky Linfield. My sister is Susan. We're staying with our granma on Oyster Lane, the white house with green trim." I pointed back down the road.

"I'm Mrs. Windsor— Lila. I called the ambulance, but they can't help this man. What happened?"

"I think a big blue and white truck hit him. We couldn't see what happened, the truck was in the way. The truck slowed down, and then just kept going. I think the driver knew he hit the man. Can you stay here? I need to go to the lighthouse with my sister."

"Sure. I'll wait for the ambulance. You be careful walking along the road. Don't walk on the asphalt."

"Okay, we'll be careful." I yelled at Suzy, "Come on, Suzy, meet me up ahead. I'll pull the wagon." I pointed down the road a little way. Suzy could walk across a grassy area and not see the dead man.

We continued toward the lighthouse with four books. I had put the black book the man had talked about with the others. I had to remember to ask Mr. Waicukauski if he knew the name of the lady on the bicycle. I hoped it was Elena, because I knew what she looked like. I hadn't seen any other ladies near the road except for Mrs. Windsor, and her first name was Lila. Of course, I knew Mrs. Nesbitt; her name was Dorothy, but I couldn't imagine her knowing the dead man. I wondered what his name was. Maybe he had a wife and her name was Elena.

Chapter 3

Lieutenant Nesbitt

Just before getting to the lighthouse, Suzy and I heard a siren. We looked back down the road and could see an ambulance with a flashing red light stopping where the man was. We didn't have to knock on Mr. Waicukauski's door, he was already outside.

He was looking at the ambulance and said, "Hi, kids. Did you see what happened down the road?"

I answered, "Yes, sir. A man got hit by a truck. Mrs. Windsor said he was *d-e-a-d*" I spelled out the word so Suzy wouldn't know. I told Mr. W I thought they would take the man to the hospital.

Mr. W said, "That's too bad. We haven't had many accidents along that road. That's the first one in the last four years. That's how long I've been here."

"I'm ten," I said.

Suzy walked up to Mr. W and said, "I'm five," and held up her left hand to show Mr. W her fingers and thumb.

Mr. W said, "How many will you be at your next birthday, young lady?"

Suzy held up one hand and extended one finger on the other hand, and said, "Six."

Mr. W asked, "How many is Rocky?"

Suzy looked at her fingers for a moment and said, "I don't know." *"Well, that's all right. Maybe you'll know next year. Tell me about the books. I see four books in your wagon."*

"One book is from that man. It's the black one." Suzy looked at me to take over; she didn't know what to say about the other books.

I explained, "We have a book on Queensland; that's in Australia, one on walruses, and one on zebras. Our pay is seventy-five cents, isn't it? We can't give you the black one, we have to give it to Elena. Do you know who Elena is, Mr. W?"

"I'm afraid I don't know Elena. May I look at the black book?"

I gave Mr. W the book and he looked at the cover. Then he opened it up and glanced at the pages. "It's a Russian to English dictionary." He flipped through the pages and then looked at the last page.

I asked, "How can you read those words with the funny letters?"

"I lived in Poland at the start of the big war. Poland is next to Russia. It's between Russia and Germany. We studied Russian and German in school."

"Oh. What does *da* mean? The man said da when I asked him if he wanted me to give the book to Elena. I didn't know what language he was using."

"He said yes, Rocky. Da means yes in Russian. So, we have to find a lady named Elena. I'll try to help you find her. Shall we put the book on the shelf for Russian, or dictionary, or do you want me to keep it for her in the house? Maybe you want to keep it for her?"

"I think you'd better keep it here with the other books. Maybe Elena will look for the book and come here. She won't know where to go if Suzy and I have the book."

"All right. I'll put the book on the top step, next to the maintenance opening. Did you look at the book, Rocky—I mean the pages inside?"

"A little bit. I saw some letters circled on the pages I looked at and the numbers of some pages were circled. I remember the page forty-nine number was circled, and I think fifty-two, but I didn't look at all the pages."

Mr. W said, "I saw the same thing. Some letters are marked on different pages."

I got excited. "Maybe it's a code! We should ask Mrs. Nesbitt's son to look at it. He's a Lieutenant in the Navy. I'll tell Mrs. Nesbitt to have her son come take a look. She told me he works with codes. I think he's a secret agent."

Mr. W smiled and reached into his pocket. He pulled out a handful of coins and gave me two quarters, two dimes, and a nickel. "That's your pay for the books. You and Suzy did a good job. Do you think you can find some more?"

I was full of confidence and said, "Sure. We got those books from only one house. I think we'll find lots more. Don't you think so, Suzy?" I put the money in the little coin pocket in my pants and patted it with my hand to make sure the coins wouldn't come out.

Suzy said, "I think we can fill the whole wagon with books— more than three. Do you have lots of money Mr. W?"

"Sure do, Suzy, lots of quarters, that is."

Suzy eyes sparkled and she replied, "Oh, goody. We'll need lots of quarters."

Mr. W asked, "Are you saving for something?"

Suzy smiled, "Yes, sir; birthday presents for granma and Mommy. How much do we have, Rocky?"

"Seventy-five cents so far. We'll need a lot more, maybe three dollars total. We need to find nine more books, Suzy. What time is it, Mr. Waicukauski?"

"It's 11:30. Do you have to be home for lunch?"

"Yes, sir. We have to go now. Thank you for the money. Maybe we'll see you tomorrow. Bye."

"Bye, kids. Be careful on the way home. See you tomorrow."

Suzy sat down in the wagon and smiled at me, "Pull me, Rocky."

I thought for a second and said, "All right, but hang on." I picked up the handle and started pulling, but it was more difficult than I imagined. Suzy was a lot heavier than those four books had been. The wheels sank into the gravel. I looked ahead where the road was packed harder and decided I could do it, at least for a while. I might have to ask Suzy to get out before we get back to granma's. That's a long distance to pull a loaded wagon.

Granma was waiting outside, talking to Mrs. Nesbitt, when we got home. I had been able to pull Suzy all the way, but I was sure glad when she jumped out of the wagon and ran to granma.

"We saw an accident, granma. A man got hit by a truck. The ambulance took him to the hospital. There was a nice lady that helped Rocky, she called the ambulance."

Granma gave me a worried look. "We're you hurt, Rocky?"

"No, granma. Mrs. Windsor checked the man and put her apron over his head." I motioned for granma to come closer. I whispered in her ear, "The man was dead."

"Oh, I see. So the ambulance took the man to the hospital?"

"I guess. We saw Mr. Waicukauski after, and he said the book the man had was a Russian to English dictionary. I need to ask Mrs. Nesbitt to have her son look at the book. We left it in the lighthouse with the other books."

"Well, let's get you some lunch and then you can tell Mrs. Nesbitt all about it. Okay?"

"Okay. What's for lunch?"

"I hope you like tomato soup, crackers, and cheese."

Suzy answered, "We do, but the soup makes my nose run." Suzy grinned and looked at me.

I nodded, "Mine, too. I hope you have some Kleenex."

Granma smiled, "I have plenty of paper napkins. Those should do."

After lunch, we went next door to talk with Mrs. Nesbitt for a few minutes, and then came back home. I was really tired from pulling Suzy in the wagon and fell asleep on the sofa. I woke up when I heard a knock on the front door. I blinked my eyes and tried to see who it was through the screen door, but everything was blurry. I rubbed my eyes, but it didn't seem to help much. All I could tell was that it was a man in a uniform, and he was pretty big. I was kind of woozy—kind of sweaty, too, but I heard granma say, "Rocky is right here on the sofa, he just woke up from a nap. Come in, Lieutenant Nesbitt."

When I heard granma say Lieutenant Nesbitt, I sat up wide awake. Being a secret agent, he would know all about codes. I had to tell him about the code book. Granma walked ahead of the Lieutenant and stopped beside me, putting her hand on my shoulder. She turned toward the man in uniform and said, "This is Rocky, my grandson. Rocky, this is Lieutenant Aaron Nesbitt. He's Mrs. Nesbitt's son."

I stood up and extended my right hand. I thought about saluting, but only for a moment, I wasn't in the Navy. He shook my hand, laid his cap on the sofa, and sat down where I had been sleeping.

"It's nice to meet you, Rocky. I heard you saw the accident today."

"Yes, sir." I told the lieutenant what Suzy and I had seen. Just in case Suzy might hear us talking, I whispered, "The man died."

The lieutenant leaned closer to me and whispered, "How did you know he was dead?"

That's when I told the lieutenant about Mrs. Windsor, and what the man said before he died.

"So, he said Elena?"

"Yes, sir, but I don't know who that is. Maybe it's the lady on the bicycle."

"Can you show me the book?"

"No, sir. I don't have the book. I left it with Mr. Waicukauski at the lighthouse—on the top step. That's where Mr. Waicukauski said he was going to put it. Nobody goes that high up. There aren't any books up there."

Lieutenant Nesbitt looked away from me toward the kitchen. Suzy was standing in the doorway eating a cookie. She took a bite and part of the cookie fell on the floor. She looked at the chunk of cookie on the floor, and then looked back at the lieutenant.

The lieutenant said, "Oops. You must be Susan. I'm Lieutenant Nesbitt. I came to talk to you and Rocky about the accident."

Suzy didn't say anything, she just nodded slowly. She remembered not to talk with her mouth full. I think she was a little afraid of Lt. Nesbitt in his uniform. She probably remembered when two Navy men in uniform came to tell Mom about Dad getting shot down in Korea.

"What do you remember about the truck, Susan?" The lieutenant's voice was very calm. He looked like he wanted to help.

"Granma, I made a mess."

Granma said, "Don't worry, I'll fix it. You talk with the lieutenant." Granma came in the living room and picked up the piece of cookie with a wet paper towel and went back in the kitchen.

"It had a boat painted on it—on the back. The truck was blue and white."

I nodded in agreement with Suzy. I said, "The boat was a sailing ship painted in black."

The lieutenant drew something on a pad and held it for us to see. "Does this look like the boat?"

Suzy and I both nodded. I said, "Yes, sir."

"That was a Columbia Van Lines truck. Good work, kids. That should help the police find the truck and driver. I'll get the black book you left at the library. I'll be back in a little while, okay?"

I said, "Okay."

The lieutenant talked with granma for a minute and then drove off. Suzy and I put the wagon in the garage and then started looking for pretty rocks in the front yard near the street. Suzy had found three she liked and I had two good sized, nearly clear stones when a jeep pulled up. It was Lieutenant Nesbitt. He had come back—just like he said he would. I think he had been gone for about twenty minutes, maybe a little longer.

He got out of the jeep and walked over to us. "Hi, kids." We both said, "Hi." He was holding a black book in his left hand. He held it out and said, "Is this the book, Rocky?"

I took the book and looked at the cover and then I opened it and saw some of the letters were circled on each page. It sure looked like the book I had given to Mr. Waicukauski, but when I turned to page forty-eight, the page number wasn't circled. I couldn't see that the circle had been erased. It wasn't the same book! I told the lieutenant, "That isn't the same book, but the outside looks the same."

"You're sure about that?"

"Yes, sir. There should be a circle around the page number forty-eight. This book's different." I gave the book back to the lieutenant.

He said, "You are very observant, Rocky. Thank you for your help."

I couldn't hold back any longer. I had to ask the lieutenant, "Sir, are you a secret agent?"

He smiled and said, "No, but I know someone that is, but I can't talk about that. She wouldn't be a secret agent any longer if I told people about her."

"The secret agent is a lady?"

"Uh-huh."

I had never thought a lady would be a secret agent. I was disappointed that Lieutenant Nesbitt wasn't one, but when he said he knew a lady that was one, I was surprised. A lady would have to be strong, smart, and tricky, but she couldn't be too pretty, that would cause people to watch her, especially men. I wondered if Elena might be a secret agent, but she was too pretty.

The lieutenant talked with granma for a short time and then drove off slowly toward the lighthouse. Some blueish smoke was coming out of the tailpipe. Suzy and I hunted through the pebbles in the front yard and found some different colored rocks, some red-orange, some gray, and Suzies favorite ones, pure black. I liked the red-orange ones the best. Granma said they had iron in them. We put our rocks in a small box granma gave us. Suzy said she wanted to keep the box next to her bed. I said that was okay with me, as long as she didn't try to eat them.

Suzy said, "Why would I eat them, Rocky?"

"Those colored rocks look like candy. If you had a dream, you might get confused."

Chapter 4

More Books

Granma asked, "How would you kids like to go for a ride? I think I know where we can find some more books for the library."

Suzy was sitting on the ground, but jumped up and said excitedly, "I'm ready."

I liked watching Suzie's eyes when she got excited, they sparkled, but she started jumping around, and that made me nervous. I guess young kids get excited easily, but I was calmer. I was wondering where we would be going to get more books.

"Where are we going, granma?"

"We're going to see Mr. Sherner. His first name is Larry. He owns a bait and tackle store down on the dock. We'll have to drive; it's too far to walk. We only have an hour before we have to be back for dinner."

Granma had a four-door, light-green Desoto with a gray sun visor. The car had a drooping front bumper on the passenger side. Granma never said how the bumper got bent. Maybe Granpa was driving when it happened, but I knew granma would never tell on him. Granma locked the house front door and backed the car out of the garage. Suzy climbed in beside granma first and I got in next to the window. I told Suzy she was the meat of a sandwich, granma and I were the bread. Suzy complained, so I didn't say anything more about it. I was going to say she was hamburger and her curly reddish hair was catsup, but I have red hair, too. I smiled when I figured the catsup also got on the bread.

I think granma drove for about four or five minutes. I don't have a watch. While I looked at the water, I saw a fishing boat arriving in port, the seagulls were swooping down from all around, gliding over the water, but staying close to that boat. I could see two men on deck. It looked like they were cleaning up, throwing things into the water. I was wondering who would arrive at the dock first, the boat, or us in granma's Desoto.

Sherners Lures and Live-Bate store was painted dark-green with yellow letters. It was Suzy's and my first time at the dock; we could hear the water underneath the big beams that made up the surface like a street, but with slots, big enough to lose stuff, between the lumber. We beat the boat to the dock so I heard the water making slapping sounds when that boat came in. Suzy and I got on our hands and knees and looked through the spaces between the beams at the water slapping against the posts supporting the top of the pier.

Granma led us into Sherner's store and said, "Hi, Lawrence. How have you been?"

"Great, Marty. You look good, and who are those two fish on the line behind you?"

Granma put her hands on our shoulders and pulled us forward so Mr. Sherner could see us better. "These are my two grandchildren, Rocky and Susan. They're staying with me for six weeks. We came to see if you have any books they could have."

Suzy nodded and quickly said, "Non-fiction."

Mr. Sherner was quite a bit taller than granma and wore a green and yellow plaid shirt and black work pants. He had brown boots like loggers wear, with black laces. He looked at us and said, "Ya know, I think I have a few." He turned and yelled toward the back of the store, "Elena, could you please bring me that box of books on the back shelf?"

When he said Elena, I looked at granma. She was as surprised as I was. Suzy didn't say anything—I think she was waiting to see the box of books. A young woman, older than a high school girl, wearing jeans, a work shirt, and rubber boots, appeared carrying a small box. Suzy pointed and said excitedly, "Hey! That's the bicycle lady!"

The young lady smiled and said, "That's correct. I saw you on the road the other day; Is this your brother?"

Suzy answered with, "Uh-huh. I'm Susan and he's Rocky."

"It's nice to meet you, I'm Elena Allen. I just started working here two days ago. I go to the University of Maine, in Orono. I'm on summer vacation." She smiled at us and said, "This is my summer job for two months."

I said, "We saw you give a man a book. Did you know he was hit by a truck? He told me to give you the book, but I didn't know who you were. The book he had is gone now, someone took it from the lighthouse and put a different book in its place."

"I heard the man died, but I don't know what I would do with the book. I was just told to deliver it to the man walking along the road to the lighthouse."

Suzy's eyes got big and she looked at me. "The man died?"

Granma could see that Suzy couldn't understand what had happened. She had seen him walking at the side of the road and then he was hit and died. Granma said, "I'm sure the man went to Heaven. Granpa will be his friend."

Suzy looked at granma, "He will see Daddy, too, won't he?"

"Sure he will. Everybody in Heaven knows everyone."

"Okay, just so he won't be lonely." She smiled and looked in the box of books. "Rocky, are these non-fiction? Does Mr. W want any of them?"

Elena sat on the floor beside Suzy and said, "Are you looking for certain books?"

"Uh-huh. Rocky, tell her the letters."

I told Elena the letters we wanted and she quickly sorted through the books. There were ten of them, all about the same size, except some were thicker than others. I watched her go through the books, sorting them into two piles.

"There you go. I've got the ones you want in this pile." She pointed to the stack of books closest to Suzy, and then said, "I'll put the others back." She arranged the books in the box, picked it up and disappeared behind a curtain at the back of the store.

I sat down with Suzy and we started reading the titles. Actually, I read the titles, Suzy opened each book to look at the pictures. I had trouble with a couple of words, but granma helped me. We had five books for Mr. Waicukauski, so we should get $1.25 for them, unless Mr. Sherner wanted us to pay for them. I asked him and he said they were free; they were just gathering dust in the back room.

"Thank you, Mr. Sherner. Mr. Waicukauski will like these books. He doesn't have any of them in the lighthouse." The books were different from the ones Mrs. Nesbitt had given us. After we deliver the books, we'll have $2.00.

Mr. Sherner replied, "Glad I could help you. Its good to have a library in Crafton. Tell Wayne we should have some fiction books, too. A lot more people read fiction than non-fiction."

I told Mr. Sherner, "Mr. Waicukauski doesn't have room for many fiction books, just non-fiction."

Mr. Sherner said, "I'll bet Wayne could find some room out there. He needs to clean out some of those old buildings that are full of junk. Some of those old lighthouse parts could be thrown away— they're junk, not antiques. You can tell him I said that." Mr. Sherner had a serious face at first, but then he grinned.

"Okay, I'll tell him." I wasn't sure I would tell him his stuff was junk, antiques would be nicer.

"Let me put the books in a paper bag for you, Rocky. They'll be easier to carry." Mr. Sherner grabbed a bag from behind the counter, shook it open, and filled it with the books. The bag had a drawing of a fish on it. He hefted the bag and said, "Will this be too heavy for you?"

I took the bag with both hands. "No, I can carry them to the car. It's not that far. They aren't too heavy."

We started toward the door, but a big man filled the doorway. The man wore a dark-blue jacket with shiny-brass buttons and a white captain's hat with a fish on the front. His hat almost touched the top of the doorway. Suzy and I stepped back next to Granma so he could come into the store. He looked down at us and watched us move out of the way.

I watched him shuffle—kind of a limp, to the counter in front of Mr. Sherner and say, "Have you got any non-fishing books for sale?" He had a rough sounding voice like he was hoarse from yelling at someone. "I would also like to get a pound of those yellow candies." He pointed a big, dirty, gnarled finger at the lemon drops in a gallon jar on the counter.

Suzy ran over beside him and pulled on his pants leg. He looked down at her and said, "What is it young lady?"

Suzy replied, "Non-fiction," and smiled.

Granma said, "I'm sorry sir. She thought you meant *non-fiction*, not *non-fishing*. She just learned about fiction and non-fiction."

"Oh. That's all right. I just want to get something to read that isn't about fishing, that's all I hear about on the boat. Have you got a library?"

Granma said, "The lighthouse is a library. What boat are you from?"

He pointed outside to the vessel that had just pulled in to the dock when we arrived.

I looked out the door across the rough wooden planks and saw the name of the boat written on the side. I grabbed Granma's hand and pulled her to the door. "Look, Granma!" I pointed at the writing and said, "The boat is called Elena! Do you think the man was talking about the boat, not the lady?"

Granma looked at the boat and then the man at the counter. All she said was, "Hmm."

Mr. Sherner said, "Bye, Marty and kids."

Granma answered with, "Bye, Lawrence. Thanks for the books."

I waved and said, "Yeah, thanks for the books—and the bag."

Suzy laughed and said, "Thanks for the bag—and the books!"

Granma grabbed Suzy's hand and we left Sherner's, walking toward the parking area.

Suzy swiveled her head and asked, "How much money will we have now, Rocky?"

"Two dollars," but I wasn't thinking about the money, I was thinking about the boat called Elena. That was something I had never counted on. I had a lot to learn before I could be a secret agent. I had to go to high school and college first, and then maybe be in the military. But since I'm big for my age, maybe I could qualify for training earlier.

"Two dollars? We need lots more. Where can we get some more books?"

"I don't know, Suzy. I'm thinking about something else. We'll talk about it after dinner— okay?"

"Okay, but I don't want to go to bed early. We need to talk about how to get more books—*before* I have to go to bed."

Chapter 5

Return to the Library

When we got home, Granma started getting ready for dinner. Suzy and I took the books out of the bag and started looking through them. One of the books was about Walla Walla, a city in Washington State, clear across the country. The book said there's a state prison there. Another book was about Kentucky. The other three books were about wax, watermarks, and wasps. We thought Mr. W would like the books.

While Granma, Suzy, and I were eating dinner, the big man from the Elena was going to the lighthouse. He had walked from his boat at the dock. It had been a long distance and his leg was sore. He was in a foul mood. We didn't know the captain of the Elena had visited the lighthouse until later on.

Wayne answered a knock on the door. He recognized the man immediately; it was Dmitri Suvorov, captain of the Elena. Wayne opened the screen and invited the captain into the living room. "Can I get you a drink, Captain?"

"No. Do you have the book?"

"I wondered when you would be here, comrade. Yes, I recovered the code book. Some children brought it to me. I exchanged it with a similar book containing a meaningless code. When Uri was injured, he asked a young boy to deliver the book to Elena. The boy thought the delivery girl was to receive the book. He didn't know Elena was the name of your boat."

"Well, he knows now. He told his grandmother about it. I do not think they will cause any trouble, they are just useless pawns. I would like you to get the book."

"It's in my bedroom with the books I'm going to read. I've got a pile of them beside my bed. I'll get it for you." Wayne went to his bedroom and returned with the code book. He handed it to Captain Suvorov and watched the captain leaf through the pages. Suvorov turned to page forty-eight and noticed the page number was circled.

"This looks like it's the original."

"It has to be—that's the book the kids gave me. Unless, of course, the book was substituted before they brought it to me, but that would be highly unlikely. They brought the book here directly after getting it from Uri. Who was he supposed to deliver it to?"

"You don't need to know that, comrade. The less each of us knows, the better."

"Sure, I understand. Would you like to stay the night?"

"No, brevity of contact will keep us safe from the authorities. Let me check one other page." He flipped two pages ahead and saw that fifty-two was also circled. "All right, it checks out. I had better get back to the boat, I have several messages to decode."

The code book looked small in the captain's large hand. Suvorov placed the book into the inside pocket of his jacket and turned to leave, but hesitated and said, "Do you think the grandmother suspects anything?"

"No, she hasn't got a clue. She's just a nice lady. I kind of like her, but she's not too bright. The young boy is smarter than she is."

"All right. Keep that light functioning properly, we will need the signal the seventh of next month. Good bye, comrade Waicukauski."

"Good bye, Captain Suvorov. Have a productive journey."

Thursday morning was chilly, a light wind was blowing from the ocean causing the boats moored in the harbor to slowly and gently rise and fall. The Elena was gone. The haze would lift by noon, when sunlight was expected to shine on Crafton. The weather report was rarely wrong, except during the winter months, and usually only the wind direction.

Suzy had gotten up first, excited about getting paid for the books she and Rocky were going to take to Mr. W. She went into the kitchen to check if Granma was up. Usually Granma was first up and made coffee.

Granma wasn't up; it wasn't six o'clock yet. Suzy spotted a bristle that had fallen off Granma's broom on the floor by the trash can. She picked up the bristle and sneaked down the hall to Rocky's room. The door was open just wide enough for her to squeeze through. He was still asleep.

I felt a tickle in my ear and reached up to rub it. I was barely awake, I didn't even open my eyes. It might have been an insect. I turned my head the other way and sighed. I was so comfortable in that soft bed and the light from the outside wasn't very bright. It was too early to get up. I felt the tickle again. It must be a bug trying to get in my ear. I opened my eyes and almost jumped out of bed. Suzy screamed—and then started laughing.

"What are you doing? Why are you in here?"

She answered, "I wanted to do something—you called me a piece of hamburger with catsup. You shouldn't tease me."

"All right. I'm sorry, but don't go sticking things in my ears, okay? You might poke my eardrum and make me deaf." I looked at the alarm clock on the night stand next to my bed. It was six a.m. "You'd better get dressed, Granma will be getting up to make us breakfast. We have to get ready to see Mr. Waicukauski and get our money for the books."

"Hey! What's the yelling about? You kids had better get along or your mom will be disappointed. She told me you wouldn't be any trouble. Did you make her a promise?"

I answered, "Yes, Granma. Were all right now. I said I was sorry for teasing."

"Okay. Please get dressed so you can have breakfast. Don't you have to take some books to the lighthouse?"

"Yes, Granma. We're coming."

Suzy and I got dressed in less than a minute—maybe two, and hurried into the kitchen. Suzy was out of breath, but she smelled the eggs and said, "One egg, please; scrambled, no pepper." She got into a chair and smiled at me. "See, I can order at a restaurant."

Granma served us eggs and put a couple of pieces of bread in the toaster. I poured us some milk and the telephone rang. Granma had just taken the orange juice out of the refrigerator. She put the OJ pitcher on the counter and picked up the phone.

"Makler residence." Granma listened for a minute, and then said, "Thank you, officer."

I heard Granma say officer so I asked, "Was that Lieutenant Nesbitt?"

"No, Rocky. That was Crafton Police Sergeant Weems. He said they arrested the driver of the truck that hit the man the other day. Mr. Wills, the driver, didn't stop because he had some illegal bottles of whiskey in his truck. He was afraid if he stopped, the police would search his truck and find the stolen bottles of alcohol. He should have stopped, the penalty wouldn't have been as great as a hit-and-run offense."

I said, "So those were two mistakes. Will he go to jail?"

Granma answered, "Probably. Stealing and running away from an accident are never good."

Suzy was chewing on a piece of toast when she said, "Granma, I'm running out of socks and underwear."

"Me, too. I have one more set of underpants and socks."

"Okay. Before you leave for the lighthouse, bring me all your dirty clothes. I'll wash them while you're gone. They'll smell good after drying outside on the clothesline. Make sure you're back for lunch, okay?"

"Okay, Granma. What's for lunch?"

"It's a surprise. You'll see when you get back."

Suzy said, "Can you give me a hint?"

"I'll give you one hint, it is yellowish-orange. Now, off you go, and be very careful. Take the wagon to transport the books."

I said, "Okay, see you for lunch."

Suzy wanted me to pull her all the way to the lighthouse, but I told her I would only pull her back home. That way the books wouldn't be in the wagon, just Suzy. I thought that was pretty good thinking. As we pulled the wagon toward the lighthouse, Suzy kept asking me what we might have for lunch that was yellowish-orange. All I could think of was Velveeta cheese, but that wouldn't make a lunch. It had to be something else. All Suzy could think of was orange juice.

I grinned and said, "I don't think we'll have an orange-juice sandwich, Suzy."

Suzy laughed, "I wouldn't eat that; it would be all squishy."

The rest of the way to the lighthouse, we made up things we would never eat for lunch, like worm or butterfly sandwiches, stuff like that. Suzy made up a sandwich of ants and grass with dandelions. As we got closer to the lighthouse, we saw Mr. Waicukauski going in the front door of his house. I think he saw us coming, but he didn't wave. Suzy waved but looked disappointed when she didn't get a wave back. Mr. Waicukauski must have been thinking about something. Maybe he was going to get more quarters to pay us.

We climbed the three steps to the porch and I knocked twice on the screen door. Suzy put her nose on the screen and squinted to see inside. I pulled her back and said, "Help me get the books from the wagon." I put three books next to the screen door and Suzy made two trips to get the other, thicker books. We sat on the steps and waited.

Suzy commented, "I see a yellow rock, want me to get it for you?"

I looked in the direction she was, but I didn't see any yellow rock. "Okay."

She stood up and walked about four steps, squatted down, and picked up a small pebble. She brought it back to me and dropped it in my hand. It wasn't a rock. It was a piece of lemon-drop candy, just like the candy that big fisherman bought at Sherner's. Maybe he had come to the lighthouse to borrow some non-fishing books from Mr. W. I remembered he had asked Granma if we had a library. I stuck the candy in my pocket, to show Granma. I wasn't going to eat it; it had been on the ground, and the fisherman had probably touched it with his dirty fingers.

We heard Mr. W call out from inside his house, "Just a minute, I'm on the phone. I'll be right there."

We waited about two minutes before Mr. W came to the door and said, "Hi, kids. Have you got some more books for me?"

Suzy said, "Five, Mr. W. That's one dollar and twenty-five cents, please."

"Boy, you are becoming quite a business lady, aren't you?"

Suzy nodded, smiled, and replied, "Uh-huh."

Mr. W stepped onto the porch and picked up the books. He read the titles and said, "These are good ones, thank-you. I'll get your money."

He took the books into his house and came back with a paper dollar and a quarter.

I reached for the money, but Suzy said, "I'll take it," and stuck out her hand, palm up.

I said, "Okay, but don't lose it. Put it in a safe place."

She stuck the money in her dress pocket, closed the flap, and buttoned it. She patted her pocket and said, "There, it's safe." She smiled, proud of making the money safe. "Well, let's go, Rocky. You have to pull me in the wagon. Bye, Mr. W. We'll be back with some more books—maybe tomorrow."

I said, "Thanks, Mr. Waicukauski. Bye."

"Goodbye, kids."

Suzy got in the wagon and looked around at the ground. I think she was looking for more candy. I picked up the handle, said, "Hold on tight," and started pulling, remembering how hard it was to pull the wagon over the dirt and stones until we got to the road.

When we got to Granma's, Suzy ran into the house to show Granma the money, but when Suzy called for Granma, we heard, "Suzy, where did you get this paper?" I didn't know what Granma was talking about, but Suzy did. I could tell Suzy thought she was in trouble.

Suzy said, "What paper?" She looked at me and I just shrugged my shoulders.

I asked, "What paper, Granma?"

Suzy and I walked toward Granma's voice. It sounded like she was in the kitchen. She was doing dishes. Granma wadded up the dish rag, put it on the edge of the sink, dried her hands on her apron, and reached in the pocket of her shirt. She unfolded a sheet of white paper and held it up.

I got closer so I could see it, and said, "What does it say?" It wasn't in English; it looked like it was written with the letters like the ones on the front of the book I gave to Mr. Waicukauski, the one the man had asked me to give to Elena.

"Well, Suzy, where did you get the paper?" Granma's voice was serious.

Suzy was almost ready to cry. Her hands hung down at her sides. She answered, "I-I found it."

Granma suddenly realized that Suzy thought she was in trouble, so she said, "It's all right, Suzy, you're not in trouble. I just want to know where you got the paper."

"When the man got hurt, I found it in the field on the way to the house. I put it in my pocket. I wanted to save it to read when I got older, maybe second grade."

"I'd like to show it to Lieutenant Nesbitt. Would that be all right with you?"

"Uh-huh. Maybe he can read it to me. Some of the letters are funny—not like A-B-C."

"We'll see. How would you like to have some lunch?"

Suzy nodded and said, "Is it really yellow?"

Granma smiled and said, "Yes. It's macaroni and cheese. And— you can put catsup on it if you like, Rocky."

Chapter 6

Elena

Right after eating lunch Suzy and I lay down to take a nap. I didn't think I could go to sleep. The sun was out and it didn't feel like a time to nap, besides, I was getting too old to bother with naps. I think Granma just wanted Suzy to nap and she wouldn't want to if I didn't. The bedroom door wasn't completely shut and I heard Granma using the telephone.

"Operator, I'd like Boston, Keystone 369. Thank you, I'll wait."

I didn't hear Granma's voice for a minute and then she said, "This is Marty at Lighthouse 998. Yes sir, I can deliver the article this afternoon, about four o'clock. Thank you, goodbye."

It was quiet again and then I heard, "Operator, Harbor 92, please." I didn't hear anything else. I woke up at 2:06 and looked around. The room was getting dark. I swung my legs off the bed and took a look out the window. The sky was getting gray and there were black clouds over the water. Granma's Desoto was parked in the driveway. She must want to use it this afternoon; she usually puts it in the garage, unless she has to go somewhere. I went into the bathroom, got a drink of water, and walked into the living room. I was surprised to see Elena, the girl from Mr. Sherners store: the one that had ridden past us on the road. She was sitting in Granma's big green chair reading a book.

She looked up and smiled. "Hi, Rocky. Your grandmother had to go to Boston. She asked me to stay with you and Suzy until she gets back. She said she should be back by eight o'clock tonight. Do you and Suzy have anything planned for this afternoon?"

I sat down on the sofa and looked at my socks. "No, ma'am."

"You can call me Elena, Rocky. I could be your older sister."

I thought to myself, *Yeah, a lot older*. I was a little irritated that Granma left without saying anything to us. Then I remembered what she had said on the phone about delivering an article. I wondered what the article was.

Suzy walked into the living room, rubbing her eyes, and said, "Where's Granma?"

I looked at Suzy and answered, "She went to Boston."

Suzy frowned and said, "Why'd she go to Boston?"

Elena replied, "She told me she had forgotten about a doctor's appointment and she didn't want to miss it. She would have to reschedule it and it takes months to see the doctor; he's very busy."

I wondered what was wrong with Granma. She must be seeing a special doctor if she had to go to Boston. If she had a cold or something, she could see a doctor in Crafton. It was a two hour trip on the Greyhound bus to Boston. She could have taken her car and gotten there faster.

Elena explained, "Your grandma called me and asked me to meet her at the bus station. She told me to take her car and watch you guys until she got back. When she calls, we'll go get her at the bus station. I have a kite, would you like to go to the beach and fly the kite? I think the wind is good for flying."

Suzy and I both wanted to fly the kite. Dad once took us kite flying, but Suzy was only three and wasn't very interested. We went outside to the car. I noticed the wind was blowing stronger than in the morning. We got in the front seat, but Elena ran back in the house and returned with the car keys, holding them up and jingling them. Elena started the car and said, "Off we go!" I watched Elena driving; boy she is pretty; almost like a movie star.

I looked out the windows at the darkening eastern sky and said, "We might get a summer storm tonight, the wind from the ocean is getting stronger."

We drove south for about ten minutes along the shore road to get to a beach where we had enough room to run in the sand to get the kite into the air. Elena parked at the top of the cliffs that sheltered the beach from the cool wind coming on shore. We took a sandy trail down to the cove where Elena and I assembled the box kite. While we put the kite together, Suzy walked the beach looking for shells. We could barely see the lighthouse in the distance, just the top half. The beacon light would come on before too long, the sky was getting darker.

I said, "Let's hurry, we won't have much time to fly the kite before it gets hard to see."

Elena laughed and said, "Don't worry, we have at least an hour before the clouds get on shore. I'll hold the kite and you run along the beach letting the string out. As soon as the wind catches it, hang on tightly. The wind might pull the string out of your hands."

Suzy was watching us and when the kite rose above the cliffs, Suzy yelled, "You did it, Rocky. The kite is flying! It's beautiful!"

When I felt the kite pulling at the string, I got goose-bumps. I had forgotten what it was like when Dad and I flew a kite before. It was exciting to see the kite drifting back and forth in the wind.

Elena smiled and looked at Suzy, "Do you want to send a message?"

"Send a message? Who to?"

"We'll write on a piece of paper and put it on the kite string. The wind will take it up to the kite. If there's anyone looking at messages on kites, they'll see what is written."

Suzy was grinning and thinking about who a message should go to. "Okay! I know who to send a message to. I want to send my Daddy a message. He's in Heaven. I think he will see the message on the kite. It will be high up."

Elena took a circular piece of paper from her pocket. She had prepared several when she got the kite. She had cut a small hole in the center and cut the paper from the edge to the hole so it would fit over the string. "What do you want to say, Suzy?"

Suzy thought a moment and then stated, "I love you, Daddy."

Elena found a flat rock and placed the paper so she could write the message with a small pencil from her pocket. She printed the message and showed it to Suzy, pointing out the words.

"Okay, Suzy, let's take it to Rocky so we can send it on its way."

I was watching the kite, pulling at my arms, trying to get away from me and the ground. Suzy ran up and said, "I'm going to send a message to Daddy. Elena helped write it." She held the piece of paper so I could see the printing.

I saw the cut in the paper and said, "It'll blow off the string, Suz. It won't make it to the kite." Suzy s face turned from happy to sad for a moment—until Elena joined us.

"I have some tape. I got it from your grandmothers desk." She showed us a roll of Scotch tape and pulled off a small piece. "Okay, Suzy, put the message on the string and we'll tape the cut in the paper so it won't come off."

"Oh, what a good idea!" Suzy's excitement returned and she awkwardly slipped the paper over the string so the string was in the hole. Elena taped the paper and they stepped back as I fought to hang onto the kite string. The wind had gusted as if it knew to carry the message along the string. The paper began sliding up the string toward the kite, slowly at first, but it moved faster as it got closer and closer to the kite, dancing in the gusty wind.

"My arms are getting tired, Elena." It seemed like my hands had been holding the piece of wood with the string wrapped around it for a long time. "Can you take the string for a while?"

"Sure, Rocky." Elena stepped behind me and reached around my chest and grabbed the stick holding the string. I squatted down and let go of the stick when I thought Elena had it, but she only had one hand on it and she lost hold. The stick dropped to the ground and the last of the string unrolled from the stick. Elena tried to grab the stick, but it moved too fast and the kite went higher and higher, carrying the stick into the air. The kite was gone! We watched as the kite rose higher, becoming smaller and smaller.

"Can we get it back?" Suzy asked.

I could see the disappointment in her face. I think she wanted to send more messages, to Granma and Mom, maybe Granpa, too. I was trying to see where the kite had gone, but it was completely out of sight. "I don't think so, Suzy. The wind will blow it away so we can't find it. Did the kite and string cost a lot, Elena."

"No. Don't worry about it. I can always get another one. Just remember, we sent a message with this one, so all is not lost. We did a good thing and we had fun. You should be happy. If we do this again, we'll have to have a better way to hold the string—so the kite can't get away. Maybe we should tie the string to your belt." She grinned, "I don't think the kite could carry you away."

"Nope, I'm too heavy." I was watching the clouds coming in from the ocean; some were overhead, moving west, and the sunlight was getting dimmer.

Elena said, "We'd better go back home. We don't want to be out in a storm. What do you two want for dinner? Any ideas?"

I thought for a moment as we began walking up the sandy pathway to the car. All I could think of was macaroni and cheese, and pancakes.

Suzy said, "Hotdogs!"

Elena laughed and said, "Okay, but you have to eat some vegetables; lettuce and carrots, maybe some tomatoes, too. We'll see what your Grandma has, and if we need to, we'll go to the grocery store. Does that sound all right, Rocky?"

"Uh-huh, but I don't like mustard, just catsup." I was convinced that mustard ruined a hot dog, but catsup made it taste better. I would rather eat a hotdog without anything on it than to use mustard. It made a dry hotdog taste even drier, but Suzy liked mayonnaise and mustard. I don't know how that ever happened. "How old are you, Elena?"

Elena was watching the road very closely and didn't answer my question right away. We were about halfway back home when I noticed a boat moving toward the dock area. I couldn't read the name, but it sure looked like the Elena. It had the right colors and was about the right size. As we got closer to Crafton, I noticed something else, the top of the lighthouse had been painted red. I wondered if Mr. Waicukauski had painted it, or if he had someone do it for him.

"I'm twenty-one, Rocky. Why do you ask?" Elena glanced at me and smiled.

"When I'm twenty-one, you would be thirty-two. Would you marry me then?"

I expected Elena to laugh, but she didn't. I thought I saw the beginnings of a grin, but then she said, "I would certainly think about it, if I'm not already married to someone else."

Chapter 7

Granma Gets Back

Just as we pulled up at Granma's house, it began to rain, just a sprinkle, but Elena said to hurry. We left the car in the driveway and rushed into the house. Suzy ran into the bathroom to dry off her face, but I just pulled up my T-shirt and wiped my forehead and nose. Elena wiped a few raindrops from her face with her hand, went into the kitchen, and switched on the overhead light.

Elena said, "Rocky, would you please turn on a light in the living room?"

I was going to do that anyway; it was getting darker outside, almost as if it was 9:00 p.m. "Okay." I turned on the floor lamp beside Granma's chair, and Suzy turned on the television. Granma only let us watch TV after dinner, unless it was something special, but Elena didn't know that. The evening news from Boston was on. The weatherman was talking about the storm. It was supposed to get to Boston in two hours. I remember Granma saying Crafton almost always got a storm before Boston did. I hoped Granma was going to make it home during the storm. The telephone rang, two quick rings, a pause, and then two more quick rings.

Elena answered, "Hello, Makler residence." Elena listened for a while and said, "Mrs. Linfield, I'll let you talk to Rocky."

When I heard what Elena said, I walked over to the phone, and Elena handed it to me. "Oh! Hi, mom. I thought it was Granma calling about getting back late—because of the storm." I listened for a minute and said, "Okay. Granma will stay with you tonight and come back home tomorrow. I'll tell Suzy. All right, just a minute." Mom asked to talk to Suzy. "Suzy! It's Mom, she wants to talk to you."

Suzy ran to me smiling, reaching for the phone. I gave Suzy the phone and stood beside her, in case she didn't understand what Mom was saying. I bent down and listened to mom. Suzy surprised me; she answered Mom's questions and started telling her about the kite, the books, and the lighthouse. When Suzy talked, her eyes moved all over, like mine did when I was trying to do a problem in arithmetic. I guess that is part of the thinking process. When Suzy ran out of breath, and things to say, she gave the phone back to me and went back to the TV.

Mom told me to listen to Elena; do what she said.

"Mom, is Granma all right? What did the doctor say?"

Mom surprised me when she said, "Granma didn't go to that type of doctor; she went to a doctor of mathematics to help her with a problem."

I asked, "Was it about her taxes?"

There was a pause and then Mom replied, "I think so, but everything is all right. They were able to figure it out. I'd better hang up now, Rocky. I love you. Goodbye."

I said, "I love you, too, mom. Bye." I hung up the phone and watched Elena put the hotdogs in the oven. "Elena, Granma puts the wieners in water and boils them on top of the stove."

"I thought we'd use the broiler and give them a good tan—makes them a little crispy. Should we try it?" Elena had put her hair down; it went to her shoulders. I think she wanted to get it dry. She was really pretty that way. The bun made her look older though.

"Okay. Do we put any sun-tan lotion on them?" I laughed and looked into the oven. I could see the top elements glowing red.

"No sun-tan lotion, but we'll have relish, mustard, mayonnaise, and your favorite, catsup, after we get them tanned." Elena placed six wieners on some metal foil and stuck them in the oven near the top. "Come on, Suzy, wash your hands. We're almost ready."

I watched Elena at the stove, watching the wieners starting to sizzle. She seemed to be having fun making the hotdogs. I hope she waits for me until I'm twenty-one. But if she happens to fall in love with someone else before then, I think it would be all right, as long as she's happy. I will probably find another girl, but I'm sure I'll miss Elena.

After dinner, we watched TV for about an hour. Suzy fell asleep on the sofa and I was sitting on the floor, almost ready to fall asleep. I was looking at the picture tube, but I couldn't understand what was being said, but I remember the little Alka-Seltzer man commercial.

Elena said, "Time for bed. You guys are tired after all that activity on the beach. Get into your PJs." Elena picked Suzy up and carried her into the bedroom, helped her undress, and put her in bed. I got into bed in my undies after quickly brushing my teeth. I could hear the rain hitting the bedroom window. The next thing I heard was a man's gravelly voice coming from the living room.

"Where's the note?"

Elena said, "What note are you talking about? I don't have any note."

"There was a note in the book you delivered on the road to the lighthouse."

"I didn't see any note. I gave the man a book and peddled back to Sherner's on the cove road. I didn't look in the book, Mr. Sherner said to deliver it. That's what I did."

I got out of bed and tip-toed into the kitchen where I could see the man and Elena. He was a little taller than Elena. The man was dressed in black pants, a brown sweater, and had a gray knit cap on his head. He needed a shave. His raincoat was all wet. Water was dripping on the hardwood floor. Granma wasn't going to like that. The man turned and I saw he had a gun pointing at Elena, who was standing in front of the TV. The man had his back to me. I looked around for a knife but I saw the big barbeque fork next to the sink. Elena had used it to turn the wieners in the oven. I picked up the fork and sneaked over to the doorway to the living room. Elena saw me, but the man didn't know I was there.

The man said, "Maybe the kid knows about the note. Get him up."

"Okay, let me turn off the TV." When she moved toward the TV, she limped, reached down to massage her calf and said, "I have a cramp in my leg."

I figured Elena was trying to make some noise so he wouldn't hear me. She wanted me to stab the guy in the leg. I snuck up behind him and jammed the fork into the back of the man's leg and twisted it. He yelled and that's when Elena attacked. She Judo chopped him in the neck and kneed him in the crotch. He fell to the floor, dropping his gun. Elena moved like a cat, picked up the gun, and when he tried to grab her, she shot him, twice.

"Go in the bedroom with your sister, Rocky. Don't let her see the blood."

All I could say is, "Okay," and followed her orders. I went in Suzy's bedroom and closed the door.

Suzy sat up in bed, rubbed her eyes, yawned, and said, "What's all the noise, Rocky?" I told her what happened. Then, I was thinking about Elena. *I don't think she is a regular babysitter. Maybe she's a secret agent after all, but she said she was a college student. Did she lie to me? Maybe that's her cover.* I could hear her talking on the phone and after about ten minutes a car arrived. It was still raining, but the wind had let up a bit. The rain wasn't hitting the window any more. Suzy had gone back to sleep, but I sat near the door so I could hear what was going on.

I heard Elena's voice and the voices of two different men. One of the men called her Agent Hill. So she is an agent. I wondered if she's from the FBI, or the Navy. Maybe she worked with Lt. Nesbitt. I opened the door just a crack so I could hear more clearly.

One of the men said, "I'll get a body bag. This guy just croaked. Too bad you weren't able to avoid killing him, but you had to react quickly to protect the kids. Good job, agent. We should give the kid a medal. He might have saved your bacon, too."

"Thanks. Rocky reacted perfectly on cue. He seemed to have read my mind. Take all the pictures you need, and I'll clean up the floor after you're out of here. Mrs. Makler will be back from Boston in the morning. I don't want her to think the kids were in any danger."

"You got it."

I listened as there was some movement in the living room. I think the two men were removing the body. I heard one of the men say goodnight, and then I heard the click of the door lock. It was quiet again, so I went out to see Elena. She was sitting on the sofa, leaning back against a pillow, with her feet up on the coffee table. Her right hand was on her forehead. Her eyes were closed. She was holding a wet rag with blood stains on it.

I was in the kitchen doorway where I had moved to stab the guy in the leg. I said, "Are you all right, Elena?"

"Oh! Hi, Rocky. I'm just fine. I thought you might have fallen asleep. Are you and Suzy okay?"

"Uh-huh. She's asleep, but I couldn't go back to sleep after what happened. You sure took care of that guy. Who was he?"

"I don't know. Those two men that just left will figure that out. I want to thank you for sticking him in the leg. You did just what I had hoped. Thank you very much."

"You're welcome. I figured you wanted me to stick him when you moved toward the TV. He was watching you. We did a good job, didn't we?"

Elena smiled, "We sure did. I have to tell you something, Rocky. I'm sorry I lied to you before. I work for the FBI, and I'm not twenty-one, I'm twenty-seven. My cover story is that I am a college girl on a summer job, but that isn't true. I graduated from college six years ago."

I couldn't think of what to say, so I said, "I look like I'm eleven or twelve, but I'm really ten. I'm taller than most kids my age."

Elena grinned. "What you did tonight was very courageous; more like something a twenty-year-old would have done. I'm glad you helped me. If you hadn't stabbed him, I don't know what he would have done to us. I had to get his gun." She looked at me for a moment, and then said, "I think you'd better go to bed now. Good night."

I started walking toward my bedroom, but paused, "I'm sure glad you were here. I don't think Granma would have known what to do. Good night, Elena."

When we got up in the morning, Suzy said she had a scary dream. She told me about it and I said, "That would have scared me, too." I decided not to tell her it wasn't a dream. I told Elena that Suzy thought the fight had been a dream, so we said nothing more about it. Elena would explain it all to Granma.

Later In the morning, we picked up Granma at the bus station at nine o'clock. Granma took over driving her Desoto, and we took Elena to Sherner's. She said she would talk to Granma on the phone at noon. Granma drove us home and we told her about our kite flying trip. Suzy told Granma how the kite was lost in the wind, and about the shells she found on the beach.

"Granma, what did you talk to the doctor about?" I was curious because Mom had said the doctor Granma had gone to see was a doctor of mathematics, not a medical doctor.

Granma said, "The note Suzy found was written in code, Rocky. Dr. Newton is an expert in the study of codes."

I asked, "Is he related to Isaac Newton?" I knew that Isaac Newton was a famous mathematician that figured out the Law of Gravity and something called calculus.

"Maybe, but I don't really know. He figured out the message Suzy found was written in a code, but he is still working on it. When he figures it out, he will tell the authorities."

"Granma, did you know Elena works for the FBI?" I thought I would be telling Granma something she didn't know, but she wasn't surprised.

"Yes, Rocky. That's the reason I had her stay with you while I was in Boston. Lt. Nesbitt told me about her a few days ago when he came here to talk to you about the accident."

I remembered the lieutenant saying he knew a woman that was a secret agent; it must have been Elena, but I thought she was too pretty to be one. I guess secret agents can look like anyone, good looking or not, a woman or a man.

"Oh—Rocky, your mom is coming to visit the third week of August. She has a week off from work. We'll take a trip in my Desoto, maybe visit New Hampshire, or northern Maine. She and I want us to go camping. Maybe we can ask Elena to come, too. That would be a car full. There are some maps in the car. We can look at them and pick a place to go."

Granma sounded kind of excited about taking a trip. I wonder if there is a reason she wants us to be out of Crafton. Mom has never liked camping. Once, when Suzy was little, Dad drove us to Canada, but Suzy's dirty diapers stunk up the car. But now that Suzy is older, it might be fun to go on an adventure. "That sounds like fun, Granma. Suzy would like it, too. I bet she could add to her rock collection."

Chapter 8

Another Shooting

Granma had seen a notice in the newspaper about a garage sale a couple of days ago. It was almost ten o'clock; she was looking through the newspaper to find the location. She found the notice, folded the newspaper back, and lay it on the kitchen table. "Rocky, please hand me a pencil. There's one on the coffee table."

I had just gotten comfortable on the sofa. "I see it, just a second." I grabbed the pencil and took it to Granma. She wrote something on a tablet she kept near the telephone on a little round table with three legs. It has a glass top.

"Let's go to a garage sale. We'll see if we can get some more books for you and Suzy."

She put the pencil on the table, stood up, and paused. She looked at what she had written on the paper and said, "Oh, I know where that is. That's Kitty Whitcom's address. I'll bet we can get a few books from her—but she reads mostly fiction. Well, we'll see what she has. I haven't talked with her in some time. Where's Suzy?"

"She's looking for pebbles by the car. She found a nice one when we got home from Sherner's. She likes the almost transparent ones. I think they're called agates."

"Okay. You'd better bring fifty cents with you. Kitty might not want to give you the books. She might want a dime apiece."

I got two quarters from my sock drawer in the bedroom. I kept the quarters in a black sock, there was only one, so it was easy to find. I don't know where the other black sock went. Most of my socks were white, but there were a few brown ones. Granma was waiting at the door to lock up. She usually didn't lock the door, but after the shooting, she locked it. Suzy was standing beside the car, holding a couple of small stones, but when she saw us walking toward the car, she dropped them on the ground.

I said, "We're going to a garage sale to see if we can get some more books for the library."

"Oh, good, we need lots more." She walked over to the car and stood there.

I opened the door for her and we both climbed in the front seat. Granma slid into the driver's seat and started the car. "We're going to have to get some more gas soon. Ten gallons will cost S2.90 at the Mobil station. I've got about five dollars in my purse. We'll get gas on the way back from Whitcoms'."

It only took about five minutes to get to Whitcoms' house. It was pretty far from the dock area, up on a hill with some other big houses with white columns and big porches. The white two-story house had gray-brown shingles and some evergreen trees near the front door. At each end of the house a chimney stuck above the roof. The house looked much bigger than Granma's. I wondered if there were any kids. *I guess I'll find out before long.* Granma parked in front of the house and we walked on a long sidewalk and then up six steps to the porch. I looked at the metal door-knocker and then at Granma. She nodded and I whacked the door-knocker. It looked like a fat bulldog—kind of ugly, but it was shiny. Granma said it was made from brass.

Mrs. Whitcom answered the door, a bit surprised to see Granma, or maybe she was surprised to see Suzy and me. "Well, hello, Marty. Are these your grandchildren?"

Granma introduced us and I told her what we were looking for. Mrs. Whitcom disappeared for a few minutes and then reappeared carrying five books. One of the books was thick and fairly heavy, the others were just average size. The big book was an atlas she didn't want anymore; it was free. She wanted ten cents each for two of the others and fifteen cents each for the last two. I told her I had fifty cents and gave her the two quarters I had in my pocket. I figured we would get back a dollar, or double our money when we sold them. If Mr. Waicukauski wanted the atlas, we would get a total of $1.15, more than double our money.

Granma was talking to Mrs. Whitcom about something else when we heard a siren. Granma opened the front door and said, "That sounds like it's coming from the dock area. Kitty; may I borrow your phone?"

"You may." Mrs. Whitcom pointed at the phone.

Granma closed the door, went to the phone, and called Mr. Sherner. She told me later that his nickname is Ike.

"Ike, has something happened on the dock? Did someone get hurt?" Granma sat down in a chair next to the phone and said, "Oh, no! How bad is it?" Granma listened for a bit and then said, "I'm at Whitcoms' with the kids. I'll call you again when we get home. Bye." Granma looked kind of pale and hung up the phone.

Mrs. Whitcom asked, "What happened, Marty?"

"That pretty young lady, Elena—works for Sherner on the dock. She was badly hurt and is being flown to a hospital in Boston. She took care of Rocky and Suzy while I was in Boston yesterday."

"Granma! Will she be all right? How'd Elena get hurt?" I felt like Granma knew more about Elena, but didn't want to say anything that Suzy could hear, so I was satisfied with what Granma said next.

"As soon as we get home, I'll call Ike and find out more. Get your books and get in the car. Did you thank Mrs. Whitcom?" Granma was upset and giving us orders like never before.

Suzy and I both said, "Thank you for the books."

Mrs. Whitcomb replied with a smile and, "You are very welcome."

Suzy picked up the atlas, and I took the other four books to the car. After we put them on the floor behind the front seat, we jumped in the Desoto and Granma drove off, waving to Mrs. Whitcomb.

I couldn't see the speedometer, but Granma was driving pretty fast; I don't think she was speeding. As soon as we got home, Granma was on the phone calling Ike Sherner. As we brought the books in from the car, we could hear engines getting louder and louder and then we saw a two-engine seaplane climbing into the sky from the bay area.

Suzy ran inside and told Granma about the airplane taking off from the water. I had told Suzy it was a seaplane. When I got inside, Granma was hanging up the phone. She looked worried.

"I have something to tell you. Elena was shot—she's being flown to a special hospital in Boston. One of the bullets punctured her right lung and the other one hit her in the head. The emergency doctor in the airplane thinks she will be all right though. The bullet that hit her head glanced off. She'll have a scar, but it will be hidden by her hair. They'll have to operate on her to fix her lung. That airplane was taking Elena to the hospital emergency room."

Suzy was crying and my eyes were beginning to water, but I was so mad I didn't cry much. All I could think was who would do such a thing? I guess it was time to say a prayer. I went outside and asked God to help Elena. If God had made the earth, the sky, the stars, and the animals, I thought God would understand that Elena was on the earth to do good things. She had already made our lives better. God should help Elena get well and punish the bad guys. Before I went back inside, I thought I should ask Granma if we could visit Elena in the hospital. Maybe Granma couldn't afford another trip to Boston so soon, but I had to ask her.

Suzy was in her room on her bed crying. I went in and sat on the edge of the bed.

"Did you ask God to help Elena, Suzy?"

Suzy stopped crying and shook her head, sat up, and wiped her eyes with the pillow slip.

"No," she answered. "I guess I should do that." She thought for a minute and said, "God, please help Elena get better, and stop bad things from happening to her. She's our best friend in the whole world." She paused, looked at me, and then added, "Amen."

I told Suzy, "I think that should help. Let's talk to Granma."

When we went in the living room, Granma was on the phone. She didn't say much, just some yeses, all right, and I'll talk with Lieutenant Nesbitt. After she said goodbye, she hung up and looked at us. She tried to smile and said, "How about some lunch?"

Suzy said, "I'm not very hungry, Granma. I'm worried about Elena."

I said, "Me, too. We asked God to take care of Elena. Do you know if she will be all right? Do you think God will answer our prayers?"

"Maybe He will, I said a prayer for her, too."

Granma made Suzy and I feel safe; we always depended on her when Mom wasn't around. Granma went in the kitchen, opened a cabinet, and looked in the refrigerator. I heard a sigh, and she came back in the living room.

"Let's take the books to the Lighthouse and then we'll come back and have something to eat. Maybe we'll be hungry then. What do you think?"

I looked at Suzy and she nodded. I said, "That's a good idea, Granma," and grinned. I think Granma wanted to get our minds off of Elena for a while. It was working. Suzy and I both wanted to earn some more money. We took the books to Mr. Waicukauski and he gave us a quarter each for all five books, even the atlas. He didn't have one like it, so he paid full price instead of fifteen cents like we expected. So, now our total was $3.25, more than half-way to $5.00. I had thought we needed three dollars, but I raised it to five. Five dollars would buy better birthday presents than three dollars would.

On the way back home, Suzy poked me in the side and said, "Look at me, Rocky."

I had been watching for boats on the water, but I wasn't really looking at anything, not paying any attention, but when Suzy poked me, I blinked, and came out of my trance. I looked at her and said, "Okay, I'm looking."

"We need more than $5.00. Don't you think we should send some flowers to Elena, or maybe a Teddy bear? How much is a Teddy bear?"

I had never heard the price of a Teddy bear, but I had seen some almost as big as Suzy at the state fair. They were prizes for throwing baseballs at milk bottles, so they must cost at least a dollar. I thought we'd better ask Granma. I figured she had heard what Suzy said, so I asked, "How much does a Teddy bear cost, Granma?"

Granma said, "Probably several dollars. They don't give them away. If you're thinking about getting one for Elena, we can call the store on Brindle Avenue and ask them. Theirs would be the lowest price. What about sending flowers instead, or maybe some balloons?"

Suzy said, "Yeah, balloons!"

I said, "But balloons pop or shrink, and flowers wilt and have to be thrown away. A Teddy bear can be taken home from the hospital. I think she'd like a Teddy bear."

Granma said, "We'll check on prices when we get home. Lets not worry about it now."

We were almost home, I could see Granma's house. There was a brown Navy car parked in front in the gravel. Granma pulled into the driveway. I saw a man sitting on the front porch at the top of the steps. It was Lt. Nesbitt. He stood up and walked toward the car as Granma shut off the engine.

As we got out of the car, the lieutenant said, "I came over to tell you about Elena."

Granma was worried, I could see it in her face. We didn't move from beside the car, not knowing what he was going to tell us. I didn't know then that the Navy sends an officer to give bad news.

"Don't worry, I have good news." He smiled. "Elena will be all right, but she has to stay in the hospital for a few days. The doctors have to make sure her chest wound doesn't get infected. Her head wound isn't serious, it was just bloody; Her hair will hide the small scar." Granma sighed, put her hands on Suzy's and my shoulders, and said, "That's a relief. We were all worried."

I was happy, but curious, and asked, "How did you find out about Elena, Lieutenant?"

"They took her to the Navy hospital. I have some friends there. They knew that Elena and I have been dating, so they told me about her condition."

I suddenly realized who the woman was the lieutenant knew was a secret agent; *it was Elena.* I blurted out, "Oh! Elena *is* a secret agent.

"Not really, Rocky; she's a regular agent for the FBI."

"So Elena isn't the woman you know is a secret agent?"

"That's correct."

"But Elena is your girlfriend?"

"That's correct, too. We've been going together for almost two years.

"Are you going to marry her?"

"Boy, Rocky, you are sure full of questions. Elena and I have been so busy, we haven't had much time to get to know each other very well. I'm not sure how she feels about me."

"But you really like her?"

"That's correct."

"Suzy and I were wondering what to get for Elena: a Teddy bear, some flowers, or balloons. Isn't that right, Suzy?"

Suzy had been listening to Granma and me talk to Lt. Nesbitt and she walked over next to me. She looked up at the lieutenant, smiled and said, "Uh-huh. We don't know how much a Teddy bear costs. We have $3.25. Should we buy flowers, balloons, or a just a Teddy bear?"

Lieutenant Nesbitt smiled, his eyes were moving around as he was thinking. "Why don't each of you give me a quarter and I'll do the rest. I'll get some flowers, some balloons, and a Teddy bear. Then, if it's all right with your grandmother, I'll take you to Boston to see Elena. We'll go in a Navy vehicle with a driver. In fact, your grandmother can come with us."

Suzy reacted immediately, "Oh! That would be fun! We could all see Elena, and Mom could come to the hospital, too. Mom could meet Elena, and you, Lt. Nesbitt."

Chapter 9

The Trip to Boston

"If we're going to ride together, I think you should use my first name. You don't need to call me Lieutenant. My name is Aaron," Lieutenant Nesbitt told us as we climbed into the Navy car. The driver's name was Ensign Lucas Thorndike, fairly new to the Navy, and had just recently been assigned to Lt. Nesbitt. I could tell he was in good shape, his arm and neck muscles pulled his shirt tightly. He had crew-cut light-brown hair, and looked like he had just gotten out of high school. He might have been a wrestler, one of his ears was funny looking. He wasn't quite as good looking as Lt. Nesbitt, but he looked strong.

Aaron helped Granma get in the back seat; Suzy and I were the bread. Aaron closed Suzy's door and I pulled mine shut, hard. Granma said not to slam the door after I had already slammed it. I thought that was funny and smiled. Aaron got in front with Ensign Thorndike, and we were on our way downtown. Aaron and Granma went shopping while Suzy and I waited in the car with Ensign Thorndike. We found out his nick-name was Thorny. Suzy laughed when she heard the name. It took about twenty minutes to buy three balloons, a small bunch of flowers, and a Teddy bear. I was keeping time with the bank clock on the corner tower.

Aaron kept the flowers in the front seat, Granma held the bear and Suzy had the balloons. She made the balloons squeak with her fingers. Granma lightly slapped her hands and said, "You can do that at home, but not in the car, please."

I could see Lt. Nesbitt's face in the rear-view mirror. He grinned when Granma scolded Suzy.

We had been travelling for about ten minutes when Thorny said, "We've got a tail, Lieutenant. It's a black sedan two cars back."

I watched Aaron look into the side and rear-view mirrors for about a minute before he said, "There's a small town coming up, pull off and get some gas at the Mobil station. Let's see if they follow us."

I could see a Mobil sign ahead of us on the right, not far off the highway, but a Dairy Queen sign made me lick my lips. It looked like it was across the road from the service station, or maybe next to it, I couldn't tell yet. I turned around and got on my knees to look out the back window at the car following us. Granma grabbed my belt and pulled me down onto the seat and said, "If that car is really following us, I want you and Suzy to get down on the floor behind the front seats. We don't know what the people in that car are up to, but I don't want you kids to be in any danger."

Suzy and I said in unison, "Okay, Granma." Suzy's eyes were big and she was clenching her teeth.

Aaron said, "It looks like they're tailing us, all right."

I said, "Do what Granma said, Suzy." We got down on the floor and waited. Suzy reached under Thorny's seat and pulled out a piece of paper. She looked at it and handed it to me. It was a receipt from Dairy Queen dated June 23, 1951. I stuck it in my pocket.

Granma leaned forward and spoke to the Navy men, "What weapons do you men have?"

Aaron answered, "We both have forty-fives, and there is another one locked in the glove compartment. There are two M-ls in the trunk."

"Unlock the glove compartment and give me the other forty-five." Aaron shook his head and replied, "I don't think so, Mrs. Makler."

"It's all right, Lieutenant, I outshot my husband when he was in the service. I'll bet I can handle a handgun just as well, or better than you."

There was a pause and then I heard the lieutenant insert the key in the glove box. Granma reached over the front seat. She sat back and smiled at me as she checked the gun and stuck it behind the teddy bear where Suzy had been sitting. I was surprised to see how Granma held the gun, it seemed too big for her hands, but she didn't think about it, gripping it like she knew how to use it—-just like she said. She had a determined look on her face. I smiled as I imagined her telling someone to drop their gun or she'd shoot them dead. I sure wouldn't want to mess with Granma if she held a gun pointed at me; she could accidently pull the trigger.

I could feel the car slowing down, and then I heard the tires make a different sound as we left the highway and pulled into the gas station. Ensign Thorndike waited a few seconds before getting out of the car. Aaron opened his door, but sat on the seat, watching out the windows. I raised my head up and saw a black car roll by on the street, but it didn't stop. I saw two men in the front. One man wore a hat. He looked like a gangster the FBI was hunting for robbing banks. I remembered seeing some pictures of wanted men on the post office bulletin board. Thorny pumped some gas and went in to pay for it as Granma and Aaron watched the cars near the gas station. I didn't see any more black ones.

Suzy saw me looking out the window so she stuck her head up, looked out, and saw the Dairy Queen sign. She grabbed Granma's arm and pointed, "Look, Granma, ice cream. Can we get some? I'm hungry."

Granma looked at her watch and nodded to Aaron when he heard what Suzy said. The danger had passed, so he said, "I'll be right back," and headed across the street.

I figured Aaron was going to get some ice cream, but I didn't say anything. Suzy gets too excited sometimes, and after eating, throws up in a car. Mom has cleaned up vomit a couple of times when Suzy was riding in the back seat of our car after eating, but maybe ice cream wouldn't cause any problems. I never get car sick.

Suzy saw Aaron first and started singing, "We're going to have ice cream," over and over until Aaron returned to the car. We all got cones. The soft ice cream was really good. I got one drop on my pants. Granma gave her handkerchief to Thorny and he got it wet in the men's room so Granma could wipe Suzy's face and hands. She rubbed the spot on my pants, even though I told her it was okay. It was only a tiny spot. I thought getting it wet was unnecessary, I had already wiped it off with my finger.

We were back on the road for about ten minutes when Thorny said, "The tail has returned."

Aaron replied, "I see him. Let's not get into a confrontation on the highway, too many people could get hurt. If they pull up beside us with guns drawn, shoot the driver and the tires, whichever presents a clear shot. If they try to force us off the road, Ensign, use evasive tactics to get us out of trouble."

"Yes, Sir."

I could feel the tension in the voices as I listened to the men talking. They had plans to deal with everything I could think of. Part of what they said was in code, and I couldn't figure out what they were saying, but I think it had to do with Granma, Suzy, and me. We continued watching the black car, but it stayed behind us all the way to Boston. The traffic in the city was pretty heavy and we lost our tail. The suspicious black car was gone. Suzy didn't get car sick, neither did I, but I was pretty sure I wouldn't.

The hospital was a gray concrete building four-stories high. It was a whole block long, with American flags and trees lining the walk to the entrance. Thorny parked the car near the entrance by the sidewalk and let us out. We walked up twelve steps to the front door. Suzy counted them aloud as we approached the big doors. Aaron opened one of the doors and we entered the hospital. It smelled clean. He asked a lady in uniform at the information counter where Elena was.

"Elena Harris, Lieutenant?"

"Yes, ma'am," Aaron answered.

"She has restricted visitation. Do you have authority'?"

"Well, no."

"I'm sorry, you will have to get clearance first."

Granma stepped up to the counter and said, "Please contact Admiral Secor. Tell him Marty Makler, her grandchildren, and Lt. Nesbitt would like to visit Miss Harris."

"I can't disturb the Admiral, Mrs. Makler."

"Yes you can. He will talk to me. Tell him Lighthouse 1 needs assistance.

The lady dialed a number and said, "Lighthouse 1." Then she said, "The admiral will speak with you, Mrs. Makler."

I couldn't hear what Granma was saying; she was talking very quietly, with her hand covering her mouth and the phone. Granma gave the phone to the lady at the counter and stepped back with Suzy and me.

The lady at the counter listened for a moment, looked at Granma, and said, "You'll have to wear ID badges if you want to visit Miss

Harris. I will give them to you here. You'll need four badges, numbered consecutively. Please write your names on them and pin them to your clothing in plain sight."

Granma helped Suzy, and the rest of us followed the instructions. The lady checked the badges and said with a smile, "Okay, you are all legal. Miss Harris is on the third floor, room 317. The elevator is right over there." She pointed across the lobby with a pencil to four elevators with green doors. They were labelled A to D. After we were all in the elevator, Aaron pressed 3, and we started up, very slowly. The elevator had the shakes. I think it was getting old.

We walked down a long hallway, finally stopping in front of room 317. There was an armed guard sitting beside the door reading a magazine. He looked up, saw Lt. Nesbitt, jumped to his feet, and saluted. "Sir."

Aaron said, "We're here to see Miss Harris."

"Sir. You will all have to sign in." The guard held out a clipboard with a place for each of us to sign our name, ID number, and time of arrival. We all signed the form. Granma helped Suzy. The guard glanced over the form and said, "You may all enter, but don't stay longer than ten minutes. Miss Harris is partly sedated; she may be a little sluggish trying to carry on a conversation. It's hard for her to speak."

Aaron walked up to the bed and took hold of Elena's right hand. She turned her head slowly and smiled up at the lieutenant, trying to talk. Her lips moved slightly, but no sounds came out of her mouth. Aaron bent down and kissed her on the forehead.

Aaron said, "I brought you some visitors," and motioned for us to come over beside the bed. Suzy gave her the Teddy bear. Elena raised her hand a little bit so she could hold the bear next to her. I tied the balloons to the foot of the bed; they were full of helium. I could see tears in her eyes, and her lips moved when she tried to say thank you. Aaron took some old flowers out of a vase next to the bed and threw them in the trash, then replaced them with the fresh flowers we had brought with us.

Granma held both of Elena's hands and said, "I'm so sorry you got hurt, but you should make a full recovery. We'll celebrate when you get out of the hospital." Elena nodded and closed her eyes. Granma said,

"We'd better go now, kids. Elena is going to sleep for a while. We'll see her when she comes back to Crafton."

We stopped on the way home and had some sandwiches; the ice cream hadn't been much of a lunch. It was very quiet in the car until I could see the red top of the lighthouse. Suzy saw it at the same time I did.

"Rocky, is that the lighthouse?"

"Uh-huh." I glanced out the other windows. When I got on my knees and looked out the rear window, I saw that black car again. "Thorny, is that our tail again?"

Aaron and Thorny both said, "Yes."

Suzy said, "Why is that car following us?"

Aaron answered, "We're going to find out in just a minute. Ensign, there's a wide spot in the road coming up. Pull over and we'll check the occupants. Mrs. Makler, keep that forty-five handy."

"Suzy, you and Rocky get on the floor like you did before." We could tell by the tone of Granma's voice it was an order. Nearly as soon as we hit the floor, Thorny slowed down. We could hear the gravel under the wheels as he left the asphalt roadway. When the car stopped, Aaron and Thorny flung open the car doors. Aaron said, "You take the driver, I'll take the passenger."

I could see Granma holding the gun; she was looking out the back window. I couldn't help but join Granma to watch what Thorny and Aaron were doing. They were pointing their guns at the men in the black car. It had pulled off the road behind us. Granma pushed me back down on the floor; I didn't know she was that strong. I tried to get back up to see what was happening, but she held me down and put her leg on top of me. I was pinned to the floor. It seemed like a long time, but I heard Aaron walking in the gravel saying to Granma, "It's all right, they're on our side—they're FBI."

Granma said, "Kids, you can get up now." Granma took her leg off me and I got back up on the seat. Thorny had put his gun away, was smiling, and talking to the driver of the black car. He shook hands with the driver, came back to our car, got in, and drove the rest of the way to Crafton. The tail was right behind us, but by the time we reached Granma's, the black car had disappeared.

It was getting dark as we arrived back home. Thorny pointed the car lights at the porch so Granma could see to unlock the front door. Aaron walked with us to the door carrying a heavy box. I don't know where it came from, but it had to have been in the trunk of the car. I wondered if it was full of guns and bullets. As the door opened and we got inside, Aaron set the box on the floor and said, "Good night everybody, I'll talk with you tomorrow. Thank you for being so good on the trip." He saluted me as he backed out the door, pulling it shut.

Suzy and I ran to the door, opened it, and Suzy yelled, "Good night, Aaron and Thorny." "I yelled, "Thank you for taking us to see Elena."

We shut the door and Suzy said, "What's in the box, Rocky?"

"I don't know. Granma, what's in the big box?"

Chapter 10

Lighthouse Repairs

Granma was in the kitchen putting on the tea kettle. She replied, "Open the box and take a look. After you look, wash your hands. Dinner will be ready in a few minutes."

Suzy dropped to her knees next to the cardboard box and began to unfold the flaps. She was having trouble; tape was holding it closed. She tried to pull the box away from the wall, but she wasn't strong enough. "Rocky, help me. It's real heavy. I think it's full of rocks."

I grabbed the box by the corner next to the wall and gave a tug. It moved a little bit. Now, I was wondering what was in the box. Before, I thought it was Granma's stuff, so I had ignored it. I pulled off the tape and lifted the flaps. The box popped open. It was full of books, packed clear to the top. No wonder it was so heavy! I bet the box weighed more than Suzy did.

Suzy stuck her head above the box right in front of me so I couldn't see. I gave her a little shove and she said, "Don't push me!"

"Look, you don't have to put your head in the box. Sit beside me and we'll take the books out and look at them. I'll get a pencil and paper so we can write the titles down. Take some of the books out and start a pile on the floor, but not in front of the door. Okay?"

She had already taken out three books and was going for another when I jumped up and got some paper and a pencil from Granma's desk. Now Suzy had six books on the floor, in two piles. Suzy was reacting like it was Christmas, scattering things all over, with no order at all. She was acting like a five-year-old.

Granma came in the living room and said, "I think you two had better eat something; it sounds like you need a nap. It's been a long day."

That's when I said, "Where did all the books come from? How did Aaron get them?"

"Come and eat some dinner. I'll tell you about the box."

I could hardly eat, but Suzy was stuffing things into her mouth before I even picked up my fork. Granma told me to eat a little bit before she would answer any questions. I started on a big meatball with catsup, of course, following that with some carrot sticks, French bread, and a glass of milk. I kept looking at Granma to see if I had eaten enough for her to answer questions, but she wouldn't look at me. I finished off the meatball and put my fork down on my plate.

"Is that enough?" I asked.

Granma looked at our plates and said, "Okay, what's your first question?"

"Where did Aaron get the books?" I quizzed.

"Ensign Thorndike."

"Thorny?" Suzy laughed. She thought Thorny was funny. "What's for dessert, Granma?"

"Strawberry shortcake."

Suzy said, "Yummy. How did Thorny get the books?" She laughed when she said Thorny.

"While we were in the hospital seeing Elena, Ensign Thorndike went to his Aunt Ester's house. She used to work at the Harvard bookstore and bought books at low prices for many years. Thorny said she had a garage full and she wanted to get rid of some of them."

I asked, "What is Aunt Ester's last name?"

"Biddle."

Suzy started laughing again, until her face was turning red. She finally stopped, but when she started to talk, she started laughing again. She had a case of the giggles.

Granma looked at her and said, "What is wrong with you? What is so funny?"

Suzy pinched herself on the arm and said, "Did Ester Biddle play the fiddle?" She started laughing again, and so did I, and then Granma started laughing.

I said, "I'll bet she played the tuba."

Suzy quit laughing, frowned, and said, "That's not even funny."

Granma started laughing again, got up, and went in the kitchen. I saw her smiling, wiping her eyes with a napkin.

Suzy and I went back to the books and emptied the box. We had four piles, each about ten books high. What surprised me was the titles of the books. Granma must have told Thorny about the letters we wanted for Mr. Waicukauski. Each book with those titles would earn us twenty-five cents, and there was no duplication. Suzy and I will have to thank Thorny next time we see him. I hope Mr. W has ten dollars to pay for all the books. Now I'm afraid he won't want any more; they're gunna cost him lots of money.

I started writing down the book titles and after a couple of minutes, Granma called us, "Strawberry shortcake is served. Come and get it." Suzy beat me to the table. She already had whipped cream on her chin when I was taking my first bite. I sure hope she doesn't throw up.

The books were in the piles as we had left them the night before. Granma had left them in front of the door. She hadn't expected anyone to come calling. I was the first one up and still in my pajamas when Granma got up and was making coffee. Suzy came into the living room and said, "Lots of books."

I said, "Good morning," but she just turned around and went back to her room. I don't think she was wide awake yet.

I was eating Wheaties with slices of bananas on top when I heard Suzy say, "Granma, I feel sick." Granma started toward Suzy's room, but suddenly stopped. I could hear Suzy's bare feet as she ran to the bathroom.

Granma said, "Oh, dear," and followed Suzy. The door closed, but I could hear Suzy throwing up. The bananas and Wheaties didn't taste so good anymore. I got up, drank the rest of my milk and took the dishes to the kitchen sink. I didn't finish the Wheaties; they were getting too soggy. I guess Suzy wasn't going to the lighthouse with me today. I decided to take only half the books to Mr. W. Suzy could go with me when she felt better, probably tomorrow.

About halfway to the lighthouse, I was joined by a boy on a girl's bike. I didn't say anything about the bike, but he was riding with a wobble. I realized he was having a hard time going so slow, matching my walking speed, so I suggested he ride in small circles so we could talk.

He said, "I'm Jerry. What's your name?"

Jerry was about my size, but sported long, almost black, hair. He wore a yellow T-shirt with the letters CGH on it, and khakis. His belt had a big silver buckle of a gorilla on it. I decided not to tease him about riding a girl's bike. I didn't have any friends in Crafton.

"I'm Rocky. Where're you goin'?"

"I want to see the lighthouse close up. You?"

"Same here. I'm taking these books to Mr. Waicukauski."

"Mr. who?"

"He runs the lighthouse and the library. He pays me a quarter for each of these books. My sister usually goes with me, but she got sick this morning."

"Mind if I go with you?"

"Nope. We can talk; it'll take my mind off pulling the wagon."

"I'm new in town, been here three weeks—from London."

"London, England?"

"Nope. London, Ontario, Canada. Lived there about two years."

"I live in Boston with my mom and sister. We're here for two weeks; not my mom, just me and my sister." I stopped pulling and switched hands on the handle. I didn't want any blisters.

"I'll help with the wagon, if you don't mind riding a girl's bike."

"Uh, okay. Let's trade places." I was glad to drop the wagon handle. I shook out my arm and grabbed the handlebars of the bike. Jerry was almost my height—about an inch shorter, but I could tell he had more muscles than I did. His shoulders were wider, and he wasn't as skinny as me. He didn't have any trouble pulling the fully-loaded wagon. His bike was a little hard to steer, the handlebars were kinda loose. No wonder he wobbled some as he rode—the same thing happened to me.

Jerry told me he moved to Canada when he was nine. When Jerry was three, his father was killed fighting Germans in WWII. His mother, Natalya, worked at the Crafton hospital in the laboratory. Their last name used to be Tukynov, but when his mom remarried, two years ago in England, his name became Morgan. His first name was changed from Yuri to Jerry when he came to the US, two months ago. His mom thought it would be better to have an American name; there were some suspicions of Russians. I would have been suspicious of Germans, not Russians, but what did I know? I had just started reading the newspaper, but I had read the comics since the first grade.

I pointed at his chest and asked, "What are those letters on your shirt for?"

"Crafton General Hospital—that's where my mom works. Where does your mom work?"

"In Boston at the parachute factory. I'm living with my granma for a couple of weeks. My mom will come and get us in August. We're going on a trip." I told Jerry about Dad. That was something we had in common; both of our dads had died in war. I wasn't sure about my dad, he could still be alive. We didn't know.

When we got to the lighthouse, we found Mr. Waicukauski inside, sitting at the desk next to the door. He had on glasses and was reading a book. He looked at us and said, "Hello, boys. Where's your sister, Rocky?"

"Suzy's at home, sick. She threw up this morning. This is my new friend, Jerry Morgan. We just met."

"Welcome to the library, Mr. Morgan." They shook hands and Mr. W said, "Take a look around, but don't go up top on the gallery; Some workers are installing some new equipment; you might get in their way."

Jerry said, "Glad to meet you, Sir."

"Come on, Jerry. I'll show you some of the books Mr. W has. They're all non-fiction. Oh, Mr. W, I have a wagon full of books outside. You can pay me when we come back down from looking around. Okay?"

"Sounds good. You boys hang on to the railing up there. We don't need any accidents."

Jerry was already passing by the letter G books when I started up the metal steps or shelves. As he approached the top of the lighthouse, I could see him slowing down. I think he looked down and decided to hang on to the railing tighter than he had when he was closer to the ground. I caught up to him as he passed the letter Z.

"Jerry, give me a chance to get my breath. I almost had to run to catch up to you."

"I want to look out the opening up there." Jerry pointed to the gallery access door, which was open.

"Okay, but don't go through the opening. Remember, Mr. W. said not to go out on the gallery."

"Yeah, I remember."

I watched Jerry climb up the steps to the opening, and then he suddenly crouched down and put his right index finger to his lips. He didn't want me to talk to him. He listened for nearly a minute before slowly sneaking down to where I was, five steps below him.

"Let's get out of here, Rocky," he whispered, and started pushing me to go down to ground level.

"Don't push me!" I whispered, "I might trip. What did you hear?" I was moving as fast as I could, without stumbling.

Jerry said, "I'll tell you when we get down. It's kind of scary."

We were both breathing hard when we hit the concrete floor of the lighthouse. Mr. W. looked up from the books on his desk—the ones he had removed from my wagon.

"Next time, boys, when you go up there, I don't want you to come down so fast. Okay?"

I said, "Sorry, Mr. Waicukauski, we won't do that again. I guess it is kind of dangerous."

"You got that right. It looks like I owe you $3.00. You brought me some good books." He took out his wallet, counted out three dollars, in ones, and handed them to me.

"I'll have some more tomorrow. Will you have enough money to pay us?" I grinned and he grinned back.

"Yes, as long as you don't go over $20.00; that's my limit for a whole week."

"Don't worry, Mr. W., we don't have that many books. Thanks for the money."

Jerry was pulling on my shirt to get me to follow him outside. "Geez, Jerry, don't pull on my shirt."

He whispered, "Come outside! I have to tell you something." He let go of my shirt and I followed him out to the wagon. He picked up his bike, I grabbed the wagon handle and we started back toward the road. Pulling the wagon was easy now; it was empty.

"What do you want to tell me?" Jerry was so insistent a couple of minutes ago, but now he wasn't saying anything. *What was he thinking?*

Jerry stopped riding and stood next to me at the side of the road. He said, "There were two men on the gallery. One of the men said he shot a woman on the dock—twice, but she didn't die. He will shoot her again if she ever comes back. When his cousin went searching for a note about a submarine, the woman killed him. They don't know I speak Russian. Those guys were talking in Russian, and I don't want them to come after me or my family. I didn't want anybody to hear me tell you what I heard. I don't know if Mr. Waicukauski can be trusted."

"Geez, Jerry, we have to tell Lt. Nesbitt about this; his girlfriend, Elena, is the one that got shot. I was there when she shot that guy's cousin. I stuck him in the leg with a Bar-B-Que fork and Elena, our baby-sitter, shot him dead. Lt. Nesbitt's mom lives next door to my granma. Granma will call Lt. Nesbitt. You'd better come home with me. Could you see the men on the gallery that were talking?"

"Nope, and I'm sure they didn't see me. I was thinking we could wait for them to come down. We could follow them and see where they go. If I hear their voices, I can tell which one shot the woman."

"I don't think we can follow them, but I think that brown truck must be theirs. We can't follow them with a bike and a wagon." I laughed, thinking of what it would look like—two boys, one with a girl's bike, and one pulling a wagon, following an old, brown, pickup truck.

Jerry laughed, too. I think he had the same mental picture. "Okay, let's go talk to your grandma."

Chapter 11

At the Dock

Jerry and I got to Granma's in about eight minutes. I had to run to keep up with Jerry, but he didn't have to pull a wagon, just ride that wobbly girl's bicycle. He would get ahead of me and then wait until I caught up. When we reached Granma's, I left the wagon in the yard and we went in the house.

"Granma!"

"What is it, Rocky?" She came from the kitchen holding a dishtowel. I didn't see Suzy.

"Granma, this is Jerry Morgan. Jerry heard a man say he shot Elena."

"Where did you hear that, Jerry?" Granma put the dishtowel on the back of the sofa and sat down looking up at Jerry.

"There were two men working at the top of the lighthouse. I was listening to them. They didn't know I was there. They were talking in Russian."

"And you speak Russian?"

"Yes, ma'am. My mother is from Russia. I was born there. When the Germans were coming, my family tried to leave, but I don't remember that; I was too little. The Germans killed my father. I was nine when we got to Canada. I understand Russian but I talk mostly in English. At home I sometimes talk to my mom in Russian."

"Can you tell me what you heard?"

"Sure. One guy said he shot the woman but she didn't die. He would try again. They said something about a big fish. I don't know what that was about. I got scared and we came down to the ground and left the lighthouse."

"I got three dollars for the books, Granma. Do you have a bicycle I can use?"

"I sure do, but it's a woman's bike and the tires are flat. It's out in the garage—hanging on the wall."

"Do you have a pump?"

"No, but I think the Nesbitt's have one; Aaron used to ride his bike all over town and he had flat tires all the time. He had a patching kit and a pump."

Jerry scrunched up his face and asked, "Who is Aaron?"

"That's Lt. Nesbitt. I told you about him. His mom lives next door. Granma, are you going to tell the lieutenant what Jerry heard?"

"Yes. I'll call him this afternoon. Do you want to fix the bike? You don't mind if it's a girl's bike?"

"I don't mind, Granma. Jerry has a girl's bike. We want to ride around and look at stuff."

"Okay. You boys will have to help me get it off the wall. It's too heavy for me."

Granma, Jerry, and I went to the Nesbitts' and borrowed the tire pump. To Jerry's and my surprise, Granma showed us how to remove the inner tubes and check for leaks. She used the garden hose and added water to a washtub so we could put the tubes under water and look for bubbles as we pumped air in them. One tire had a small hole, but the other one just needed air. It was time for lunch, but Jerry couldn't stay. His mom had told him to come home to eat. He said he would try to come back in the afternoon.

Granma asked me to check on Suzy. I went in her bedroom and she was sitting on top of the bed coloring in a Roy Rogers and Dale Evans coloring book. She wasn't staying in the lines but I didn't say anything about that. She had chosen colors that made the pictures look pretty good.

"Hey Suz, are you going to have lunch with Granma and me?"

"What are we having?"

"I don't know. I s'pose sandwiches." I hadn't smelled anything like soup or chili. I hoped we weren't having macaroni and cheese; I knew Granma was out of catsup.

"What kind of sandwiches?"

"I don't know. Why don't you come and see. I don't think you'll throw up any more. Maybe we'll have some Jell-O."

"Orange?"

"Maybe, but I like strawberry better. I hope it's not lemon." I didn't even know if Granma had any Jell-O. "You can wear the rabbit-jammies you have on. I think Granma will have some carrots." I laughed, but Suzy didn't think it was funny. She crawled out of bed, put on her slippers, and followed me into the kitchen.

"Well, young lady, it looks like you're feeling better. How would you like some toast with strawberry jam on it? Maybe some saltines? Those shouldn't upset your tummy. Rocky and I are going to have toasted cheese sandwiches, but I don't think you should have cheese— it doesn't digest very well after an upset stomach."

Suzy said, "Okay." She sat in a chair, laid her head on the table, and looked at Granma. "Do we have any Jell-O?" she asked.

"I think I'm all out, but I'll take a look." Granma opened the cupboard next to the sink, stood on her tiptoes, and felt on the second shelf. "Nope. No Jello-O today. We're going to the hardware store this afternoon. We can stop by the grocery and get some. What is your favorite flavor?"

Suz sat up straight and said, "Orange." She smiled at Granma, picked up a spoon, and tapped it on her napkin. She picked up a saltine, smeared some jam on it, and began nibbling at the edges.

Right after lunch, Suzy got dressed and we took the Desoto to get some tire patches, glue, and Jell-O. We were gone for about an hour. When we got back home, Jerry was waiting on the porch.

Suzy saw Jerry sitting on the porch and said, "Who's that boy?"

"That's Jerry Morgan. He speaks Russian. We met on the road to the lighthouse."

Suz frowned, "You went to the lighthouse without me?"

"Yep. I took twelve books and got three dollars from Mr. W. He didn't have any of them."

"So, can I go with you this afternoon?"

"We'll go tomorrow, Suz. You can carry the money on the way back. Okay?"

"Uh, all right. But don't go without me. Promise?"

"I promise."

Suzy went in the house with Granma and the Jello-O and I took the glue and tire patches out to the back yard where Granma's bike was. Jerry joined me with his bike. He had seen an inner tube patched before, so Granma didn't need to help us. We worked together and an hour later, after getting permission from Granma, we started riding toward the lighthouse. Suzy and Granma had made orange Jell-O with fruit in it. Suzy said we'd have it for dessert.

When we got to the lighthouse turnoff road, Jerry put on his breaks and skidded to a stop in the gravel. I was already turning, so as soon as I was going straight, I put on my brakes and walked my bike back to where Jerry had stopped.

"Hey, Rock, I've been thinking. Let's go to the pier and see if we can hear any of those crewmen talking—you know, the guys from that Elena ship."

I thought to myself, *maybe he's right. Those men said something about a bigfish. I'll bet they 'work on the Elena; it's afishing boat.* "I don't know if I should go to the pier; I told Granma we were going to the lighthouse."

"C'mon, Rock. We'll ride down there and look around, listen for men talking, and then ride back to the lighthouse. You'll get more experience riding that bike; it'll be good for you."

"Okay, but I don't want to stay down there very long. We can go in the bait and tackle store and listen and then check out the Elena. If Mr. Sherner sees me, he might tell my granma I was there."

"That's okay. You don't have to go in the store; you can wait outside and listen while I'm inside. Let's go."

It was downhill most of the way, so we had to use our breaks to slow down and not lose control. Jerry stayed ahead of me; going pretty fast. I guess I was over-cautious, but I didn't fall. It seemed like it took about five minutes to arrive at the pier from the lighthouse turnoff, but it could have been longer. We figured it was about two miles to the dock.

We left our bikes at the end of the dock beside the Ohlands' fish market and walked toward Mr. Sherner's store. Two men, not very old, dressed in blue jeans, T-shirts, and wearing boots passed us. They both had tattoos of girls on their forearms. I figured they were motorcycle riders, but I hadn't heard any motors. I think they were going toward the C-Side Pool Hall and Tavern. One of the men said, "Having a nice day, girls?" They both laughed. They must have seen our bicycles.

Jerry said, "Those guys probably didn't make it through the second grade."

"I smiled and replied, "Maybe they didn't go to school." They both had packages of cigarettes in their shirt sleeves and were very muscular. Both Mom and Grandma told me not to smoke—many times. Mom said it was a disgusting habit and Granma said it was low-class. I told them not to worry; I didn't like the smell of the smoke, and I couldn't imagine smoke being good for a person's lungs. Most of the smokers I knew of coughed a lot, their breath smelled, and their clothes stunk.

I waited for Jerry outside of Sherner's. I sat down on the dock and dangled my legs over the edge. The water was about ten feet below me. It must have been at least ten minutes before Jerry came out of the store and joined me. He sat beside me and said, with some disappointment, "Nobody in there sounded like those guys in the lighthouse. Maybe they're at work on the boat. I think we should go down to the Elena and watch for people to come ashore."

I looked down at the end of the pier at the Elena. It was about a hundred yards away in a different place than when I first saw it. I thought about what Jerry said, but we had been gone from Granma's for about a-half-hour. We had to ride uphill to get back to the lighthouse, so it was going to take a lot of peddling and time to climb the hill. I thought we had better start back; we would have to return to the dock some other time. I told Jerry, "I have to go back. Granma will be worried if I'm gone too long. Let's figure out another time to watch for those guys; maybe we can come back tomorrow after Suzy and I take those other books to Mr. W."

"Okay. I don't want to go down to that boat alone, but I sure would like to see the faces that belong to the voices I heard."

We got on our bikes and started back to the lighthouse. It wasn't too hard to peddle until we got out of the downtown area; then it got harder. Climbing the hill toward the lighthouse about wore me out. When we could see the top of the lighthouse, I got off my bike and pushed it the rest of the way to the top of the hill. Jerry was able to ride all the way up, but he waited for me. He was out of breath but proud that he peddled all the way to the top. Since he is older and more muscular than I am it was easier for him. When we arrived at the turnoff, we decided to continue to Granma's without stopping.

Granma came out of the house when we rode up. She wasn't smiling as usual, so I knew I was in big trouble. Suzy stepped out of the house onto the porch beside Granma. She had a partially eaten cookie in her hand.

"Where have you been, Rocky?"

"Yeah, Rocky. Where have you been?" Suzy parroted.

Granma gave Suzy a dirty look. Suzy hid behind Granma. Granma said, "You didn't go to the lighthouse. I called Mr. W. after you had been gone for almost an hour. He said he hadn't seen you."

"We rode down to the dock, Granma. We wanted to see if we could tell who had spoken in the lighthouse about shooting Elena. We checked out people in Sherner's store and then came back. I knew you would worry if we were gone too long."

"Well, I have to give you credit for thinking about that. But you are not off the hook. No riding tomorrow. Leave the bike in the garage for one day."

I looked at Jerry and shrugged my shoulders. We wouldn't be checking out the boat until day after tomorrow. I asked Granma, "Can Jerry and I go to the pier on Tuesday?"

"Okay, but you have to check in with Mr. Sherner."

I thought for a minute and said, "All right. Will you call him and say we're coming to the pier?"

"Yes. I'll call him Tuesday morning and ask him to keep an eye on you.

Chapter 12

Monday at the Library

Suzy got up before I did on Monday. I heard her and Granma talking in the kitchen, a cupboard door banging shut, and a chair being pushed across the floor. It had to be Suzy getting ready to eat breakfast. Then I smelled toast, so I threw back my covers, got up and put on some jeans and a T-shirt. I knew Granma had some plum jam that was really good; she called it plum butter. My mouth watered as I tied the laces on my sneakers.

"Good morning, sleepy head," Granma said when I sat down at the kitchen table next to the wall. Suzy laughed and said, "Sleepy head." I just gave her a dirty look. I wasn't ready for any goofing-off yet. It took me a few minutes to get wide awake.

I said, "Good morning, Granma," but I didn't say anything to Suzy. Out of the corner of my eye, I could see her watching me and then she looked away at her orange juice.

Suzy had eaten some eggs and toast, so I said, "Two eggs, please; scrambled." I looked for the pepper and salt shakers. They were on the counter top next to the stove.

Suzy got out of her chair, went to the counter, brought me the salt and pepper, and asked, "Are you mad at me?"

I replied, "No, I'm just not awake yet. Thanks for getting the salt and pepper."

"Welcome," she said.

"You're welcome," I said.

She looked kind of funny at me and I said, "When somebody says thank you, you say you're welcome, not just welcome."

"Oh, thanks." She smiled.

"You're welcome." I laughed and then Suzy did too.

"Are we going to the lighthouse today with the rest of the books?" she asked.

"That's the plan," I said. Granma gave me a plate with eggs and two pieces of toast. I had to butter the toast and lather on the plum butter. As I was eating the toast, Granma gave me a glass of milk and some orange juice. Suzy just sat there making faces and watching me eat. I told her if she didn't quit making faces, one day her face would stay ugly.

As I got up from the table, I burped, and said, "Excuse me."

Suzy said, "You're welcome," and giggled. Granma and I started laughing. I could tell it was going to be a good day.

We sorted the remaining books and found one fiction book. Granma told me it's a good book; I should read it. It was White Fang by Jack London. I put it beside my bed and would start reading it tonight.

Suzy and I loaded the books in the wagon and started toward the Lighthouse. Granma told us not to mess around. After we got paid, we should come right back home. The sun was out and it was muggy so we took our time. I wished Suzy could pull the wagon, but she just wasn't strong enough, although she did try it once, but whined that it was too hard.

We were almost to the turn off when I heard someone call my name. It was Jerry on his bike coming towards us pretty fast. A cloth bag was hanging from the handlebars, swinging back and forth. He slammed on the breaks, skidded off the asphalt, and stopped on the gravel. Suzy stepped behind me thinking he might run into her. Jerry was really excited.

"Hey, Rock! I've got something." He let the bike fall to the ground, but he held on to the bag. He untied the bag, reached in, and pulled out a small camera. His eyes were big and he was smiling.

I had seen one like it before. A boy in my home room brought a camera to school once. I had to ask, "Does it work?"

"Sure, it's a Brownie. They always work."

Suzy stuck her head up close and said, "It's black, not brown!"

Jerry replied, "Yeah, they come in different colors, but they're all called Brownies. Maybe the first one was brown. I've got film in it. When we go to the pier tomorrow, we can take it with us. Maybe we can get a picture of you know who." He put the camera back in the bag and tied it to the handlebars.

Suzy frowned and asked, "Who?"

I thought quickly and replied, "Elena. You know—the ship."

"Oh. Let's sell the books to Mr. W." She pointed at Jerry and asked, "Is he coming with us?"

Jerry looked at me and said, "If it's all right with you and Rocky."

Suzy nodded and pushed on the wagon. "Well, let's go. We don't need these old books."

When we were about thirty yards from the lighthouse parking area, where there was enough space for about eight cars, Suzy saw it; a Navy car, just like the one Thorny had driven. It was the only car in the lot.

Suzy squinted and asked, "Is that Thorny's car?"

"Maybe. Thorny and Lt. Nesbitt might be here talking to Mr. W. Let's go see. Could be somebody else though."

Two minutes later, we were at Mr. W's door. Suzy ran up on the porch and knocked, but no one answered. I stepped on the porch and noticed a paper, taped to the window on the inside, saying Mr. W. was at the lighthouse, working on the gallery.

I told Suzy what was written on the sign. I had to smile when she commented, "I wish I could read."

I told her I would help her get started reading with a book about a dog in Alaska.

She said, "Oh, thank you."

I replied, "You're welcome," and she started laughing.

Jerry asked, "What's so funny?"

"Nothing, Jerry. Let's go see Mr. W. He's at the top of the lighthouse. You can go up on the gallery and look down. It's kind of scary; Lt. Nesbitt might be there."

Suzy entered the library first. I was close behind and I turned to see where Jerry was. I watched him get his camera out of the bag tied to his handlebars. Suzy looked around and said, "Where is Mr. W?"

I pointed up and she looked to the top of the stairs. "I don't see him," she remarked.

I explained, "He's up at the top on the gallery landing; you can't see him from here."

"When will he be here? I want him to give us the money."

Jerry announced, "I'm going up there. I want to get a picture from the top. I bet I can see my house from that high up." He started up the steps and Suzy walked over to the steps, stopped, and looked back at me. I shook my head and told her, "It's dangerous up there, you'll get scared and start to cry." She thought about it for a second, then walked back where I was, reached for my hand and looked up at me.

"Will you take me up there? I can hold onto you."

"We better not, Suzy. If you got hurt, I would feel bad and Granma would get mad at both of us. What would Granma tell Mom?"

Suz let go of my hand and replied, "I don't know. I want to go up there someday."

"Maybe when Mom comes, she'll take you up there. Mom isn't scared of heights."

I looked up and saw Jerry at the top, climbing the ladder to the access hole in the gallery floor. Normally the light was dim up there, but I could see his bright yellow T-shirt very clearly because sunlight was shining through the gallery floor opening. I watched him going up one step at a time, holding the camera with one hand and the ladder with the other.

I looked at Suzy and said, "Let's get the wagon and bring in the books. We can stack them over there on the desk."

We started toward the door but had to stop to allow a really big woman to enter. She smiled when she saw us and said, "Hello, children, are you borrowing a book from the library?"

Suzy answered as she shook her head, "No. We're selling books to Mr. W. They're in our wagon."

"I see. I'm returning a book and getting another."

Suzy stepped around the lady and said, "C'mon, Rocky."

I followed Suzy to the wagon, parked next to Mr. W's front door. I noticed a white car parked next to the Navy car. It was a Cadillac. A man was sitting behind the steering wheel.

I grabbed the wagon handle and started pulling; Suzy pushed. We had started through the gravel toward the lighthouse when the man got out of the car and came over to us.

He asked, "May I help you?" He was tall, but not as tall as Mr. W, and skinny. His hair was gray and short and his black shoes looked shiny as glass.

I replied, "That would be nice of you."

He then said, "I'll carry the wagon and the books. Do you want them in the library?"

"Yes, please," I responded. "Is that lady your wife?" I asked.

"Yes, she is Mrs. Griffith. My name is Oscar."

"We are Rocky and Suzy Linfield. Thanks for helping with the books."

Mr. Griffith had carried the books and set them down next to the library door.

Suzy said, "Thank you."

"That's quite all right," Mr. Griffith responded and smiled.

Suzy frowned, looked up at Mr. Griffith and said, "You're s'posed to say you're welcome."

"Well, young lady, you have very good manners."

Suzy said, "Thank you."

Mr. Griffith smiled and said, "You're welcome."

Suzy nodded, smiled, picked up two books, and carried them into the library. I followed her with four more books, two in each hand. I saw Mrs. Griffith looking at books in the G section. I wondered what she was looking for. Suzy and I made another trip before Mrs. Griffith came down to the desk holding a gardening book. She laid it on the desk next to the books Suzy and I had brought in. She looked around and said, "Where is Wayne—Mr. Waicukauski?"

Suzy pointed up at the ceiling and I said, "He's up there with someone.

"Did you find the book you wanted, Ellen?" It was Mr. Griffith talking to his wife.

"I did," she replied. "I guess I can check it out by myself. I know what to do." She sat down at the desk, took the card out of the pocket in the back of the book and wrote her name on it. Then she pulled out the desk drawer and found the date stamp, checked the calendar, and stamped the due date in the book and on the card. As she put the stamp back in the desk drawer and dropped the card in the out box, we heard a voice from above. It was Mr. W., Aaron Nesbitt, and Jerry coming down the book shelves. Sandwiched between Aaron and Mr. W, Jerry was carrying his camera.

"I'll be right there. I can't move as fast as I used to."

Mrs. Griffith said, "That's okay, Wayne. I've taken care of the check out."

We all waited for Wayne and the others to arrive at the desk. As Lt. Nesbitt got closer to us, he saluted. I looked up at Mr. Griffith and he saluted back.

Lt. Nesbitt said, "Nice to see you and your wife, Sir. Have you met these young people?"

"I have, Lieutenant, but I don't know the young gentleman with the camera."

Aaron said, "Jerry, this is Captain Griffith and his wife Ellen. Captain Griffith is the commander of the submarine, Deep Fathom."

Jerry smiled and said, "Hi," and then stepped forward and shook hands with Captain Griffith. Mrs. Griffith asked where his father worked and Jerry told them his mother worked at the hospital, his father died fighting Germany. Jerry said he liked his step-father, an engine mechanic.

I told them about Suzy and me and after that, Mrs. Griffith said they had better go. While we were talking to Mrs. Griffith, Aaron was talking to Captain Griffith and Mr. W.

Mrs. Griffith got in their car and slammed the door. I saw the captain look at his wife, say something to Wayne and Aaron, and walk to his car. He got in, started the engine, waved to all of us and drove slowly away. Mrs. Griffith waved to us, too.

Suzy waved to the Griffiths as they drove away, turned to me and said, "She's nice. How much money do we get?"

"Three dollars for twelve books. Ask Mr. W for the money. Thank him and then we can go home." She went into the library with Mr. W and I asked Lt. Nesbitt what he and Mr. W were doing on the gallery.

"I had him show me what those men were doing when Jerry heard them talking about shooting Elena. They had installed some electronics to adjust the power that runs the light, to make it more efficient. I don't know enough about the equipment to judge if it does what they told him. I'll have to ask one of the Navy technicians to check it out."

I asked, "Did you find out if they were from the Elena?"

I didn't hear what the Lieutenant said, but I saw him nod his head. Suzy had come running out of the lighthouse waving three-one dollar bills and almost yelling, "I got the money! How much do we have now?" She stood in front of me breathing hard.

"We have $9.25 now, but I don't think that's enough. Presents are going to cost more than we have, Suz."

Suzy was very serious. She wasn't goofing around as usual. As she folded the money and put it in her pocket, the one with the button, she commented, "Well, then. We'll just have to get more books."

Jerry had gotten on his bike and ridden over to talk. I could tell he was pretty excited as he put on the breaks and skidded to a stop next to me. He straddled the pedals and said, "I took three pictures from the gallery: one shows your grandmother's house, one shows my house, and I got one of the pier. The Elena is docked. I hope she stays there so we can check out the crew tomorrow."

"What did you think of being on the gallery? Were you a little scared?"

Jerry looked at Lt. Nesbitt before he answered me. I wondered if the lieutenant hadn't been there, would Jerry have said what he did, but I hoped Jerry wouldn't lie.

"Yeah, it was a little scary. I stood next to the lieutenant so he could grab me if I started to fall. After I took the pictures, I sat down on the floor with my back against the bottom of the light."

Lt. Nesbitt nodded his head, so I knew Jerry was telling the truth.

"Well, boys, I have to start back to Groton. I'm going to check on Elena on the way."

I asked, "How is she doing?"

"She's getting better every day. She'll be up and around in another week or so, then she will go to Groton for a couple of weeks before coming back here."

"Is something going on in Groton?" I asked. I knew it was a naval base, but I didn't know much more. Then the lieutenant told us something I had never heard of before.

"I guess you know that is where they are building the first atomic powered submarine. There's a lot of security there these days. Captain Griffith's submarine is there getting some instruments overhauled. I'd like to show you around there sometime."

That sounded exciting, but all I could say was, "That would be neat! Can Jerry go, too?"

"Can I go, too?" Suzy was looking up at the lieutenant, smiling, with her eye lashes flickering. I wondered if the lieutenant would tell her she was too little, but he surprised me.

"Sure you can all go, but we'll have to ask your grandmother. I'll bet she'll want to go, too."

Chapter 13

The Elena

When we got home, Jerry and I asked granma how early I could get up in the morning. She asked us why and we told her we wanted to go down to the pier and take some pictures of the boats leaving the harbor. That wasn't exactly true, but I thought it was close enough; we could say we changed our minds once we got to the pier.

Granma looked at both of us and said, "Well, Ike Sherner's shop isn't open until eight o'clock. I want to tell him you'll be coming down there. I guess if you get up at seven that will be early enough. You have to dress and eat before you go."

"Can I take the bike? I didn't ride it all day yesterday—just like you said."

"You're going with Jerry?"

Jerry answered quickly, "Yes, ma'am."

"Okay, then. How long will you be gone?"

I looked at Jerry and he just looked back at me. We hadn't talked about that. I smiled at granma and said, "Until noon, I guess."

"Okay, boys. I'll make you some sandwiches to take with you. You might not get home in time for lunch. It takes a while to ride up the hill. Maybe you'll want to stop to rest and have a sandwich."

"That sounds like a good idea. Thanks, Granma."

"You're welcome."

I looked at Suzy. She was smiling, happy that Granma did it right.

Granma started in the house but stopped at the door, turned, and asked, "Would you like to eat lunch with us, Jerry?"

Jerry nodded his head and replied, "Sure, thank you. I'll have to call my dad and tell him what I'm doing. He expects me to meet him for lunch on Mondays."

Granma said, "Where is he working?"

"He's down at the school bus garage this week."

"Well, come in and wash your hands—all of you." Granma clapped her hands like she wanted us to hurry.

After lunch, Jerry said he had to go home. His parents had given him a list of things to do. He was supposed to clean his room and vacuum the floor in the living/dining room, then take out the trash. He said thanks to Granma, climbed on his bike and rode off. As he began to pump the pedals, he yelled to me, "See you tomorrow at eight o'clock."

I yelled, "See ya!"

Granma commented, "Jerry is a nice boy. I think you can depend on him, Rocky."

I replied, "Uh-huh." He was my only friend in Crafton. I wondered if we would still be friends after Suzy and I returned to Boston. Maybe we could write to each other.

Jerry came over right at eight o'clock. Two paper bags of sandwiches were beside me and Granma's bike was leaning against the railing, ready to be ridden to the pier. I had checked the tires, but they didn't need to be pumped up. As usual, it was humid and already getting warm.

"Are you ready?" Jerry asked as he put on his breaks and came to a stop.

"Sure am. I've been sittin' here for a-half-hour." I lied to see what he would say.

"You are full of beans, Rocky. I bet you just sat down about the time I saw your house."

"Yeah, I was just pulling your leg. Let's go. Oh, here's a sandwich for you." I stood up and gave him one of the paper bags. He opened his camera bag and stuck it in with his Brownie. I started to put my bag in my right front pocket, but he stopped me, saying, "Put it in with mine. It'll get squished in your pocket."

The lighthouse, just standing there above the rocks, looked kind of lonely as we passed by. The light, housed in the red dome was turned off to rest during the day. I wondered what Mr. W was doing; probably having coffee and reading yesterday's Search-Light, the Crafton newspaper. The only things I ever read in the paper are the funnies and sometimes the sports. I'm a Brooklyn Dodgers fan.

As we rode, sometimes coasting, sometimes pedaling, the air, rushing noisily past my ears, felt cool, goose bumps forming on my arms, but the sun felt warm on my back and neck, almost like a warm blanket. Jerry led the way, being more daring and more reckless than I, but when he got too far ahead, he slowed down a little so I could catch up.

We arrived at the pier, parked our bikes, and walked to Sherner's, the fourth store along the top of the dock, between a law office and a boat store. The door was locked but we could see the twenty-four hour clock through the windows. It was eight-twelve; Mr. Sherner was late. Maybe Granma called him at home and they got to talking, forgetting the time. Granma does that to people sometimes. Jerry and I waited a couple of minutes and then began walking down the pier toward the Elena, about the length of a football field from Sherner's. The pier was quiet, Jerry and I were the only people walking on the timbers, but as we approached the Elena, we could see a crewman on the deck moving some boxes with a large, red, hand truck. He wore black work pants, a white T-shirt with armpit stains, and a black sailors cap.

We crouched behind some big metal barrels and watched the guy move the boxes from the side of the boat to a spot closer to the bow. As he tried to get the hand truck from under the boxes he had just moved, the box on top fell to the deck. We could hear him yelling, but I couldn't tell what he was saying. He took off his hat, pulled up his shirt, and wiped his forehead: he was shaved bald.

Jerry smiled and said softly, "He was cussing in Russian." We watched him move three more boxes and then he disappeared in the superstructure at the front of the boat. Jerry pulled on my shirt and said, "C'mon."

"What are we gunna do?" I asked.

"We're going on board."

Before I could think about it, I was on Jerry's tail, following so closely, I could have easily tripped him. The wood ramp to the gangway looked old and worn so I grabbed the back of Jerry's belt to stop him.

I was afraid running across the ramp might make noise and we would be discovered.

"What's wrong," he whispered.

"Sneak across the ramp to the boat so we don't make any noise, then get behind those boxes and listen. Get your camera ready." I had to take over from Jerry, he was too excited to be careful and I didn't want to get caught. What would happen if they caught us? I began to think of an excuse for being aboard the boat as we crouched behind those heavy boxes. The boxes were stacked in two layers, and just our heads showed above them when we were standing. Kneeling, I couldn't help noticing the deck was really dirty, which was not what I expected. I had always thought the deck of a boat was kept clean, and there was something else: I couldn't detect any smell of fish.

Jerry and I moved to the sides of the door where the crewman had disappeared. Jerry and I looked at each other, not knowing what to do next. We stood there for maybe thirty seconds, kind of scared, listening to the sounds from inside the boat. Jerry whispered, "I can hear somebody talking in Russian; something about a radio room."

I took a chance and slowly moved my head so I could see through the door with my right eye, exposing less than half of my head. There was a hallway with an overhead light only giving enough light to see where a person was going in the dark green walkway. I could see the back of a man in a doorway about twenty feet down the corridor. He was big, his right bicep and his chest stretching the shirt material. It looked like the guy we had seen on deck. He stepped back into the hallway and said something, then turned and walked farther down the hall, holding his right hand with his left.

Jerry whispered, "He's going below to get medical aid. When he dropped that box, he hurt his finger; he thinks he broke it." When he was gone, we went into the hallway and slowly moved toward the open door where we knew someone else was. This time Jerry went first, moving slowly with me directly behind. He stopped at the door and peeked in, then we moved past the door, down the hall and turned left, the opposite direction from the guy that hurt his hand. We went upstairs to the second level and stopped.

We saw a large room with desks in the center, bright lights overhead. Along the walls, benches were piled about six feet high with equipment, lights blinking. There were three men with their backs to us looking at paper rolling out of a noisy typewriter, the biggest typewriter I had ever seen. Jerry stood up, took a picture of one wall of equipment, and squatted. The three men were huddled together. Jerry turned and pulled on my shirt. We went back down the stairs and back on the deck without being seen.

"Hey! What are you kids doing on board?" a loud raspy voice came from above us. I looked up to see the giant of a man I had seen at Sherner's buying candy, putting a whistle to his lips and blowing. The shrill sound hurt my ears. Jerry yelled, "Run, Rocky, run!" but it was too late. Two crewmen were standing at the gangway, blocking us from getting off the ship. Jerry spun around and ran for the opposite side of the ship, ready to jump overboard, but a third crewman grabbed him by his left arm near the shoulder before he could get to another gangway. I was too scared to move. I just stood there wondering what was going to happen to us.

Another man clamped his rough fingers around my neck and forced me to follow Jerry and the guy that had grabbed him; he smelled like sweat, his shirt was greasy, and his breath stunk of beer. Both guys had tattoos of daggers through hearts and lightning strikes on their necks and forearms. Neither man said anything as they forced us up to the third level above deck, pushed us into a small room, and made us sit down at a table across from the big man that had yelled at us and blown his whistle.

"What are you doing on The Elena?" he shouted as he leaned toward us, his left eye only about halfway open and bloodshot.

Jerry and I leaned back in our chairs to get as far as possible from him. He looked about as mean as anyone I had ever seen. Earlier, I had planned an excuse if we were caught, so I said, "When school starts in the fall, our teachers always ask us to write a paper about what we did during the summer. We thought it would be fun to see what a big boat was like so we came on board. We weren't trying to do anything but see what was in the boat. It's the biggest one we have ever seen at the pier."

Jerry nodded and the man sat back and smiled a little bit, but then he looked at Jerry, frowned, and said, "What's in that there bag?"

"Sandwiches," Jerry answered.

The man leaned back in his chair, reached into his jacket pocket, pulled out a lemon drop, and popped it in his mouth. "Show me."

Jerry had the bag in his lap, hoping he wouldn't have to show the guy the camera. Jerry reached into the bag and pulled out a sandwich bag and laid it on the table.

"That's all you got in that bag?" the man closed his left eye and twisted his mouth, lifting his left cheek. "Show me what else you got in there, or I'll look for m'self."

Jerry looked at me and then slowly put the second sandwich bag on the table, looking up at the man. I think Jerry and I both wanted him to think that was all there was in the bag, but when I looked at the man, I could tell he knew there was more in the bag.

He stood up and ordered, "Gimme that bag!" He reached across the table and wiggled his fingers. Jerry stood up and held the bag so the man had to reach out for it. I was hoping Jerry wasn't making him mad.

He took the bag and dropped it on the table. Everyone in the room could hear the thud.

As he opened the bag and pulled out the camera, he whistled and said, "Well, looky here, a camera. Who belongs to this camera?" He raised his eye lids, looked at me, and then slowly let his eyes drift over to Jerry. "So it's yours. What pictures did you take? Any of things on the boat?"

I don't know how he knew the camera belonged to Jerry, but maybe he saw something in our eyes that gave it away. Jerry said, "I took some pictures from the top of the lighthouse, so I could show my mom."

"Anything else?" he kind of growled.

"Two of the boat from the pier," Jerry fibbed, but the lie seemed very convincing to me. I would have believed what Jerry said.

"Huh. We don't have time to fool around with pictures." The boss man opened the camera and unrolled the film, tossed it on the floor, and ground the heel of his boot into it. "Now pick up that garbage and throw it in the wastebasket over there." He pointed to a square metal container in the corner. I was closer, so I bent down to pick it up, but the guy stopped me.

"Not you! Him!" I jerked and stood up when he yelled. He pointed his big, right, dirty forefinger at Jerry.

I sat down, dropping into my chair. Jerry shrugged his shoulders, got up and carefully, as if it were an injured pet, put the destroyed roll of film in the trash.

"You can have your sandwiches." We were frozen like statues, not knowing what to do. Then he said, "Go ahead—pick 'em up."

We each took a bag and sat looking at the boss man. I wondered what was next. He gave the empty camera back to Jerry and called to one of the men standing outside the room.

"Russell, put this riffraff in cargo hold three."

Chapter 14

Cargo Hold Three

Russell, the guy that had grabbed me around the neck, took us down three flights of stairs so we were below the main deck. It was dimly lit but our eyes were getting adjusted when he stopped us in front of a big metal door. In the center of the door there was a wheel that he rotated counterclockwise and pushed with his shoulder after hearing a metallic noise; kind of a thud. The right-half of the door swung open. It was very dark in there, the only light was coming from the open door to the dimly lit hallway. I was afraid we were going to be in complete darkness when he closed the door, but he flipped a switch on the wall and a light bulb, hanging about a foot down from the ceiling, came on. Jerry whispered, "Nice." I knew what he meant but I was afraid to laugh.

"Make yourselves comfy, boys, I'll be back to check on you in about an hour. Eat your sandwiches and I'll bring you something to drink, maybe a shot of whisky to warm your guts." He laughed and slammed the door shut. We could hear the wheel turning on the outside of the door, but there wasn't any way to open the door from the inside.

Jerry said, "Boy, we're up shit creek. I wonder what they're going to do with us."

"I wonder what time it is." I was thinking Granma would come looking for us, but that wouldn't be 'til after maybe one o'clock.

Jerry guessed, "About ten o'clock, I think."

I told Jerry to look around and see if there was a way out of the big room. All I could see was empty wooden crates and a pile of boards along one wall. I sat down on one of the crates, looked at Jerry and asked, "See anything?"

"Nope, we're sunk." He looked at the floor, slowly came over, and sat beside me, laid back on the big box, and unwrapped his sandwich.

He chewed for a few seconds and said, "Hey, this sandwich is all right; peanut butter and jelly, but I don't know what kind of jelly."

I took out my sandwich, lifted the bread, and licked the jelly. "It's prune butter jam. Granma makes some of the best." I took a bite of sandwich and leaned back, looking up at the ceiling. That's when I saw our way out of the cargo hold, or least I thought I did.

"Hey, Rock, I think I see something." Jerry had seen the same thing!

"How do we get up there?" I asked.

"It's only ten or twelve feet—we can pile some of these boxes and climb to the ceiling. Where do you think that hole goes?" Jerry took another bite and was chewing as he looked around at the boxes on the floor and stacked against the wall.

That's when I remembered—that guy, Russell, said he would be back in an hour to check on us. We couldn't move any boxes until he wasn't coming back for a while. I told Jerry what I thought and he agreed.

He asked me again, "Where do think that hole goes?"

"I think it must be for ventilation—probably goes up to the deck, or out the side of the boat."

Jerry swallowed and said, "I'll bet it goes to one of those curved pipes sticking up above the deck, they're about the same diameter."

"Yeah, I think you're right. I think I can get through that pipe, but I don't know if you can. Your shoulders are wider than mine." I glanced at Jerry and then said, "Maybe if we wait until the crew is asleep, I can crawl up there and come back and unlock the door; all I have to do is turn that wheel."

"Okay, but if they see you, you'd better get to the pier, or jump overboard, and go for help."

"Hey, Jerry, do you feel that rumble?"

We held our breath for a few seconds, listening to the boat, before Jerry said, "The boat is moving—stand up and face the bow. Maybe we can tell where were going if we can feel what direction the boat is moving.

"Geez, I hope we don't go far. If I have to jump over the side, I might not make it back to land. I've never swum even close to a mile."

"We'd better watch for something that floats so we can hang onto it. I'm not a very good swimmer either. I've never tried to swim in the ocean, just the public swimming pool."

I heard a noise coming from the door. It sounded like the wheel was turning—a grinding, creaking noise, metal on metal. I said, "Somebody's opening the door!"

"Yeah, I heard it."

We focused our eyes on the door, watching to see who would appear. Russell stepped into the hold carrying a tray. He looked around and then walked over to the box, where we had been sitting, and put the tray down.

"I've brought you some chow. It will be several hours before we transfer you to the sub. We wouldn't want you to be hungry when you become torpedoes, would we?"

Jerry's voice cracked when he quizzed, "What do you mean torpedoes?"

Russell smiled, but it was more than a smile, he was trying to be cruel. He knew we were scared already. He was probably a bully when he was a kid. "I might as well tell you. We're going out about a mile and make some noises underwater so one of our subs can listen with their sonar. We'll be sending them a message to come closer so we can put you on the sub. They'll take you out into deep water, tie some bricks to you and shoot you out their torpedo tubes. Don't worry, drowning in deep water ain't so bad." He gave us that sick smile again.

I couldn't think of much to say but I blurted out, "I know a guy that would tear your arms off, smear your blood all over the deck, and throw you to the sharks." I was thinking of Thorny; he had arm muscles twice as big as Russell's.

"Yeah, kid. You ain't scaring me. You'll have to try harder than that." He laughed as he stepped back toward the door and turned to leave the hold.

That's when Jerry saw his chance. He slipped behind Russell and started running down the corridor. Jerry's footsteps echoed down the hallway and then I heard Russell say, "Damn! Now I have to go get that little shit." I tried to get out the door, too, but Russell's big, dirty, meat hook pushed me back in the hold. "Nope! You're stayin' right here."

He slammed the door and turned the wheel; I recognized that grinding noise; he had locked me in.

I went over to the tray of food and looked to see what was there, all the while hoping Jerry had gotten over the side and was swimming toward shore. I was praying that they wouldn't man a lifeboat and go after him. But as I took a bite of a pickle and bit off some cheese from one of two large chunks, I heard that familiar grinding sound. The door opened and Jerry flew into the hold and rolled across the floor.

"Now, don't try that again, you little ship rat! If ya run again, I'll hogtie ya both."

The door slammed shut and that wheel locked us in the cargo hold.

I helped Jerry off the floor and asked, "What happened?"

"They caught me just as I was going to get on deck. A big oaf blocked the door and Russel grabbed me from behind. I tried to kick him in the balls, but he was squeezing me too tight to his side. I couldn't get room to plant my foot in his crotch."

"Good try, Jerry. Our escape plan might work later when it gets dark, okay?"

Jerry hung his head, disappointed with his lack of success at escaping. He looked up and answered, "Yeah. What are you chewing on?"

I smiled, "A dill pickle and some cheese. Better try some, it's not bad."

Jerry and I sat on the floor beside the tray of food, picking at it as we talked. We peeled oranges and ate the rest of the cheese, but we avoided the pickles, their taste didn't seem to go very well with the oranges. When we finished the fruit, our hands were sticky, so we rubbed them on the dirty floor and wiped them on our jeans.

"I have to pee. Is there a bucket, a can, or a bottle to pee into?"

Jerry replied, "There's a five gallon can over there in the corner behind a box. Do you think you can fill it up?" We both started laughing as I walked over to check out the large can. It was an old paint can. I pried the lid off. It was nearly empty; a little dark-green paint was still in the can, but it had a dried layer on top; the can had never been closed properly. As I stood over the can trying to relax so I could go, Jerry said, "Why would they feed us if they're going to use us as human torpedoes?"

I finished and zipped up. "Yeah. Russell must have been trying to scare us.

Jerry commented, "Well, it worked. I was scared."

"Me, too. I wonder what time it is." I was thinking Granma was going to be worried soon and she would be calling Ike at the pier to find out where we are."

"I think the boat stopped; I don't feel the engines anymore." Jerry smiled, picked up our orange peels and dropped them in the open paint can. "I'll bet that's going to really stink pretty soon, especially after I add to it; I had asparagus last night."

I offered a suggestion. "Put the lid on after you take a leak."

We both fell asleep on top of two boxes, longer than we were tall. Russell woke us up when he came in with another tray of food. I asked, "What time is it?"

"Eighteen-hundred hours. We'll move out about five miles to transfer you to the sub at twenty-four-hundred hours. If you're bored, practice holding your breath." He laughed as he backed out of the hold, stopped for a moment, and said, "Next time I see you will be six hours from now, enjoy your prison cell." Then he relocked the cargo hold and pounded on the door.

Jerry looked at me and grinned. "Did you hear what he said, Rock? We're going to be alone for slx hours. It's time to pile up some boxes to see if you can get out through that big pipe."

"Uh-huh, I've been planning which boxes to stack up so I can get into the hole."

It only took us about ten minutes, being careful to keep the noise down, to build a pyramid of boxes so we could reach the ventilation shaft. I stuck my head and shoulders into the tube and looked up. It was a tight fit; I had to have my right shoulder higher than my left, but that was actually a good thing, I was my own wedge. I could reach up with my right hand and pull while pushing with my left hand, but there wasn't much room to move and I slipped a little. After a couple of minutes, I had only moved about three feet, so I slid back down.

"What's wrong?" Jerry asked.

"My hands and shirt slip and it's hard to keep moving up. It looks like I have to go about ten feet to get out."

Jerry and I sat there looking at each other, wondering what we could do without more things to work with. We sat there, probably for a couple of hours, brainstorming, but without any results. All of a sudden, Jerry was excited and got to his feet, stepped in front of me, and said, "I've figured it out, but you're not gunna like it." I watched him go to the can we had peed in, take off the lid, reach in, and pull out part of the orange he hadn't eaten. I was glad I wasn't reaching into that unflushed toilet.

His idea popped into my mind, so I stripped off my T-shirt, preparing my mind and body for getting sticky. He gave me the chunk of orange. I shook off the drops of pee, and squeezed some of the juice on my hands. I covered my sides, shoulders, and forearms, but couldn't reach my back, so Jerry gave the remaining pulp a final couple of squeezes and rubbed the juice on my back. I couldn't smell the asparagus, just the orange. I figured I was going to itch, but as soon as I was in the water, the juice would wash off. I had never heard of sharks attacking anyone covered with orange juice, maybe it would be a repellant.

After removing my shoes and socks, I climbed on top of the boxes and looked into the tube, thinking of getting on deck, hoping no one would see me and searching for something I could use as a float. The scariest part was going to be dropping into the water. I was as ready as I could be. I looked back at Jerry and said, "If I can't come around and get you, I'll get the coast guard or the navy to rescue you."

Jerry crossed his fingers, said, "Good luck," and I started up the pipe. This time, with the added friction, I was able to move up, kind of like a caterpillar, without slipping back. I had gone about halfway when I noticed a light coming from above. I stopped moving, holding my breath, thinking someone was shining a light down the ventilation shaft. When I couldn't hold my breath any longer, I gasped for more air, and then I realized the light was coming from the lighthouse library beacon, reflecting down the tube.

I continued moving upward, the air smelling fresher as I neared the top of the tube. I stopped moving as I got close to the opening and listened for voices. I heard some very faint noises, almost whispers, of two or more men talking. I thought they must be pretty far away, maybe on the third level above the deck, so I slid out of the tube and dropped about four feet to the deck.

When I peeked around the tube, I saw two men on the second level smoking, the burning tobacco making a small red glows in the darkness. It must have been a couple of minutes before they went out of sight. As I waited, my eyes fully adjusting to the dark, I saw a board close by. I wanted to use it as a float when I went over the side. I hoped it wasn't too heavy or fastened to the deck. I decided not to try to get to Jerry. If I got caught we were goners.

Chapter 15

Escape

I crawled across the deck to the board, got my fingers under it, and lifted. It wasn't too heavy and about five feet long—about my height. I sat there against the side of the boat for a minute, thinking about diving into the water. I took off my pants and tied the legs around my waist, not wanting to be kicking with wet pants covering my legs; it would tire me out faster than with bare legs. I didn't think any fish would try to bite me during the night, they probably couldn't see as well as I could. I sat there for a moment, but knew I had to get off the boat.

It was time to go. I looked over the side, but I couldn't even see the water. Fearing that I might hit my head and drown, I tossed the board over the side, far enough away so I wouldn't whack into it when I jumped. I heard a splash and listened to see if anyone else had detected the noise. After half-a-minute or so, no one had appeared from the bow, so I sat on the raised edge of the deck, prayed I wouldn't hit the board, and even though I was afraid, I held my nose and dropped into the water, just like I had seen a kid jump from the high board at the swimming pool.

My whole body tightened up when I felt the cold water going over my head. I moved my arms and popped to the surface. Pushing away from the boat, I took two strokes and ran into the board. At first I thought it was a fish, but it didn't wiggle or swim away, so I put my left arm over it and looked around. I could see the lighthouse light clearly in the distance. That was my goal; the lighthouse or bust. I used my right arm and left leg to swim away from the boat, and after about ten minutes, I held the board with both hands and began kicking, occasionally looking back to see the boat getting smaller.

As I was kicking, I figured the trip to shore was like a long distance race; I had to pace myself, or I would get pooped before long, but that's when I got a good idea. I laid on top of the board, and even when it sank under the water, I rested my legs. I used my arms to paddle forward, looking at the lighthouse as often as I could, using it as my compass. As soon as my arms got tired, I continued paddling for a bit longer, then I slid back off the board, and kicked some more. I felt all alone when I couldn't even see any stars, the Big Dipper being hidden by thin clouds, but I knew if I just kept moving toward the lighthouse, everything would work out.

When I thought half-an-hour had passed, I raised my head as high as I could, and looked back at the boat, but I couldn't see it anymore; it was too dark and it must have blended into the ocean. If it had lights, I couldn't see them. I could tell the lighthouse light was getting brighter and higher in the sky, and I began to look forward to climbing over the sand and rocks on the beach and knocking on Mr. W's door. He would call Granma for me and maybe give me something to eat. The cheese, pickle, and orange hadn't been much of a dinner compared to Granma's dinners. Her sandwich was only supposed to tide us over until we got home at one o'clock. Gosh, that was nine or ten hours ago.

It wasn't long before I could hear waves hitting the shore. I paddled faster, even though my arms were getting really tired, but I was nearing the finish line, so I seemed to have more energy stored in my batteries. I rode the waves hanging onto the board until I could stand in the foamy surf. I carried the board to the beach, almost falling in the shallow water, and then I dropped my poor excuse for a surfboard on the sand and rocks far enough from the water so it wouldn't float away when the tide came in. I didn't want a small boat to hit it.

Even though I was running out of energy, I climbed over some layers of rocks, skinning my legs, but I didn't want to stop to put on my wet pants. I was starting to shiver, my teeth chattering, but I was now getting close to the seaside wall of the lighthouse. I leaned my back against the concrete, feeling the slight warmth the sun had left during the day. The shivers were going away, but I still had to get to Mr. W's house. I untied my pants from my waist so they could dry faster, using my left arm as a towel rack. I worked my way around the lighthouse, through rocks and weeds, and was able to see cars in the lighted parking lot.

I was surprised when I saw Granma's car. *Why would Granma's car be at the lighthouse?* I thought she would be on the pier, maybe at Sherner's looking for me, but Sherner's would be closed now. The gravel hurt my feet, but I walked slowly across it to the concrete, and then moved faster to Mr. W's house. The door was open; I could see Granma sitting on a chair talking on the phone. I knocked twice.

Suzy came running to the door yelling, "It's Rocky! It's Rocky!" She pushed the screen door open, hugged me, and said, "Rocky, you're in your underpants and they're all wet."

Granma dropped the phone, like it was too hot to hold any longer, and ran to me, saying, "Oh, my God, you're all right." She threw her arms around me and bear hugged me so hard I could barely breathe. Then she said something that really surprised me. "Jerry said you were going to swim to the lighthouse. We've been waiting for you, talking to your mother. Why did you do such a crazy thing?"

"I feel kind of naked, can I get some clothes, and something to eat?"

Mr. W wrapped me in a blanket and helped me to the sofa. He noticed the scratches on my legs and got some Mercurochrome and Band-Aids. I sat down, trying to figure out how she had talked to Jerry. He was on the boat in cargo hold three. As Mr. W. began fixing my scratches, I looked at Granma and Suzy with disbelief. "You talked to Jerry—Jerry Morgan? When did you see him?"

Granma sat beside me, put her arm around my shoulders, and said, "Jerry came by the house with your bicycle and clothes about thirty-five minutes ago. He said those men were just teasing you and were trying to teach you a lesson. They weren't going to hurt either of you."

"I don't believe that, Granma, and I don't think the Elena is a fishing boat. It's full of radio equipment, not the kind a fishing boat would have. And there was a big typewriter machine printing on paper being pulled out of a big cardboard box."

Mr. W brought me a hot dog with mustard on it and I ate it, even though I don't like mustard. It was hot and helped warm me up, so I didn't ask him to put catsup on it. Suzy kept looking at me in a funny way, and finally she said, "I didn't think you could swim so far in the ocean."

I smiled as if I had used trickery and said, "I had a big board for help, otherwise, I would have had to walk."

Suzy observed, "No one can walk on water—you're crazy."

"Jesus walked on water, Suz."

"But Jesus was the son of God. We're not even related to God. Granma, what is God's last name?"

Granma glanced at Mr. W and smiled, then she answered, "God doesn't have a last name, Susan, his whole name is just God."

Suzy looked at me and said, "See, we're not even related."

I wanted to tell her that we are all children of God, but I wanted Mom to explain all that. All I could think of to say to Suzy was, "Aren't you up awfully late?"

She dropped to the floor on her knees in front of me, touched my bare feet with her little right hand, and said, "I had a nap this afternoon. I'm glad you're all right." She rumpled up her nose and said, "You smell funny."

"I know. I need a bath and some clean clothes. Granma, can we go home?" I looked at her for some support, having worn myself out, wanting to get in a nice warm bed and go to sleep. I had to talk to Jerry tomorrow to see what happened on the boat. I wondered how he got home before I got to the lighthouse.

She stood up and said, "Well, we'd better get home so you two can go to bed. We'll talk about all this tomorrow, after a good night's sleep. Thank Mr. Waicukauski for the hotdog and blanket and we'll be off."

I said thanks and shook his hand. Granma handed me my shoes, socks and T-shirt. I put on my T-shirt—backwards, but I didn't care, and I pulled on my sneakers. I gave the socks back to Granma, who asked, "You don't want to put on your socks?"

"No, Granma, I'll just have to take them off in a few minutes, and besides, they're all dirty."

I fell asleep in the bathtub; the warm water felt so good, and I didn't have to talk, to anyone, so my brain could rest. I heard Granma knock on the bathroom door before I had a chance to use any of the bar of Ivory soap floating next to my toes which were sticking out of the water. I shifted my eyes to see the door open about six inches and I watched Granma's hand put a clean T-shirt and underpants on the hand-towel rack.

"It's almost mid-night, Rocky. You should be in bed. We'll talk in the morning. Don't forget to brush your teeth."

"Okay, Granma. Thank you for the clean undies."

"Remember to turn off the hall light, I'm going to bed."

"Okay, good night."

After washing my skin, and then my hair with soap, I stood up, pulled the shower curtain around the inside off the tub and removed the plug with my toes, letting all the soapy water drain from the tub. As the grayish-white water disappeared, I turned on the shower and rinsed off all the leftover suds. Five minutes later I was in bed, having remembered to turn off the hall light. In my bed with my eyes closed, I was trying to figure out how Jerry got home ahead of me. That was the last thing I remember thinking about.

"So tell me the whole story, Rocky. What happened to you and Jerry?" Granma began questioning me as she was frying some eggs. Suzy was sitting next to me for breakfast, her hair all messed up, but she seemed pretty happy. We were both dressed except for shoes and socks, having left our slippers in Boston, we ran around barefoot inside Granma's house.

I started telling them the story of how we got on the boat and were caught and put in the hold below the main deck. When I mentioned the wheel and the sounds it made, Suzy ground her teeth together and shook her shoulders, then she started asking questions about how dark it was in the cargo hold. I told her I would answer her questions after I finished telling my story to Granma.

As I was explaining about dropping into the water and using a piece of wood to help me float, I watched Suzy playing with her Cheerios, pushing around the little doughnuts with her spoon as they floated, and trying to sink them with teaspoons of milk. They were like miniature life preservers. That made me think of how nice it would have been if I had used a life preserver last night; it would have given me more confidence than that old board. I think I'll get that board and have Mr. W cut it up for firewood for use during the winter. If Granma had a fireplace, I'd bring it home. When I finished my story, Suzy asked, "Did you have a lamp in that room?"

"Yes, and we even had a bathroom." I didn't tell her about the can in the corner, or how Jerry fished the orange sections out of the pee.

Granma didn't say Jerry had lied, she just said that he didn't tell her the whole story. She thought it was a clever idea to use the orange juice to get sticky. I told her it had been Jerry's idea. I hoped that I would never do that again.

After eating a fried egg and two pieces of toast with plum jam, I put on clean socks and my sneakers, then I checked the bicycle to see if anyone had messed with it. I looked it over and couldn't see anything wrong, so I was going to ride around the house to make sure it still worked. Just as I got on the bike, Jerry rode up calling to me and got off his bike, smiling.

"Hi, Rocky. Looks like you made it home without any problems. I was afraid you wouldn't make it; those guys said we were over a mile offshore. How'd you swim so far?"

I was serious, a little mad at him, and replied, "You lied to my Granma. I thought we were friends."

"That's why I came over early. I had to find out if you were okay and tell you what happened."

"So, what happened? Why did they let you go?"

Jerry was straddling his bike as we were talking, so he put it down and sat on the ground. I laid my bike down and sat next to him, silently, waiting for him to give me a good explanation. It only took him a couple of seconds before he started talking again.

"About ten minutes after you left, one of the crewmen came down to the hold to get us. When he saw that you were gone, he asked me where you were. I just pointed up at the ventilation shaft. He cussed in Russian, locked the door, and I heard him run down the hall. A minute, or so later, he came back with Russell, and they asked me how long you had been gone. I thought they would look for you if it hadn't been long, so I told them at least an hour, and they cussed some more. Then they hauled me up to the captain's room and after they talked, he told me they were going to let me go. They didn't know I could understand them, so I knew their plans."

"What were they going to do if they let you go? Weren't they worried you'd tell about the stuff on the boat?"

"Yeah. They were afraid if both of us talked about the equipment, the authorities would search the boat, but if it was only you and I said it wasn't true, they would be all right. They said I had to lie or they would kill my mom and dad, so I had no choice; I agreed."

"That's all?"

"No. I'm supposed to listen for talk about the nuclear submarine and tell them anything I hear. Each week I'm supposed to go to the boat and talk to the captain. They even gave me another roll of film for my camera. They said I wasn't supposed to take any more pictures of their boat, and not tell anyone what had happened.

"Then they brought you back to the pier?"

"Uh-huh. One of the crew rode your bike back here. He was one of the guys I heard talking in the lighthouse. I shouldn't have shown him where you live. I should have stopped at another house along the way, but I didn't think of it until it was too late."

"I hope he doesn't know I was the one that stabbed his buddy; the one Elena shot."

Jerry thought for a moment and said, "I don't think so. He looked at your house number, but didn't seem to react at all. I was watching him in the porch light. Then he took off running toward the lighthouse, but it was too dark to tell if he was going there."

"So what did your parents say when you got home late?"

"I told them the whole story, but they didn't think those guys on the boat were serious. They just said not to stay out so late next time, but since I was with adults, they weren't worried."

I laughed and said, "If they had seen those guys, I think they would be worried, especially your mom. Let's go in and talk to my granma."

"No! I can't tell anyone!"

I looked Jerry in the eyes, but he looked away as if he had let me down. I told him, "Granma knows people in the FBI. I bet they can tell you something worthless to tell the captain of the Elena. He'll think it's good stuff, not fake." I smiled and added, "Maybe they'll give you another roll of film."

"I don't think so. Okay, let's talk to your granma."

Chapter 16

Another Camera

Together, Jerry and I told Granma the whole story of our time on The Elena; what one of us forgot, the other remembered. She asked us questions as we explained the part when we were together in the cargo hold. Granma listened closely to what happened to Jerry after I left the boat, but she started doing dishes as I told her about swimming to the lighthouse. She had heard my part before. I hadn't remembered anything new since last night. In fact, the only thing new about me was my sore arms. My legs weren't sore though, probably because I had been riding Granma's bike for a couple of days. I bet I could outrun Curtis Logan right now. He's the only kid my age that can beat me when we run at school.

"What are we going to do for Jerry, Granma? Can we get something about the Groton submarine base to mess up the captain and his crew? Maybe Lt. Nesbitt can get some stuff to tell the captain."

"I'll talk with some friends and see if they can help us. But today I don't want you to go to the pier. I want you to help me clean up the yard. Remember, your mom will be here on Friday. I don't want her to work on my yard when she's supposed to be on vacation."

"Is Suzy going to help?" I asked. I was thinking she might get in the way. Anyway, after a few minutes of work, she'd find something else to do. Her attention span is pretty short for most things, unless it's baking cookies, especially if they have chocolate in them. She really likes fudge brownies, 'course I do too. I teased her the other day, accidently. She had made orange Jello-O with Granma's help and they put slices of oranges in the Jell-O. I said it looked like goldfish were swimming in the Jell-O, but Suzy got mad and said I couldn't have any. I said I was sorry. I just thought what I said was clever. The Jello-O was pretty good.

"Everyone will do something, even Jerry—if he wants to. Then, we'll take a trip to the lighthouse."

I looked at Jerry, he shrugged, and said, "It's okay by me."

It only took us about thirty minutes to clean up the yard, the leaves hadn't started to fall from the three maple trees, but there were a few small limbs that had broken off during the last good wind. That was the day we had gone kite flying with Elena. We threw all the junk from the yard into a big barrel at the side of the garage. Granma said she would add leaves and burn everything in October after raking. There was only a small patch of grass to mow; most of the yard was dirt mixed with gravel except for the area between the house and the garage. Jerry and I took turns pushing the mower while Suzy and Granma cleaned up the flower beds surrounding the house.

We put the lawn mower back in the garage and sat down on the porch with Suzy.

"Where'd Granma go, Suz?"

"In the house. She's getting something."

"Maybe she's returning a book to Mr. W." I couldn't think of anything else she would be getting before we went to the lighthouse. But a moment later, Granma came out the front door holding a fancy camera, looking like something from a science laboratory, at least three times the size of Jerry's Brownie. The front of the camera had a silvery-metal telescope sticking out from the part that held the film.

Jerry and I were both staring at the camera, a spectacular looking instrument, when Jerry whistled, like the older guys do when they see a pretty girl. Granma smiled and turned the camera around so we could see the whole thing.

I asked, "Where did *that* come from, Granma?"

"This was your Grandpa's. We used to take our bicycles, a picnic lunch, and this camera and photograph birds that had nests high in the trees at North Woodland Park. I'll have to show you some of our pictures. We developed the film in our bedroom closet. I think I remember how to do it."

"Are you going to take pictures from the lighthouse?" My eyes were still focused on the beautiful camera and lens.

"I thought I would show you and Jerry how to use the camera. What do you think?"

Jerry answered quickly, "That would be really neat!"

I thought about it for a second longer and said, "Let's go to the lighthouse!" My fingers were itching to get on this thing of beauty Granma was holding. I had seen some pictures of cameras like this, but never thought I'd get so close, or even better, to touch it and take pictures with it. It was like I had been starving for a week and someone put a hamburger and a bottle of catsup in front of me. I couldn't wait to hear the click of the shutter.

I was holding the camera as we drove to the lighthouse. It was pretty heavy and I was trying to see if I could hold it steady, but that didn't seem possible with the car bumping along, especially on the uneven gravel road from the highway to the parking lot. Granma was going to have to show me how to hold it to get good pictures. I think it will be easier once we are on steady ground. I don't think Jerry took his eyes off the camera during the whole drive to Mr. W's house. A couple of minutes after leaving Granma's, we piled out of the Desoto and knocked on his door.

Suzy had gotten there first and had banged with her fists on the screen door, the entrance door was open. As Jerry and I arrived, a couple of steps behind Suzy; we heard, "Just a minute, I'm shaving. Be right there."

When Granma climbed the two steps to the porch and stood behind us, Mr. W appeared behind the screen door wiping spots of shaving cream from his neck and slightly in front of his ears. He spoke as he tossed the blue washrag over his shoulder, "Hi, Martha. What can I do for you today? The youngsters don't seem to have any books to sell."

"We wanted to ask permission to go up to the gallery and take some pictures. I want the boys to try out my husband's old camera." I held it up so Mr. W could see what I had.

I watched his eyes as he studied it, almost like he was afraid it might expose some hidden facts about the lighthouse. Then he looked at Granma and said, "Sure, I opened the door to the gallery early this morning to let in some fresh air. It gets a little stuffy during the night.

I close the trapdoor at night in case it rains. But the library door is locked." He reached into his pocket, feeling among the contents, which jingled as he searched for the right item, and pulled out a key. Mr. W pushed the screen door open just a crack, so not to make Suzy back up, and gave her the key. Suzy glanced at the piece of metal and gave it to Granma.

"I'll be out in a minute, but you can climb up to the top, just be careful."

Granma replied, "Thanks, Wayne. We'll wait at the bottom for you. I don't want Susan to go up there, but I want to go up with the boys, so I'd like you to watch her for a few minutes."

"You're not afraid of heights, are you?"

"A little, but I need to show the boys how to operate the camera. They want to take some long distance shots of birds flying around the boats in the harbor."

"Okay. You can't see all of the harbor from the gallery, only about two-thirds. I'll just put my shaving gear away and slip on a clean shirt. Be right with you."

Granma, Jerry, and I wound our way around the inside of the lighthouse to the gallery ladder. Jerry went up first, and as I got close to the top rung, I handed him the camera, and crawled through the opening. I watched Granma climb the ladder and stick her head above the gallery floor. I thought I would have to help her up, but her flexibility surprised me, and in a couple of seconds we were all looking out over the railing toward the harbor. There was a little breeze that stirred some of the cottony wisps of Granma's hair on her forehead, but it didn't seem to bother her one bit. She held out her hands to Jerry and he handed her the camera.

Holding the camera steady was very important, so she showed us how to use the top of the railing to support the weight of the heavy lens system. Fortunately, we didn't have to fight with the wind for control, the camera was shielded by three bodies. Granma focused the lens on the harbor buoys; we couldn't see the Elena, it was hidden behind the buildings along the pier. Jerry and I each took a look and then adjusted the lens on several different structures to gain experience. We each took one picture before we went back down to ground level. Mr. W had given

Suzy a piece of paper so she could draw while we were high up next to the lighthouse lamp.

We thanked Mr. W for letting us in the lighthouse and keeping Suzy entertained while we were on the gallery. As we drove away from the lighthouse, Jerry suggested, "I think we need to get closer to the Elena so we can get pictures of the crew."

Granma commented, "Exactly what I was thinking, Jerry. I have an idea that should work."

Then we walked to the car and made the short drive to the pier. Granma had to park the car about a block from Sherner's shop. She didn't want to drive on the dock; most people frowned on that behavior. Cars got in the way of free passage for pedestrians and bikers, plus the exhaust fumes were stinky, adding to the smell from the few dead fish and slight oil slicks in the harbor.

Granma's nose was a lot more sensitive than mine; she could smell my dirty socks when I still had my shoes on. I think Mom inherited that from her. Granma identified the odors as we made our way to the bait and tackle shop. We could see the Elena tied up to the pier about half-a-football field away, but we were so far from the boat, we couldn't see if any of the crew were on deck. Sherner's door was open but no one was shopping, he was there alone, unless someone was using the bathroom. Mr. Sherner was walking around carrying a fly swatter whacking at flies that had invaded his store. Killing flies was one of the jobs having a store on the waterfront brought with it. I wondered why he didn't close the screen door.

Granma said, "Hi, Lawrence. How do we get on your roof?"

Mr. Sherner quit hunting flies, raised his left cheek up to hide his eye and said, "What do you want on the roof? That's a new one. No one has ever asked me that."

I didn't know what Granma was going to say, but I had an idea, so I said, "Granma and I want to get some pictures of the harbor so I can show them to my class in the fall."

Granma put her hand on my shoulder and added, "That's right. I want him to have pictures for his show-and-tell."

I turned my head to Granma and said quietly, "Show-and-tell is for little kids, Granma, we write reports and read them in front of the class."

She asked Mr. Sherner, "So how do we get on the roof?"

He pointed to the back of the store and said, "There's a fire escape outside in back, but you'll have to pull down the steps. I'll help one of the boys do it."

"Oh, thank you, Lawrence." Granma started walking through the store with us following.

I looked back to see if Mr. Sherner was coming. He was looking around the store, I guess to see if there were any customers. He threw his hands in the air and followed me out the back door. Granma was holding on to Suzy as they looked at the fire escape. Jerry tried to jump up and grab the rope hanging from the steps, but he wasn't even close to reaching it.

Mr. Sherner motioned for Jerry to come over to him and they moved under the steps where the rope hung down. "You have to grab that rope and hang on, son." Mr. Sherner made a stirrup with his hands, Jerry stepped into it, went straight up and got a good grip on the rope. Mr. Sherner moved quickly away from the building and Jerry rode the fire escape rope until his feet hit the ground. Mr. Sherner pulled the steps all the way to the ground and said, "There you go. That wasn't too hard, was it?"

Granma grinned and looked down at Suzy. "That was easy, we didn't have to do anything." Suzy had just removed her hands from covering her ears, and giggled. The fire escape had made a loud grinding noise as it came down from above. The whole fire escape moved as if there had been an earthquake. I was holding the camera and waiting to see who was going up the steps first. I didn't have to wait long, Mr. Sherner went up to the first landing, and then up the second flight of stairs to the top of the building, and disappeared over the edge.

"Let's go!" Granma ushered us up the stairs; Jerry first, then Granma, as she held on to Suzy's hand, helping her climb the fairly steep metal steps, and then me with the camera. When we were all on top, Mr. Sherner looked around, I guess to check for bad spots in the flat roof, and then said, "Stay away from the sides, there's no railing. I don't want any of you to fall off. My insurance probably won't cover all the medical bills. I have to go back down to the keep an eye on the merchandise. Good luck with your pictures."

Granma and Suzy walked to the front of the roof, where it stuck up about four feet above the tarred roof which had a slope toward the rear of the building. Granma mentioned that was to carry off rain water. It made sense to me. Suzy was too short to see over the top, but she told Granma she didn't want to look. I guess she didn't like high places.

The front of the building sticking above the roof reminded me of western movies when a deputy was on the roof with a gun to ambush a robber as he tried to leave town with bank money. I was the lawman and the camera was my gun. I rested the lens on the building top and focused on the Elena. I could see the captain and Russell very easily. There were two other men that I didn't recognize. "Jerry, come take a look." Jerry took my place and moved the camera a little bit and said, "I remember one of those two guys, but not the other one."

Granma joined us and said, "Jerry, why don't you go to the boat and tell the captain you haven't heard anything, but you think you will by next week, your friend's neighbor is a Navy lieutenant that works in Groton. If you recognize any of the voices, scratch your butt like you do when something itches."

I said, "You know, Jerry, like this." I raised my left leg and scratched my butt so he would know exactly what I would be watching for.

"Rocky, you take a picture of the crewmen when Jerry scratches. Okay? Jerry, don't scratch more than twice, they might think something is not right."

"Good idea, Granma. Did Mom ever do that when she was little, or have you only seen boys do it?"

Granma didn't answer my question. She moved her fingers in the air to help push him toward the fire escape and said, "Go, Jerry— we'll be watching. Oh, Jerry—when you come back from the boat, don't stop here, just continue on as if you are going home. We'll pick you up when we leave in the car."

Jerry nodded, then ran across the roof and dropped out of sight on the fire escape. I could hear the sounds of his feet hitting the metal steps as he went down to ground level. The next time I saw him, he was walking along the pier toward the Elena. He never looked back, just moseyed down the dock as if he had no care in the world; he even skipped a few times. Granma smiled when she saw how he was moving toward the big boat. Jerry sure was a good actor; there is no reason the captain won't believe what Jerry tells him.

Granma pulled me down below the edge of the building as Jerry got close to the boat. I think she didn't want two heads, sticking above the building, to be seen by any of the crew. We looked at each other for a few seconds, giving Jerry time to get aboard. Granma slowly rose up, just enough to peek at the boat, and then said, "Okay, Rocky, get the camera ready."

Just as I had focused on Jerry, he scratched. I moved the camera, just a fraction of an inch and snapped a picture of the three men in focus. One of the men was Russell, but I had never seen the other two. Russell took Jerry by the arm and they went into the structure at the front of the boat. We watched for a couple of minutes, hoping Jerry was all right, and then Jerry reappeared with Russell, Jerry's escort to the gangplank. Jerry waved to Russell as he left the Elena and started down the pier toward Sherner's. Granma and I got away from the front of the store as soon as we saw Jerry walking toward us.

Suzy was sitting in the middle of the roof looking up at the clouds, humming and pointing her right index finger into the air. I asked what she was doing.

"I'm moving clouds so the pictures will look better."

I looked up at the clouds and said, "What pictures?"

"Don't you see the animals? There's a dog without a tail, so I borrow some of another cloud and put on a tail. There's a bird with only one wing, so I put on another wing. It's fun Rocky, but you have to imagine."

"We're going back down the fire escape, Suz, so you'd better get up, dust yourself off, and come with us. You can paint some more with clouds at Granma's."

We made our way down the metal steps and into the store. Mr. Sherner was waiting on a customer, so Granma told us to go wait by the car. In a few minutes she unlocked the car doors and we climbed in. About a minute later, we saw Jerry walking slowly along the road, kicking at small rocks. Granma stopped the Desoto; the breaks squeaked a little. I opened the door, and Jerry hopped in beside me. He slammed the door and said, "I was hoping you would come for me. I didn't feel like walking all the way home."

Granma said, "How about some ice cream? You boys did a fine job."

"Do I get some, too?" Suzy quizzed.

Chapter 17

Surprise Visitors

After getting back home, we had some lunch—tuna fish sandwiches. Then Suzy took a nap, Granma went into her closet to develop the film, and Jerry and I rode our bikes to the lighthouse. We left our bikes leaning against Mr. W's porch. There was a note posted on his door saying he was in the library shelving books. We entered the lighthouse and saw Mr. W about halfway up the winding stairway, slowly climbing up the steps as if he was carrying something heavy, but with only a couple of books in each hand. Maybe he had bad knees.

"I'll be down in a minute, boys. I've got a few more books to shelve."

Jerry leaned against the desk and I sat down in the librarian's chair. It was a big wooden chair with varnished arms and a thick cushion tied to the seat. It was very comfortable—kind of like the chair my fourth grade teacher, Miss Worthington, used, but this one didn't have wheels. She used to read stories to us in the afternoon after lunch. A classmate, Steve Teel, and I drew murals showing the animals of Australia while she read Dr. Dolittle to the class.

Jerry turned sideways, looked at me, and said, "What are we going to talk to him about, Rock?"

"Let's tell him about taking pictures at the pier. We won't say anything about the crew."

Jerry nodded and we watched Mr. W come down the steps from the letter *M.* When he got to the desk, he asked, "What can I help you boys with today? Did you bring me some more books? I've still got lots of quarters." He smiled and jingled the coins in his right-hand pants' pocket.

I asked, "Do you have a book on photography? We took some pictures at the pier earlier today, but we aren't sure how to adjust the shutter speed." Granma had told me the camera shutter speed was already adjusted for today's light conditions, but I just wanted to say something that made sense.

"I'm not sure there is one that isn't checked out. You can look though. Did you get some good pictures of the birds?" Mr. W quizzed.

I answered, "Nah, we changed our minds and took some shots of that fishing boat, The Elena." I had been thinking that we should make Mr. W think we might have taken pictures of the crew. Ever since that black dictionary had been changed, I've been suspicious of Mr. W. He might be involved with some bad guys. I'll tell Granma what we're telling Mr. W when we get back home.

Jerry said, "I did get one good picture of a seagull with a fish in its beak. With that special lens, I could see the eyes of the fish and its tail was wiggling around. It was pretty neat." Jerry seemed to know what I was trying to do; it was almost like he was reading my mind.

I smiled, slapped Jerry on the back, and said, "Let's see if there's a book on photography, then we can go home." We climbed the shelves to the P section and looked, but we didn't see anything about taking pictures, so we told Mr. W that we would check another time.

"Okay, boys. If I get in a photography book, I'll set it aside for yrou. Be careful riding along that road."

I was following Jerry out the door, but I stopped at the top step, turned, and said, "Thanks, Mr. Waicukauski. We'll be back—maybe tomorrow." Jerry and I got on our bikes and waved to Mr. W as we rode on the gravel road from the parking lot to the asphalt road.

In a couple of minutes we could see Granma's house with a darkblue car parked in front. It sure looked familiar, but it couldn't be the car I thought it was; Mom's '49 Ford was in Boston. She wouldn't be here for three or four more days. As we got closer to the car, I noticed the Massachusetts license plate was red with white numbers, the last two being seven and four, the month and day of my birthday. It was Mom's car! I hopped off the bike while it was still rolling and ran up onto the front porch. As I opened the screen, I heard the bike crash to the ground.

"Mom! Mom!" I yelled as I got in the living room and then I saw her sitting on the sofa talking to Granma. She stood up and we hugged.

It had been about two weeks since she had dropped us off at Granma's, but it had seemed much longer. I had so many things to tell her.

Her hair was different and it smelled like flowers; I don't know what kind. She had on a light-blue skirt with small, dark-blue flowers in little clusters, black shoes with heels, but not like the ones models wore in ladies' magazines, these were shorter. Her white blouse was cool looking and she wore a small silver chain around her neck. She looked very nice, her red hair had been shortened and she looked quite different than when she would come home from the factory after a long day.

"Who's the boy outside?" she asked.

"That's Jerry Morgan, my best friend." I went to the door and said, "Come in, Jerry. I want you to meet my mom."

Jerry put down his bike and came to the door. I pushed the screen door open and he came in, smoothing his hair with his right palm, and looking down to make sure his fly wasn't open, just the things I would have done.

I said, "This is my mom. Her name is Sandra. Mom, this is Jerry Morgan."

Jerry came over to Mom and extended his hand. Mom shook his hand and said, "It's nice to meet you, Jerry. I'm glad that Rocky has met a well-mannered, nice young man."

"Thank you, Mrs. Linfield. How are you?"

"Just fine. My mother says you and Rocky had a close call on a boat the other day."

"Yes, ma'am, but Rocky and I think that Mr. Waicukauski is involved in something."

Granma said, "Oh, you do? You boys will have to tell me what you think. I developed the film from this morning. Let me get it." Granma got up and started toward her bedroom just as Suzy came running down the hall, almost knocking Granma over. She had heard Mom's voice and rushed from the hall like the wind from a thunderstorm. Suzy launched herself from about a yard away from Mom, but Mom had seen her coming, and to avoid a collision, moved sidewise so Suz would land on the sofa cushions.

Mom grabbed Suzy and gave her a big hug. Suzy said, "Oh, Mama, I've missed you so much!" Suzy stood up on the sofa, threw her arms around mom's neck and kissed her left ear. I think she tried to kiss her on the cheek, but missed. She'll get better with practice.

"Here they are." Granma came from the hallway holding two pictures, looking closely at them as she walked. "Jerry, take a look at these. Can you identify these men?"

The pictures were much bigger than I expected, being about half the size of writing tablet paper. I had imagined they would be about the size of my wallet. Jerry took the first picture pointed, and said, "That's the captain—and that is Russell, the guy that scared us when we were in the hold." He handed the picture to me and I agreed. Jerry reacted differently to the second picture. "Yeah, that's the guy that said he shot your friend, Elena."

I looked at the black-and-white photo. The captain, Russell, and the third man was the one that shot Elena. I studied his face closely, in case I had to identify him without the picture. I said, "Look, Granma! He's the one!" I looked at Granma and almost shouted, "We have to show it to Lt. Nesbitt. Now the FBI can arrest him."

Sandra said, "Mother, what are you all talking about? What have these boys gotten into? Who is Elena, and how did she get shot? Were any of you involved?" Mom was frowning as she looked around the room at everyone.

I could tell Granma was thinking of something to say as she moved to the sofa and sat down beside mom. She took a deep breath and began the whole story from the truck killing the man on the highway to our trip to Sherner's roof to get the pictures. Jerry and I listened intently to see if Granma left anything out. She didn't. I was surprised that her memory was so good.

Then the questions started. Mom seemed to want to get everything straight, not knowing all the people involved in what Granma had told her. I think Mom felt like she was a kid going to a new school on the first day. Every once in a while I would add to something Granma said. Mom would look back and forth from Granma to me like she was watching a tennis match. Suzy got down from the sofa and walked over to the window facing Nesbitts' house. She pushed back the curtains and put her nose on the window pane.

"Hey, Rocky! The lieutenant is home. He's got someone with him and he's got a suitcase. It's a lady. She has a hat. Do you think he has a new girlfriend? He has his arm around her waist."

Granma and I had finished answering Mom's questions, so I got up from the floor and went to the window, but I was too late to see who the lieutenant was with. All I saw was the lieutenant's back as he went into the house. "Come on, Suz. Let's take the picture and go see who the lieutenant is with."

Suz was looking at the Navy car and said, "I don't see Thorny." She looked up at me, "Do you see Thorny?"

I shook my head and said, "I think the lieutenant drove the car today. Let's go."

I heard Mom's voice. "You guys stay right here. Let those people get settled before you go over there." I looked at Mom and then at Granma, who was nodding that she agreed with mom.

Jerry was sitting in Granpa's chair looking at a LIFE magazine. He looked little in that big, old, brown chair. His feet were sticking straight out in the air as he turned the pages looking at the pictures. He looked at me and said, "Are we going next door?"

"Yeah—in a few minutes. We're s'posed to wait a little to let them get settled. Maybe they had a long trip." He nodded, turned a couple of pages, and put the book back on the coffee table. I could see why he was looking at that magazine, there was a picture of Marilyn Monroe on the cover. She is supposed to be dating Joe DiMaggio. I hadn't seen that magazine in Granma's stack of books, or I would have looked at it before. I wonder how a baseball player met an actress. I'll check it out later, after we get back from the Nesbitts'.

Suzy was still watching the Nesbitts' house from the window when I looked away from Jerry. She spun around and said, "Mom, can we go now?"

Mom looked at her wristwatch and said, "You'd better wait another five minutes, dear."

It was kind of like waiting for Christmas morning so I could get under the tree and open presents, but in this case, I wanted to see who the lieutenant had brought home with him. I wondered if it really was a new girlfriend. Maybe he got tired of waiting for Elena to get out of the hospital. But if he loved Elena, he wouldn't be bringing another girl home with him. I listened to Mom and Granma talk about what to cook for dinner for a couple of minutes and then I told Suzy and Jerry to come outside and wait on the front porch.

We had been there less than a minute when Lt. Nesbitt came out of the house and walked to his car, opened the trunk and pulled out another light-tan suitcase.

Suzy yelled, "Hi, Lieutenant," and waved. I think Suzy just wanted to show off her ponytail with the white ribbon tied in a bow.

The lieutenant waved back, then carried the suitcase to his mom's porch, set it down, and walked toward us. We stood up and walked toward him, meeting about half-way between the porches.

"Hi, kids. Rocky, who is this young man?" Lt. Nesbitt pointed at Jerry.

"Jerry Morgan. He's my new friend. Were working together to figure out who shot Elena."

The lieutenant put out his hand and shook with Jerry. "I'm Lt. Nesbitt, Jerry. How are you?"

"Nice to meet you, Sir. Rocky's told me all about you."

The lieutenant turned toward his house, took a step, looked back at us, and said, "Come with me—I want you all to meet someone." He motioned for us to follow him.

Jerry and I had to move our legs faster than normal to keep up, but Suzy skipped. She would have gotten ahead of us if she had run. The lieutenant picked up the suitcase on the porch and opened the front door, holding the screen door open for us, as we filed into the living room. Jerry took a sniff and whispered, "What's that smell, Rock?"

"Mrs. Nesbitt puts some stuff on her joints. She has arthritis— like my granma."

Lt. Nesbitt said, "Take a seat on the sofa. I'll put this in the bedroom and be right back."

The Nesbitts' living room was a little more colorful than Granma's. The coffee table had a glass top with a tall glass flower bowl in the middle, full of flowers. Suzy got up from the sofa and smelled the flowers. She looked at me, raised her eyebrows, and said, "They're real."

Then she spun around slowly, looking at all the furniture and pictures on the walls.

There was a TV set, a big radio and a small book shelf on one wall. A floor lamp stood beside a chair, like Granpa's, and a small piano was against another wall. In Granma's there was a big display case with her collection of tea cups and saucers. Just next to the hallway, where the lieutenant had gone, was a small round table with a telephone and a pencil on top.

The lieutenant was coming down the hallway with someone following him. I wondered if it was his mother or the lady he brought home. All three of us were moving our heads, trying to see around the lieutenant to identify the mystery woman.

Suzy was the first to see the person behind Lt. Nesbitt and yelled, "It's Elena!" She jumped to her feet and ran toward Elena, but the lieutenant put out his arm and grabbed Suzy just as she was about to leave her feet and fly into Elena's arms.

"Whoa, young lady. Elena is not very stable on her feet yet. You might knock her down."

Elena had the biggest smile on her face, but she was moving slowly. She was watching the floor to make sure she didn't trip on the edge of the rug. She stopped next to Lt. Nesbitt and reached out to grab his arm. The lieutenant put his arm around her waist and said, "Elena, I want to introduce you to Rocky's new friend, Jerry Morgan."

Jerry was already standing, he walked slowly towards Elena, and shook hands. After shaking hands, he said, "We have a picture of the man who shot you. Rocky told me you were still in the hospital. I guess you're feeling better. It's nice to meet you."

Lieutenant Nesbitt said, "What? You have his picture? How did you get it?"

"I'll get the picture. Tell them how we got it, Jerry."

I went out the door and back to granma's to get the two pictures. When I got back, Jerry was telling about scratching himself to signal me to take the picture. Elena and the lieutenant were laughing about our signal. I gave the pictures to the lieutenant and pointed out the shooter. The lieutenant held up the pictures for Elena to see. She squinted, pulled the pictures closer, frowned, and shook her head. Then she gave the pictures back to me saying, "I don't recognize any of those men. I'm sorry. I can't remember being shot."

When I heard that, I realized Elena had been injured more than from the bullet wounds, but maybe she would remember later on. I had heard about soldiers from Korea not remembering how they were injured, but I knew she had seen the captain before in Sherner's store. How could she forget about things that happened before she got shot? She remembered Suzy and me. I wanted to give her a hug, but I was a little afraid to squeeze her, fearing I might hurt her. I didn't have to think about it very long, she came over to me and gave me a hug, so I hugged her back. I guess she wasn't as delicate as I had thought.

Chapter 18

Vacation Trip

"Elena, I have to tell Granma that you're here. Don't go any place, okay?" Suzy spun around, ran out of the Nesbitts', jumped from the porch, and disappeared.

Elena sat down between Jerry and me and said, "I want you boys to tell me everything that you've done since you met. Don't leave out anything, okay?"

I said, "Okay," and Jerry nodded. I thought for a minute and then started telling her about the days after we had visited her in the hospital. When I came to the part about meeting Jerry, he and I pretty much took turns telling about everything we had done and heard, especially about Jerry hearing the guy in the lighthouse speaking Russian, telling about shooting Elena. She was really interested about what we saw on the boat and the deal Jerry made with the crew. When we told her what we had said to Mr. Waicukauski, she looked worried. She looked over at the lieutenant and he nodded, as if he had read her mind.

The lieutenant looked at me. "Rocky, we need to talk to your grandmother. She's at home?"

Before I could say anything, Suzy came back, nearly out of breath, almost yelling, "Granma and Mom want you all to come to dinner—Mrs. Nesbitt and everybody, Jerry, too. Mom said she wants to talk to Lieutenant Nesbitt and Elena, 'specially."

The lieutenant smiled, glanced at Elena, looked at me, and said, "I guess you don't have to answer my question." He called to his mom, "Mother, we are going to the Maklers' for dinner. I'm sure we don't have to dress up. What time does your grandmother want us to come to dinner, Suzy?"

Suzy was just inside the screen door standing at attention with her hands behind her back, looking like she was waiting for orders, but I think she was trying to remember what to say. "Granma said we'd eat at slx o'clock—sharp. Please bring some paper napkins. That's all." She grinned, turned around, pushed open the screen door, and jumped off the porch.

I smiled when it entered my mind that she had become the ponytailed express. Maybe in the future, she will ride a bike, instead of a horse, and deliver the mail or maybe newspapers. Then I remembered what Suz had said about the clouds—imagine. That s just what I was doing, but if I tell her what I've been thinking, she'll whine and say I'm teasing her. I'd better keep my thoughts to myself.

Jerry leaned forward, reached across Elena's lap and poked my leg. "I have to ask my parents, and they're both at work. Mom gets off at five-thirty and Dad at six. Let's go to your grandma's and I can call them, okay?"

I said, "Okay," and then looked at Elena. "We have to go. We'll see you later at dinner."

Elena smiled and said, "Okay, boys. After dinner, I want you to tell me more about getting out of the hold of that boat and swimming ashore."

We left the Nesbitts' and walked across the grass to Granma's. As we walked, Jerry said, "Elena is really pretty, isn't she?"

"You bet. I asked her to wait for me until I'm twenty-one and we can get married."

Jerry started to laugh, but he realized I was serious and said, "Don't you think she is going to marry Lt. Nesbitt?"

"Probably. When I thought she was twenty-one, I asked her, but later on she told me she's twenty-seven."

"She doesn't look that old. Geez, Rock, she's almost old enough to be your mother."

"Yeah, I know. My mom is in her thirties." We were on the front porch now, and I opened the screen door. With Jerry directly behind me we went into the living room and saw Granma on the phone.

"Okay, Natalie, we'll see you a few minutes after six. We'll eat as soon as you arrive. Goodbye."

We stood there listening to Granma, knowing we shouldn't be eavesdropping, but ignoring the guilty feeling. When she hung up, Jerry glanced at me, and said, "My mom's name is Natalie."

Granma heard what he said and commented, "Yes, Jerry. That was your mother. Your parents will be here for dinner."

"How did you know the number to call for my mother? Oh, you must have called the hospital."

Granma smiled and said, "I've got my ways," then she winked at me. Sometimes I think Granma is a magician; when something needs to be done, she finds a way to do it, even if it seems to be impossible.

Mom asked Jerry and me to help with the dining room table. We opened the table in the middle and inserted two leaves so there would be enough room for everyone. Granma unfolded a long, very fancy, white tablecloth and smoothed it out, making adjustments so the parts hanging over the edges were equal. Then Mom and Suzy began setting places. When seven places had been set, using almost all the room at the table, I asked, "Mom, we need three more places at the table, there will be ten of us, seven grownups and three kids."

"You're right, Rocky. Would you boys please get the card table from the hall closet?"

At first, I thought Jerry, Suzy, and I were considered to be less important than the adults, being separated from them, and having to eat from a chintzy, old, card table. Granma appeared from the hallway and tossed me a folded piece of colorful material. "Put that over the card table, Rocky. It's my best fall tablecloth." Jerry grabbed one edge, I held the opposite edge, and we put the unfolded material over the card table. Suzy looked at it, shook her head, and began smoothing out the folds; then she went to the kitchen and came back with three plates and a handful of silverware. Jerry and I drifted into the kitchen and got three glasses, three napkins, and the salt-and-pepper shakers, which were both about half-full.

As we were completing the table setting, Jerry leaned over to me and whispered, "I'm glad were not sitting with them. If I do something wrong, Mom slaps my hand—it's embarrassing."

I replied, "I know what you mean. My mom gives me a dirty look. Sometimes I don't even know what I did wrong—until later, when we're alone, she explains it to me. But even then, I don't know what I did."

"Yeah. Sometimes it's hard to understand manners, but I don't burp or fart at the table. My grandfather used to do that in Russia." We both laughed. I was thinking about what would happen to me if I did that. Though I remember one time I laughed so hard at the dinner table that I farted, but no one could hear it; it just sneaked out.

I checked the grandfather clock beside the teacup display to see when we would be eating. I was getting hungry and smells from the kitchen were getting stronger. It was five-fifty and there was a knock at the front door. Mom and Suzy were at the door before I could get up from one of the fold-up chairs at the card table. After Jerry and I had finished getting our table ready, we had sat down and talked.

I was surprised when Suzy took over and introduced the Nesbitts and Elena to mom. Mom had heard all about Elena from Suzy, Granma, and me. She had known the Nesbitts for several years, having talked with them during previous summer visits to Granma's. I learned all about that stuff as I listened to the talking as the neighbors arrived.

Mom asked the three visitors to have a seat, the Morgans would be here shortly; dinner was almost ready to be served. Elena surprised me and came toward the card table. Jerry and I both stood up and said, "Hi."

"Hi, gentlemen. May I take a seat with you?"

Jerry and I both reached for the same chair and slid it away from the table to make room for her. Boy she smelled good, not enough perfume to act as deodorant, but I could imagine her putting just a touch of it behind each ear. I had seen Mom do that before.

Jerry commented, "You sure smell good, Elena. I bet you are happy to get out of the hospital."

"Thank you, Jerry. Aaron gave me some new perfume, but I wasn't sure how much to use." She looked at me and said, "Your grandmother's house is very nice, Rocky, and it sure doesn't smell like the hospital."

I had my chance, so I said, "I know, it smells like Bengay and roast beef." There was a slight pause and then Elena started laughing— just what I wanted to happen. When she laughed, her eyes sparkled, little dimples appeared, and her right hand moved up to cover her mouth as if to hide the surprise at the funny thing I said. Mom's laugh is similar to Elena's except Mom's eyes don't sparkle as much: maybe because Mom is older.

We heard another knock at the door. Jerry jumped up and hurried to be with his parents as Suzy and Mom welcomed them. Jerry put his arm around his mother's waist and said, "These are my parents Mrs. Linfield: Natalie and Steven Morgan."

His dad said, "It's nice to meet you. Please call me Steve. Jerry has been talking about doing things with your son. Is this Rocky?" He pointed at me as I joined Mom and Suzy.

I shook hands with his mom, a blonde about as tall as Granma; maybe a little taller, an inch or two. She was nice looking, but not as pretty as Elena. Her hands were soft, but she had a firm grip. Mr. Morgan is about the same height as Lt. Nesbitt, but more muscular. He looks like he could work for a circus, putting up tents, or maybe being in charge of the wild animals. I would want him on my side in a fight. The Morgans look nice together, and with Jerry, they make a nice-looking family.

Granma came into the living room wearing an apron, a wisp of hair hanging down to her left eyebrow. She wiped the sweat from her forehead with a napkin before her face lit up with a big grin. The Morgans spent about a minute talking with her. Mrs. Morgan volunteered to help put the food on the table, and Mom started seating guests.

Suzy, Jerry, and I sat down at the card table, watching the seating process. Elena was placed closest to us at the end of the big table, with the lieutenant to her left, and Mrs. Nesbitt to her right. The Morgans sat to the left of Lieutenant Nesbitt. Granma and Mom were going to sit to the right of Mrs. Nesbitt so they could easily get to the kitchen. Just before Granma brought in the last dish, a big bowl of mashed potatoes, Mom asked us if we wanted milk or water to drink: Suzy said milk, Jerry and I chose water, just like the grownups had. Later, coffee was served, but I had tried some and hated it. Jerry said he had tried coffee once and it made him throw up.

Granma asked if anyone would like to say grace, but no one volunteered, so she said a small thank-you to God for providing the food and friendship. I don't know what I would do if someone asked me to say grace, but from now on, I will pay more attention to the offering than what I am going to eat. Maybe I won't think so much about it as I get older.

As soon as the serving dishes were being passed around, Mom came over to our table and took our plates. She returned Jerry's and Suzy's plates full of food, but I had to wait a bit longer for mine; she could only hold two plates at a time, not having been trained as a waitress. I noticed Suzy's portion of meat had been cut into bite-size pieces, but Jerry's chunk of meat had been left for him to cut. I hoped Mom wouldn't cut mine, I didn't want Jerry to think I was a little kid that couldn't use a knife and fork. When Mom gave me my dinner plate heaped with food, the meat was one big piece, just like Jerry's.

Just as I relaxed and started to eat, Suzy said, "Oh, boy! Stringy meat!" loudly enough for everyone to hear.

I held my breath, holding my fork suspended over my mashed potatoes, wondering what was going to happen. Elena was closest to us and started laughing, followed by the other adults. They weren't big laughs, more like reactions to a joke that wasn't too funny.

Granma spoke first, "You don't like stringy meat, Susan?"

"I like it, Granma. The way Mom cut it, I didn't know what kind it was until it fell apart. I was surprised. Your stringy meat is the best." I listened to some of the other comments as I shook some catsup from the bottle Mom had put on our table. She knows what I like catsup on. All the comments were compliments and Mrs. Morgan asked for Granma's recipe.

Jerry and I were hungry and shoveled the dinner in pretty fast. The only thing that slowed us down was the corn on the cob. Jerry was holding his corn in his fingers, melted butter running down towards the palms of his hands; I think he had never used holders before. I inserted the metal prongs of plastic holders into my corn and said, "Jerry, like this." I held up my corn so he could see how to use the holders.

He said, "Thanks, Rocky. I didn't know what those things were for. At home we just use our fingers. I wonder who thought of that."

When we were nearly finished eating jerry and I began listening to the conversation coming from the dining room table. Mr. Morgan said he had been a tank mechanic during the war. He met Natalie in England a few weeks before he was to take the journey stateside, but he requested an extension of his tour of duty, which was granted. After they were married in London, England, Mr. Morgan, Natalie, and Jerry, her nine-year-old, moved to Canada. We listened to the adult conversation for almost a half-hour before it was time for dessert. While we listened, Suzy walked around the dining table showing everyone her new dress Mom had brought her from Boston.

As dessert was being served, Mom asked, "Lieutenant, are you on vacation from Groton?"

"No, ma'am, I'm working on a new project for the Navy. I'm on my way to Rangeley, Maine, about twenty miles from both New Hampshire and Canada. The Navy wants me to investigate an area they could use for a survival, escape, and evasion facility. The FBI wants to know more about the area, too, so Elena is accompanying me while she continues to recuperate."

Elena added, "We have the car full of camping gear. I'm looking forward to getting out in the countryside and getting lots of fresh air. I need to build up my strength after being in that hospital bed. I'm still a bit unsteady when I'm walking."

I went over to Granma and Mom and said, "Can we go camping in that same area? Do you think Lieutenant Nesbit and Elena would mind?"

"Oh, I don't know about that, Rocky. If they are studying a site for the government and Elena is regaining her strength, we wouldn't want to be interfering."

Then I heard something I hadn't expected from the lieutenant, "You know, it might be a good idea to all go together, you know, strength in numbers. If those men on the boat have found out the boys took pictures after they were told not to, they might send some bad guys after Rocky and Jerry."

"Well, it has been slow going at the garage. Since I'm the boss, I can take a few days off from work. We haven't gone camping for two years, and that was in Canada. What about it, Natalie, can you take some time off?" Mr. Morgan looked at his wife; so did everyone else. I could see the hope in Jerry's face.

Natalie looked around, scanning the faces of everybody. "Sure, I have at least a week of vacation. It would be a good time to get away before school starts. Jerry has to start school in about three weeks."

Granma stood up from the table as she swallowed her last bite of dessert. "Okay. Can we meet here tomorrow at one o'clock? Sandra and I can get the car packed in the morning. Our caravan will leave for the hinterland right after lunch—after we do the dishes, of course.

Suzy pulled at Granma's dress and said, "What's the hinterland, Granma?"

Chapter 19

On the Road

After all the dishes were cleared from the table, coffee was served while the adults planned the course of travel and decided which vehicles were to be taken on the adventure. I think Jerry called it an adventure first, and I agreed, since it might be dangerous or risky, or both. We didn't know for sure where we were going or what we would be doing when we got there, but as we listened to the different adult voices when the lieutenant brought out a map, I began to feel like it was kind of like Christmas Eve. Lieutenant Nesbitt had drawn over the shortest route with a red pencil. Mom got some tracing paper from Granma and drew two copies of the roads we would take. Towns, rivers, state roads, lakes, and mountains were marked on the paper. Mom gave one copy to Natalie and the other to Granma.

Jerry and I listened closely, occasionally glancing at each other when we heard something interesting: a mountain range, lakes and rivers; especially the Dead River, almost made me shiver and Jerry clenched his teeth. Jerry and I would have a ball exploring. The Dead River sounded like it could be very dangerous, but after escaping from that Elena boat, I felt like I could handle just about any challenge. Of course, Jerry would be with me; I know I can count on him. I hope he knows he can count on me.

Aaron and Elena were going to drive the Navy car, followed by Granma, Mom, and Suzy in Granma's Desoto. Mom said she didn't trust her car on a trip into mountainous areas. Mr. and Mrs. Morgan would follow the other two cars in their pickup, with Jerry and me riding in the back. We are supposed to leave at one o'clock tomorrow afternoon. I'll offer to help with the dishes if we can leave sooner; I have a feeling everyone will be waiting for the Desoto. Sometimes, when Suz and I want to go somewhere, Mom and Granma only move at one speed: slow, but they never seem to forget anything, so that's good.

It was after nine o'clock when the meeting was over. Suzy had fallen asleep in the sofa. Mr. Morgan picked her up and Mom showed him where Suz slept. While Suzy was being moved and put to bed, the Nesbitts and Elena thanked Granma for dinner, said goodnight, and left for home. Natalie volunteered to help with the dishes and followed Granma into the kitchen. Jerry and I could hear the clanking of dishes and female voices as we looked over the map on the dining room table.

When I woke up in the morning, I looked around the bedroom to make sure I wasn't still dreaming. The picture in my mind was of Jerry and me rafting on the Dead River and both falling off into white-water. On some large rocks on the right bank, Mr. Morgan was calling to Jerry to swim to him, but I was being bashed into and over rocks in the rapids. That's when I woke up. I looked up at the white popcorn ceiling, but had to close my eyes so I couldn't see the whitewater anymore; it seemed to be stuck in my mind, even when I was awake.

Suzy squeezed her face into the bedroom, the door opened barely enough for her head, and said, "Rocky, time to get up!" When I heard the door open, I had looked for Granma or Mom, but Suzy was there.

"What time is it?"

"It's time to get up!"

The door slammed shut. I was left alone to avoid looking at the whitewater ceiling. I got dressed in about three minutes and was walking toward the kitchen when Suzy appeared in front of me. "You have a phone call, Rocky." I had heard the ring but figured it was for Granma or mom. Why would anyone be calling me?

The phone was off the hook, laying on the tabletop. I picked it up, leaned toward the base of the phone and spoke into it, "Hello?" It was Jerry.

"Hi, Jerry. What's up?"

He wanted me to come over to his house to help him and his dad load the back of the pickup. Since I had never been to his house, he gave me the address and said, "It's like two moves of a knight on a chess board: one sidewise, two up; two sidewise, one up."

"Okay. It'll be a few minutes; I have to eat breakfast first. I'll hurry."

I put on my sneakers, ate some buttered-toast, an egg, a piece of bacon, and washed it down with a glass of milk. I grabbed my jacket and told Mom I was going to Jerry's; I would be back as soon as their pickup was loaded. Mom said, "All right." I rammed my arms into the jacket, ran beside the bike, jumped on, and heard, "Did you get enough to eat?"

As I rode off, I yelled, "Yes! Mom, I'm in a hurry." I wasn't sure what Jerry meant about the knight's moves, I didn't play chess, but I knew about where Jerry lived so I headed in the general direction, making rights and lefts I thought would get me there. I was riding about as fast as I could go, but after the second turn, I saw an old pickup behind me. It looked like the one Jerry and I had seen at the lighthouse when Jerry overheard that guy say he shot Elena.

Since the pickup went so much faster than I could go on the bike, I was a little scared, but then I got an idea. I would cut through alleys and go across lawns instead of staying on the roads and sidewalks. Jerry said he lived at 711 Carnot Street, but I hadn't gotten to Carnot yet. I kept looking behind, trying to see that pickup, but I think I lost it when I turned down that last alley. At the next corner, the sign read Carnot; I felt much safer, I was close to Jerry's. I started looking at house numbers and saw 609 on the mailbox at a brown house. I peddled as hard as I could; I was almost there. Half-a-block ahead of me, I saw Jerry and his dad loading something into the pickup. Nearly out of breath, I skidded to a stop in front of the pickup, dropped my bike and took a couple of deep breaths.

"Good morning!" Mr. Morgan smiled and put some fishing poles in the pickup.

"Hi, Rocky. You sure got here fast. I thought it might be a half-hour and we'd be done by then." Jerry was handing his dad a sleeping bag. Mr. Morgan had gotten into the back of the truck.

My heart rate and breathing had slowed a bit and I said, "That pickup we saw at the lighthouse was following me, but I lost them by going down alleys and cutting across lawns."

"You mean that old, brown pickup?" Jerry quizzed.

"Yeah, that's the one. I remember the license number; it was the same—78311."

Mr. Morgan was looking down the street and asked, "Is that the truck, Rocky?" He pointed down the street to the corner. The cross street was South Eighth.

Jerry and I both said, "That's the one!"

Mr. Morgan bent over and then stood up holding a rifle. He stepped off the tailgate and dropped to the ground holding the rifle in one hand and began walking down the sidewalk. I could see the muscles of his arm bulging. He looked at Jerry and me and said, "You boys stay here."

I smiled at Jerry when I saw Mr. Morgan twirl that rifle like it was light as a feather. I think he knew how to handle that gun. As Mr. Morgan walked toward that pickup, I felt a little scared for him, but when he was about half-way to that old truck, I heard the engine start and the pickup drove away; I think they were scared of Mr. Morgan. He turned around and walked back to us.

When Mr. Morgan got back to his pickup, Jerry had a big smile and said, "Way to go, Dad."

I asked, "Would you have shot them, Mr. Morgan?"

"No, the rifle isn't loaded. It's against the law to shoot a rifle in the city limits, but I might have knocked them around a bit." He smiled as he placed the rifle back in the pickup. I wondered where he kept the bullets, probably in the cab somewhere, maybe under the seat.

I think Mr. Morgan could have beat those guys up with one arm tied behind his back. Those two men from the lighthouse weren't very big and Mr. Morgan has the muscles of a weight lifter. I can understand why Jerry likes his stepfather, if it's only because of his muscles.

He's a quiet man, but a quiet man can get mad; then it's time to get out of the way. Dad was a little like that.

In about half-an-hour, we had the pickup loaded with a big tent, and bags of other stuff that had been packed before I came over to Jerry's. Some of the stuff was pretty heavy; it took both Jerry and me to lift the bags and boxes onto the tailgate. Mr. Morgan packed everything so the boxes fit together like building blocks. There was still plenty of room for us among the bags of equipment. The sleeping bags were placed right behind the cab giving us soft seats. If we had to sit in the bed of the pickup without some padding, it wouldn't take very long before we'd have sore butts. The last thing to go into the pickup was a shovel, not a big one, but one like a soldier might have during the war. I'm thinking it was war surplus.

Mrs. Morgan came out of the house and said, "I'm ready, Steve. Is everything packed?"

She was carrying a picnic basket and it looked kind of heavy; she was holding it with both hands.

Mr. Morgan smiled and said, "Yep. I think I've got everything loaded except for two boys. Say, Rocky, should I lock your bike in our garage?" He looked at me and I nodded. He grabbed the bike with one hand and carried it into the garage, locked the door and came back to the pickup. "Climb in, boys. Let's meet up with the others at the Maklers'."

Granma's house looked like no one was home, except the lieutenant's car was parked next to Granma's Desoto with both trunks open. Elena and Lt. Nesbitt must be in the house with Mom and Granma. Jerry and I jumped from the pickup and went in the house with Mr. and Mrs. Morgan following. Suzy was sitting on the floor watching TV and Elena was on the sofa looking at a magazine. She looked up, smiled and said, "Hi, boys."

Jerry and I said, "Hi." I didn't see the lieutenant, so I asked, "Where's the lieutenant?" Mom and Granma were doing something in the kitchen, but I couldn't see Lt. Nesbitt.

"He's helping his mother with a suitcase. They'll be here in a few minutes. We're going to have a quick lunch and hit the road."

I looked at the grandfather clock by the front door. It was ten after eleven, a little early for lunch, but after all that loading, I felt that a sandwich would be good before we started the trip. I thought that we probably wouldn't stop for several hours once we were on the road heading west. I could hear Mom and Granma talking in the kitchen, but it sounded like they were saying something about bread, so I wasn't interested. I looked at the clock again; it was eleven after eleven. Why does time go so slow when you want to do something fun and you have to wait?

"Hel-loo." Mrs. Nesbitt was on the porch holding a loaf of bread. The lieutenant was right behind her.

"Go on in, mom. The ladies in the kitchen need the bread for sandwiches."

Jerry and I said, "Hi," and I asked Lt. Nesbitt, "How did you know Granma needed more bread?"

"She called my mom a few minutes ago. We finished packing and then came over."

After everybody had sandwiches, the dishes were washed, and the house was locked up tight. We climbed into the two cars and pickup and started on our adventure. As planned, Elena and the Lieutenant led the caravan and the pickup followed the Desoto packed with ladies. In a little over an hour we arrived in Augusta, but didn't stop except for red lights. We lost track of Granma's Desoto in traffic, but Mr. Morgan didn't seem to be worried. I didn't know the adults had made plans to meet in Belgrade on Route 27 if anyone got separated.

I got on my knees and looked through the rear window of the pickup cab to see where we were going. As we pulled into the little town I read the sign beside the posted speed limit of 45 mph. The sign said Belgrade had a population of 1,100, but someone had painted over the last zero with a sloppy number one. I saw Granma's Desoto and the Navy car at the first service station at the edge of town. I wondered how long they had been waiting for us. We all got out and walked around to stretch our legs while the men filled the gas tanks. Jerry and I threw a few rocks at the back of a road sign until Mom said not to. I think she was afraid we might miss and break something—like a window, or hit a car on the highway.

After the cars were gassed up, Lieutenant Nesbitt waved to Mom and Mr. Morgan and pulled out of the service station. Mom followed with Granma, Suzy, and Mrs. Nesbitt in the Desoto. Mr. Morgan yelled at Mom as she followed the Navy car, "See you in Fairbanks!" I didn't know there was a town in Maine called Fairbanks, but I knew there was one in Alaska. I looked at Jerry and said, "Fairbanks is about four-thousand miles from here. This is going to be a long ride."

Jerry laughed and replied, "It'll probably be shorter if we cut through Canada."

We sat back on the sleeping bags and watched cars pass us going in the opposite direction. Once in a while, a car would come up behind us and pass, but Mr. Morgan seemed to keep our speed constant at the speed limit. The road was smooth, the sun was out, and I began to fall asleep, but Jerry grabbed my arm and said, "There's an old brown pickup coming up on us, Rocky. It's coming pretty fast." My sleepiness vanished and I was wide awake, squinting to read the license plate. Just when I thought I could read the plate, the pickup would jiggle and the numbers bounced around so I couldn't get a clear view until the suspicious pickup was almost on top of us.

The number was 5811 and it was from Vermont, so I let out the breath I was holding and relaxed. As the brown pickup roared past us, a young lady, not as old as Elena, smiled and waved to us from the front passenger seat. We waved back, happy it hadn't been those guys from the lighthouse or the boat. In a few moments, that ugly pickup, with a bunch of old tires in the back, was gone. I'll bet they were going at least ten miles per hour over the speed limit.

"That was kind of exciting, wasn't it?" Jerry commented.

"Sure was. I was a little bit scared for a minute, but then I remembered your dad was with us, so I didn't have much to worry about."

We sat back watching small boats on the lakes on both sides of the highway. We didn't try to talk much because the air flowing over the cab was too noisy and we had to yell to be heard. My throat was getting dry so I closed my eyes and thought about a cool mountain stream, fishing, skipping rocks across the water, and wading along the banks. It would be neat to have a dog, but Jerry and Suzy will do.

The next little town we came to was New Sharon, population 761. We hardly slowed down, but I saw some nice houses with dormers as we passed through the little town. I could hear the radio when we were driving slowly. Mrs. Morgan had her window down. The announcer said we were listening to music on WFAU, 1340 kilohertz, in Augusta. As soon as we were travelling at the speed limit, I couldn't hear the radio except when I put my head against the cab of the pickup, but that didn't last long; when we hit a bump my head got whacked. Jerry though it was funny; he had tried to hear the radio before, with the same result. I gave Jerry a dirty look and said, "You could have warned me, goofball!"

"Yeah, I could have, but then it wouldn't have been so funny." He continued to laugh. I had to grin as I began thinking of pulling a fast one on him one of these days.

Farmington was a big city compared to some of the small towns we had driven through. A population of 4,677 was displayed on a road sign as we entered the city limits. The downtown area had lots of stores, many of them had signs advertising from ten to twenty percent off on school clothes. I hadn't yet thought of going back to school in Boston, I was having too much fun in Crafton, finding books to sell, riding around with Jerry, and getting kidnapped. I hope Suzy and I get to visit Granma again next summer, maybe for an even longer time.

We had hardly gotten out of Farmington, maybe only a couple of minutes, when Mr. Morgan slowed down and pulled over. Jerry and I stood up and looked over the top of the cab, but we didn't see any town. The lieutenant had stopped and Granma's Desoto was right in front of us. Mom was getting out of the driver's seat and walking ahead to talk with Lieutenant Nesbitt. Mr. Morgan just sat and waited. Jerry and I watched Mom walking back toward the pickup. Mr. Morgan stepped out, talked with Mom for a few seconds, said, "We'll follow you," and got back in the truck.

Jerry poked me and said, "See that sign? I think we're going to a picnic area." He pointed off the road to the right. Maybe Jerry saw or heard something I didn't, but Mr. Morgan followed Mom down a gravel road. We passed over a small stream, through some trees and into a clearing where there were at least a dozen tables, a fire pit, some waste containers, and two outhouses, one marked women and the other marked men. It sure looked like a picnic area.

As soon as the pickup stopped between the lieutenant's car and the Desoto, Jerry and I jumped to the ground and went to the outhouse marked men. We went in together and took a whiz. I held my breath as soon as we were in there, that outhouse really stunk. I had to get some fresh air; I didn't finish before I had to breathe again. Jerry came out blinking his eyes and I started laughing. I took a deep breath and went back in to finish. It was a quick trip. I was grateful that I didn't have to go number two, I would have thrown up if I had to smell that place any longer than I already had. That was a real adventure. I wondered what the women's outhouse smelled like, but I wasn't going to find out by myself.

It didn't take long to find out, Suzy came out of the lady's outhouse crying. "Mommy, do I have to go in there? Isn't there a regular bathroom?"

Mr. Morgan didn't have any problems with the outhouse, I think the smells from the war were worse than from that outdoor toilet, but when he came out, he warned the lieutenant. I watched the lieutenant take a deep breath and hold his nose before he went in.

When he came out, he was smiling and said, "It's not that bad."

Mrs. Nesbitt spoke up, "Aaron never did have a very good sense of smell." Everyone laughed and Elena, Mrs. Nesbitt, Granma, and Mom walked together to a big clump of trees about thirty yards from the picnic tables. Mom was carrying a roll of toilet paper. There were only two other cars in the parking area and both were empty. I figured the people must have gone hiking.

When the ladies returned from the trees, we talked for a few minutes and then got back in the cars and pickup. As Jerry and I climbed into the pickup, Mr. Morgan told us that we would meet the others in Rangeley, about an hour away on Route 4. I watched as the Navy car started down the gravel road back to the highway, suddenly stopped and backed up. Lt. Nesbitt must have forgotten something.

He didn't forget anything after all, there was a big semi pulling a flatbed trailer hauling a tractor with a scoop on one end and a bucket on the other. It was hogging the road from the highway and was followed by a dump truck, a white pickup with Franklin County decals on the doors and tailgate. Right behind the white pickup was a brown one. Though I wasn't cold, I shivered as I saw the license number. Jerry grabbed my arm and yelled, "That's the truck, Rocky!"

"I know. I hope we're getting out of here right now." The lieutenant had gotten around the trucks and was back on the gravel with Mom following him. As soon as Granma's Desoto was on the gravel, Mr. Morgan gunned the engine and we tore off leaving a shower of gravel peppering the brown pickup truck. Mr. Morgan had recognized the pickup at the same time we did. Our caravan crossed over the Sandy River on Route 4, made a sharp right-hand turn and headed toward Rangeley.

Chapter 20

Looking for a Campsite

There wasn't much traffic on Route 4, but Jerry and I watched for that ugly pickup all the way to Rangeley. A couple of cars passed us, but we didn't see that brown pickup truck again. Jerry and I kept our eyes peeled, but after a while, we started watching the streams, trees, and occasional wildlife near the road, taking turns to watch the road behind us. We saw two deer and lots of birds, probably coming to the rivers and lakes for a drink or something to eat.

When we saw a stream or a lake, we saw people fishing, even kids our age had poles. Some people wore waders and were out in the middle of the moving water or were drifting around in lakes in small boats, sometimes canoes. The first time we saw a bunch of people fishing, I asked Jerry, "Have you ever gone fishing?"

"I did once—with my stepdad. It wasn't much fun, I got bored pretty fast. I didn't catch anything."

"Do you think you would like it if you caught some fish?"

"Nah, then I'd have to clean 'em. I don't like guts all over the place. I'd rather eat a hamburger."

"And fries?"

"Uh-huh, with lots of catsup."

I smiled and said, "Me, too."

Rangeley, I found out later on, was a resort community and was exactly half-way between the North Pole and the equator. We followed the Desoto into town and ended up on the shore of Rangeley Lake where there were picnic tables and boats for rent. I was beginning to wonder where we would stop to eat lunch, my stomach was beginning to eat at my backbone, growling as if it were a dog protecting its food.

When the caravan stopped, Jerry and I jumped out of the truck and ran down to the water to look around. There were three girls in a canoe, but they ignored us and paddled along the shoreline toward a grassy area between the water and a large building that looked kind of like a clubhouse. They were probably city girls on summer vacation and were older than us. I bet they were looking for guys with cars or just someone to flirt with. I wonder what they would do when faced with Russian spies.

"Jerry—Rocky, come get some lunch." Mrs. Morgan was calling us from a picnic table near the parking area. Jerry ran over to the table, where everyone was sitting, except Granma, but I walked slowly, thinking about that brown pickup. I wondered if every time we saw that brown piece of junk the same two guys were in it. As I got to the table, Mom asked, "Are you all right, Rocky?"

"Yes, mom. What's for lunch?" I could see two big bags of potato chips and a small stack of paper plates and napkins. Granma was standing guard over a large picnic basket, handing out sandwiches. We had a choice of tuna fish, cheese, or baloney. Jerry had taken several bites of something and was trying to talk with his mouth full. I could see his chewed up food. He wasn't able to get any words past the food. He suddenly stood up and pointed toward the highway with his sandwich. I looked in the direction he was pointing and saw it; that old brown pickup, just sitting there. Somebody was watching us.

Lt. Nesbitt and Elena were both looking, too. The lieutenant stood up and began walking toward the brown truck. When he was almost close enough to see who was in the seat, the pickup backed up and drove slowly away. Lt. Nesbitt continued walking, stopped at a public telephone and made a call. I don't think the lieutenant was going to talk with the guys in the pickup. I think he might have if he had asked Mr. Morgan to go with him.

I had eaten half a cheese sandwich by the time the lieutenant returned to the table and sat down beside Elena. She said something to him and he replied, but I couldn't hear what they were talking about.

I took a big drink of Coke and asked, "Who did you call, Lieutenant?"

Mom said, "Rocky, that's none of your business."

Her tone of voice made me realize I shouldn't have asked, so I said, "Sorry."

"Well, it wasn't a personal call, Rocky. I made a call for some reinforcements. I'm beginning to get a bit irritated with that brown pickup."

I took another swallow of Coke and burped, but not loud enough for anyone to hear, except for Jerry. Jerry had just stuffed his mouth with potato chips and was trying to get them down when he decided to take a big drink of Coke. I watched his Adam's apple twitching up and down, then he let out the loudest burp I had ever heard.

"Jerry! Where are your manners?" his mom asked with almost a yell.

Jerry's eyes were watering and he said, "Excuse me. Mom, I had to do it—the gas was hurting my stomach."

"Don't drink so much so fast and that won't happen."

I poked him in the ribs and laughed.

Granma said, "Boys, tone it down a little, please."

I watched as all the adults gathered around Lt. Nesbitt. He had his map unfolded on the table top and was pointing at some of the roads, explaining something. It was all over before I could join them to see what the discussion was about. Everyone began helping Granma and Mom clean up the picnic table and check the ground for garbage to throw away. Elena stepped on a few potato chips and smashed them into the dirt. She saw me watching her, turned and smiled.

Lieutenant Nesbitt said, "Okay, folks, we'll see you in about twenty minutes, then we'll look for a camp site." Elena and the lieutenant picked up a bag of potato chips, some Cokes, a jar of pickles, and headed for the Navy car. I heard the doors slam and watched the car pull away from the parking area. We were supposed to meet them on highway sixteen where the asphalt changed to gravel, about ten miles west of Stratton, a small town near Flagstaff Lake on highway twenty-seven, but we weren't going that far. Granma showed Jerry, Suzy and me the locations on the map. In a few minutes we were travelling, mostly eastward, toward Dallas, but the little town was not on the main highway, so we weren't stopping there.

The humidity seemed to have dropped as we drove down the highway, which was cleared of trees on both sides, maybe out to 100 feet. The sky was blue and the sun was out, but I felt a little cool. I wrapped my jacket around my shoulders and tried to sink lower into the rolled-up sleeping bag as we followed the Desoto. Jerry and I were continually watching for that brown pickup but checked out the evergreen forest on both sides of the highway as the odometer kept track of our mileage. I was guessing that the few cars on the road was due to the upcoming gravel road from Stratton. From what the lieutenant said, the untreated gravel road was very bumpy and dusty. I began to think about putting my handkerchief over my mouth and nose to keep the dust out, but then I would look like a bank robber in a western movie, except I didn't have a six-shooter or a black hat.

We had been travelling for maybe ten minutes before the pickup began to slow down and pull over to the side of the road. I wondered why we were stopping, we hadn't gone far enough to get to the gravel road. Jerry was looking around the cab on the passenger side and said, "Hey, Rock! The lieutenant's car is off the road up ahead."

I stood up and looked over the cab and could see the Navy car off the shoulder turned sideways with the front pointing toward the road. The windshield was full of cracks. Granma's Desoto was stopped on the shoulder and we were slowly coming up behind her car. Elena was walking toward Granma's car, stepping around weeds and over rocks. The lieutenant had popped the trunk of his car and was holding a jack. Before Mr. Morgan had come to a stop, Jerry and I were on the ground and running toward the Navy car.

I yelled, "What happened, Lieutenant?"

"Someone shot through the front passenger side window and also punctured a tire. I almost lost control of the car. Luckily, Elena was sitting next to me and the first bullet went into the back seat. The car nearly rolled when the tire was hit, but I was able to keep control by getting into the dirt at the side of the road. We slowed down pretty fast."

Mr. Morgan had followed Jerry and me and was pulling the spare tire from the trunk. We walked around the car and could see the right front tire was completely flat, but the window surprised me. It was almost white, cracked into lots of small pieces with a bullet hole near the top. I asked, "Why is the window still in the door? Why didn't the bullet knock out the window?"

Lt. Nesbitt answered, "The side and back windows are made of tempered glass. It breaks into small pieces so large chunks can't cut anyone. It should hold its shape until someone hits it or tries to remove it. Mr. Morgan can probably tell us if we should break it out."

Jerry asked, "What about the windshield?"

Mr. Morgan told us the windshield was made of laminated glass, two sheets of glass with a polymer in between, kind of a polymer sandwich. Then he explained what a polymer was. When the windshield breaks, it cracks, but doesn't come apart or break into little pieces, so you can still see through it to drive. It sounded like we were already in school learning science.

I asked the lieutenant, "Do you think someone was shooting at Elena?"

"I don't know, Rocky, but I hope not. Say, where is your grandmother going?"

I looked around and saw Granma walking toward the trees as if she was going into the forest to meet someone, but maybe she had something else in mind. "Maybe she has to go to the bathroom," is all I could think of to say, but she didn't have any toilet paper, both her hands were empty. We watched as she began looking around on the ground behind the trees. She moved slowly, occasionally bending down and picking something up. Then she disappeared into the forest.

I asked the lieutenant, "Do you think I should go after her?"

"No. I think she can take care of herself. She'll be back in a few minutes. I think she's looking for shell casings and footprints. If you go after her, you might mess up some evidence."

I thought about what Lt. Nesbitt had said. He sounded confident. I decided he was right. But how did Granma know how to do those things? Then I remembered that she and Granpa used to go bird watching. They probably discovered animal tracks and footprints of other people when they were in the woods. I was a little bit worried that whoever shot at the Navy car had a gun, but Granma didn't. I didn't think she could do very well in hand-to-hand combat.

Mr. Morgan joined the lieutenant and me and said, "Okay, Lieutenant, your tire is ready to go. That bullet went through and through; you'll need a new spare. Let's get out of here and get more cover.

"Right, Steve, just as soon as Mrs. Makler returns." The lieutenant looked over at the edge of the forest and then said, "Thanks for taking care of the tire. I owe you one." The lieutenant walked to his car, got in and pulled the car onto the shoulder, then shut off the engine. Elena got in and they started talking. I was too far away to hear what they were saying.

I watched the trees, hoping I would see Granma walking toward us, but we had to wait for another five minutes or so before I spotted her coming out of the trees. She waved and yelled, "I found what I wanted, let's find a place to camp."

When we were all in the cars and pickup, the Navy car pulled away with the rest of us following closely. After ten minutes or so, the lieutenant turned right on a dirt road and drove south with Mom and Mr. Morgan following, driving the Desoto and the pickup. Jerry and I had to hang on tight to keep from falling out of the back of the pickup—some of the bumps shook the whole truck, especially our bones. I could hear Mrs. Morgan laughing when we hit a big hole in a washout across the road. I think she was bouncing up and down on the seat. Mom had slowed way down, trying to avoid a wreck, and Mr. Morgan almost came to a stop, afraid to run into Granma's car.

The dirt road was dry. I couldn't see any sign of water. Maybe the water had come from snow melting during the spring thaw. The trees were very close to the road and in some places branches hung down nearly touching the top of the pickup. I imagined a cowboy riding through a forest and getting knocked off his horse by a low-hanging branch. I was a little scared to stick my head above the cab to see where we were going. Jerry looked at his watch and said, "We've been on this lousy road for ten minutes. I hope we stop soon, my muscles are getting sore from fighting to stay in the truck." I felt the same way.

All of a sudden, we were in a clearing and I could see where someone else had camped. There was a fire pit with rocks surrounding it and not far down a slightly sloping area of tall grass was a small lake. Someone had left a canoe near the bank, upside down; something for Jerry and me to use to explore the lake and shoreline.

We jumped out of the pickup and headed for the lake before any of the adults were out of their cars. I though Suzy would be following us, but she hadn't gotten out of the car. She must be asleep, but how she could sleep with the car hitting all those bumps, I don't know. Jerry and I got to the canoe and looked it over. In the bottom, there were three holes in a small triangular shape. Those holes weren't made by accident.

"Darn it! Somebody shot holes in the canoe." I think my dad can fix it though; we just need to plug the holes. Why would anybody do that?"

I had the same question.

We were both disappointed so we walked slowly back toward the cars.

Chapter 21

Making Camp

Mr. Morgan stood by the fire pit, his left hand holding his chin, as he was looking around the clearing. Lieutenant Nesbitt joined him and they began pointing and walking around looking at the ground. They talked for about a minute before Jerry's dad said, "Come on boys, you have to earn your keep." He sounded serious. I knew we were going to help him unload the pickup.

Jerry's dad backed the pickup from the road to within ten feet of the fire pit and we began removing stuff from the pickup. Mr. Morgan told Jerry and me where to put certain things. A heavy burlap bag went next to the fire pit and a large, fairly heavy, canvas bag was set about twenty feet away on nearly level ground. Jerry and I were given a shovel and asked to remove all the uneven bumps to make a flat spot. We figured the tent was going to go there.

Mr. Morgan dumped the stuff in the burlap bag on the ground and put together a grill made of reinforcing steel; the metal used in concrete structures. No wonder that bag was so heavy. Following his instructions, we started erecting the tent, but we needed one more pole over eight feet long. Jerry walked over to his dad and said, "I think we're one pole short, Dad. We must have forgotten the long pole that holds up the roof in the middle."

"You know, you're right. I put that pole up in the rafters in the garage. I forgot to get it down. Get the hatchet and we'll make one."

I went with Jerry to the cab of the pickup and watched him fold down the back of the seat. There was a rifle, an ax, and a hatchet neatly stored behind the seat; so Mr. Morgan had two rifles. I wondered if they used the same ammunition, but I still hadn't seen any. Maybe the ammo is in the glove box. Jerry handed the hatchet to me and put the seat back in its normal position. I carried the hatchet to Mr. Morgan and the three of us headed towards the trees, walking through thick grass, weeds, and a few wild flowers, mostly yellow and purple, but a few blue and white ones scattered here and there. Those little flowers sure made the forested area more interesting by adding colors other than shades of green and brown.

Jerry and I followed his dad until he stopped and said, "That one will do." I thought he was pointing at a tree about six inches in diameter, but that wasn't the one. He had picked out a small tree that looked deformed and kind of scrawny. I asked, "Why that one, Mr. Morgan, it's not even straight."

He knelt next to the tree and said, "This tree will never grow up to be straight and strong. Do you know why?"

I thought for a few seconds and said, "It doesn't get enough water?"

Jerry said, "I think it doesn't get enough sunlight; it's in the shade of the bigger trees."

"Well, you're both right. Those are good answers. So, this little tree will probably struggle through life and die, adding to the debris on the forest floor. We are going to give it a purpose; it will hold up our tent while we enjoy camping. It is doing us a favor."

"Shall we cut the branches off first?" I asked.

Mr. Morgan handed the hatchet to me and stepped behind me with Jerry. "Start cutting off the branches—as close to the trunk as you can get."

I grabbed a branch, bent it back so the needles wouldn't poke me, and swung the hatchet pretty hard. It took three whacks before the branch fell to the ground. Jerry pulled it away so I wouldn't be stepping on it and I cut off three more, each one came off a little easier than the last. I was breathing hard, so I gave the hatchet to Jerry. He cut off about as many as I did before Mr. Morgan took the hatchet, and with about ten swings, cut through the trunk.

"Okay, Rocky, cut it off so the pole is seven-foot six-inches long."

I looked at Mr. Morgan and asked, "Do you have a measuring tape?" He shook his head.

Then I started thinking. What did I have with me that I knew was a certain length? My belt was about twenty-eight inches long, my shoes were about ten inches long, and my height was sixty inches plus a bit. Mr. Morgan could see I was struggling to come up with a measuring device so he said, "How about the length of the hatchet? How long is it?"

I put my foot beside it and figured it was about fifteen inches long. I asked Jerry, "How many inches in seven-foot six-inches?"

Jerry's eyes rolled back in his head, he turned in a circle and said, "Ninety."

Then I had it! Six hatchet lengths made ninety inches. I measured off six hatchet lengths, took the hatchet and cut off the top of the tree. I think Mr. Morgan would be a good teacher.

Jerry picked up the pole, I carried the hatchet and Mr. Morgan told us we had done a good job. As we walked back to the tent, Jerry and I both noticed we had sticky fingers—really sticky! I looked up at Mr. Morgan and noticed he was grinning.

"What's that sticky stuff on your fingers, Rocky?"

"I'm not sure, but it must be from those branches."

Mr. Morgan nodded and said, "It's pitch and it won't come off with soap and water."

An idea suddenly came into my mind. That pitch is sticky and it won't dissolve in water so I told Jerry, "I just got an idea of how to fix the canoe."

Jerry smiled and said, "Me, too! I bet it's the same as yours."

Mr. Morgan asked, "What are you two talking about?"

"Jerry and I discovered an old canoe down by the lake, but it's got three holes in it—right in the bottom. We're going to patch the holes with some pegs and glue them in with pitch. Right, Jerry?"

"Yep. That's what I was thinking, too. We got the same idea. I've another idea, too."

Mr. Morgan said, "I think your idea to fix the canoe is a good one. Do you have pocket knives to make some dowels?" He looked at Jerry, "Did you bring your knife, Son?"

He pulled a pocket knife from his pants and showed to his dad. I had the Boy Scout knife my dad had given me two years ago, so we were prepared to begin fixing the canoe, but first, we had to finish putting up the tent. We used the hatchet to pound in stakes to hold the tent's walls in position with attached ropes, and then we raised the roof in the center with the pole we had made. Jerry and I had to wrestle that pole into place by pushing and shoving, but we finally got it done. Mr. Morgan looked at it and told us we had done a good job.

"If you want, you can work on that canoe. The ladies, the lieutenant, and I will set up the rest of the camp."

"Come on, Rocky, let's get to work on the canoe." Jerry was rarin' to go. He was standing there like he wanted to race me, but I was sitting on the ground looking around to see the birds that were making the loud noises coming from high in the trees.

Jerry came over to me and looked around in the trees. We both spotted a bird at the same time. It looked black and was about twice the size of a robin. "Hey, Dad, is it all right to shoot those birds?" We were both pointing at the bird making the noise.

"What's wrong, boys? Don't you like that bird's song?" Mr. Morgan grinned.

"That's not a song, Mr. Morgan, that's a racket." I smiled and he laughed.

"That's a grackle, Rocky. They like to be around humans to steal food. I believe it is their mating season. We'll probably see quite a few of those birds around here. It won't hurt to throw rocks at them, I don't think you'll ever hit one. They're pretty smart birds."

Jerry leaned down and said, "Remember, I said I had another idea."

"Yeah, what is it?"

"We can make some slingshots. We'll get the inner tube from the lieutenant's punctured tire and cut some strips like rubber bands. When we're making plugs for the canoe, we can find some Y-shaped branches to make slingshots."

Now I was really interested. Having a canoe would be fun, but having a weapon other than a gun grabbed my imagination. We could hunt those noisy critters in the trees. I got to my feet and we started running toward the canoe. The sounds of our running didn't seem to bother that stupid bird. It just sat on a limb and made those awful noises. I began to wonder if more of those grackles would be showing up. I hoped so, we would have lots of targets for our rocks.

While we collected some dried twigs of different sizes to make plugs for the boat, I picked up small pebbles to use for ammunition. By the time we had wood for the plugs and a couple of Y-shaped handles for the slingshots, my right-hand pocket was half-full of small stones. All the time we were searching the ground around the trees, I kept thinking about Suzy. I was surprised she wasn't following us around asking questions. I had plenty of answers saved up. Jerry and I spent about half-an-hour whittling plugs for the holes in the canoe, and after that, we searched for a supply of pitch. We finally found a couple of blister-like bumps on trees where limbs had been sawed or broken off. The pitch oozed out when we stuck the bumps with our knives.

It took us another half-hour to cement the plugs in the holes. We stood back to admire our work and heard Mr. Morgan call us back to the fire pit area for dinner. We had trouble putting our knives back in our pockets; once we grabbed our knives and closed them, they were stuck to our fingers. Jerry knelt down and rubbed his hands in the dirt and then slid his knife into his pocket. I did the same as Jerry and we walked back to the tents wondering what our mothers would say about our dirty hands. We knew the pitch wouldn't come off with soap and water. Maybe Mr. Morgan would know what we could do. He seemed to know lots of things about the outdoors.

Just as I thought, Mom saw our dirty hands and told us to wash. We tried to get our hands clean with soap and water, but as Mr. Morgan had said, the pitch stayed on our hands like water-proof glue. Water did no good, but Granma came to our rescue.

"Here, boys, rub some baking soda on your fingers and then add some peanut butter."

I joked with her and said, "We don't want to make peanut butter cookies, Granma."

"Don't worry, Rocky, I'm not giving you any flour. Don't eat the peanut butter off your hands or you won't be able to go to the bathroom." Granma grinned as she gave Jerry a spoonful of peanut butter. Jerry had put baking soda on his hands, so he was trying the remedy first.

"Mother! You're getting to be as bad as the boys."

"It's all right, Mom, Granma is our leader." All the adults laughed. I liked causing people to laugh, but I couldn't predict when the stuff I said would be funny.

I was watching Jerry rubbing his brown hands together. "How's it working, Jerry?"

"It seems to be working. It's like greasy sandpaper stuck to my fingers. I wonder if a bit of jelly would help." He gave a slight laugh and said, "It's going to take soap and water to get the peanut butter off. It smells good though." Jerry was sniffing his hands.

"Mom, where's Suzy?"

"She's asleep in the back seat of the Desoto. She had an upset stomach and threw up."

I figured she must have gotten carsick when we were going over all those bumps in the gravel roads. Tomorrow she'll be following Jerry and me around asking questions, but I don't always have the answers. Jerry can help me explain things.

I was next to use Granma's remedy. It took about ten minutes to feel like the pitch was coming off my skin. After I washed with soap and water, almost all the stickiness was gone, except for a small amount that would probably wear off tomorrow. I kept wondering how Mom would get the pitch out of my pockets. Washing my pants with peanut butter didn't seem like a very good idea. Maybe she would take my clothes to the cleaners back in Crafton. They probably have some chemicals that will dissolve pitch. If she wanted, she could rip out the old pocket and sew in a new one, but that might be too much work.

Dinner was over by 7:00 p.m. and then we went back to work. The men asked the women where they wanted their bathroom. Elena said, "As close to the camp as possible, but far enough away so you men can't see us." She smiled and then added, "Will we have hot and cold water—and a shower?"

Lt. Nesbitt said smiling, "Fat chance, my dear. However, Mr. Morgan has a real toilet seat for you, but no flush will be provided. You'll have to use a shovel."

I was wondering where Mr. Morgan had a toilet seat, but he opened a box in the back of the pickup and pulled out a white toilet seat. I guess the lieutenant and Mr. Morgan had talked about it when Jerry and I were working on the canoe. I was trying to imagine what the men would sit on in our bathroom—probably a log. We took the hatchet, the ax, a hammer and nails, and the toilet seat and went into the trees nearest the camp—about twenty yards away. It took us an hour to build the ladies bathroom. The men made three walls from branches and a support for the seat. Mr. Morgan dug a hole beneath and leaned his war surplus shovel against the holder for toilet paper Jerry and I made. We invited the ladies to visit their open-air outhouse.

Granma looked it over and said, "Thank you, gentlemen. That should be adequate."

Suzy said, "But there isn't a door or a roof, Granma."

Everybody laughed and Mom said, "I don't think it will rain, dear. The weatherman said it would be dry for the next week."

The shadows from the trees were growing long, so we went back to the fire pit, where I imagined a pyramid of logs glowing red at their base and yellow flames crackling, rising into the air, and occasional sparks shooting from the fire. Mr. Morgan and Lt. Nesbitt carried firewood from a pile in front of the cook tent. After the fire was started, we roasted some marshmallows. Suzy's started on fire and turned black, so she didn't want it. I ate hers and she ate the one I had carefully toasted to a light-brown. I hoped she wouldn't throw up; all the care I had given that marshmallow would have been wasted.

Chapter 22

An Orphan

The next morning after eating, Lt. Nesbitt and Elena went hiking to look over the area south and east of our camp site. They said they might be gone for twenty-four hours. They both had backpacks and canteens. It looked to me like they were going to climb mountains. I noticed the lieutenant wearing a holster and handgun. Elena had a much smaller pack than Lt. Nesbitt's, probably because she wasn't very strong yet. I didn't think they would have any trouble. I couldn't tell if Elena had a gun.

Jerry and I went to the canoe, put it in the water, and checked for leaks. Jerry got in to add more pressure on our plugs, but no water came through. I was about to shove the canoe into the water and jump in, when we both realized we had no oars. I stood up and said, "We need to make some oars." Jerry took a quick look at the bottom of the canoe and said, "Yeah. There's nothing here to use for oars. Let's talk to my dad."

An hour later, we had an oar made from a good-sized limb, a green limb with the small end bent into a circle and a grease-stained piece of cloth Mr. Morgan had in his tool box. It looked like a bandaged, out-of-shape, tennis racket with a long handle, but it worked. Mrs. Morgan and Mom made us take an old, spare, collapsed, inner tube with us after we had filled it with air. She said it had a tiny hole in it, but it would hold air for a day. Jerry and I had to take turns forcing air from our lungs into that rubber tube, but we got enough air in it so we could use it as a lifesaver.

Having passed all safety tests, we set out across the lake to see what was interesting on the other side. We took turns paddling and were surprised when we found the little lake to be much bigger than we could see from camp. The water was in the shape of a lamb chop. We had only seen the smaller part from where we had found the canoe. Jerry and I guessed the bigger part of the lake was about half- a-mile across. We stayed along the shore, a little afraid that we might get out in the middle of the lake and lose our paddle or it might break apart. It would take until afternoon to paddle back to camp using only our hands. If we had to walk back, we would have to leave the canoe and climb through some thick clumps of trees and shrubs that almost grew out of the water.

As I paddled, Jerry watched the shoreline for things to investigate, just as I had done when he paddled.

"Hey, Rock! What's that over there?"

"Over where?"

Jerry was pointing at the shore about fifty yards ahead of us. I couldn't see what he was pointing at, so I paddled harder. I didn't want to stand up and tip over, so I stayed sitting down. I kept looking, squinting to improve my sight, and then I saw it. It was a small coyote or wolf sniffing along the shoreline, probably looking for something to eat— maybe a dead fish. As we approached it, the animal didn't run away; it stood there and yipped, watching us come closer. It was a little black puppy, not a coyote or wolf. Its tail was wagging, as if it was excited to see old friends.

I was first out of the canoe and into about six-inches of water. I pulled the canoe onto shore and Jerry hopped out onto dry land. The puppy wasn't very big, but it was squirming around when we tried to pet it. I tried to pick it up to see if it had a collar, but it ran to Jerry. He grabbed it by the scruff and held it up so we could examine it. It didn't have a collar. It had a white patch on its chest, like a small vest, and the white tips of its hind legs made it look like it was wearing shoes. Floppy ears made it look cuddly. Jerry and I guessed it's a Labrador retriever mix. We decided to take it back to camp and see if we can find someone who owns it. We wondered why it wasn't with another dog. Maybe its mother got hurt and it's all alone.

It was Jerry's turn to row, so I got in the canoe and Jerry gave me the puppy. He shoved off and jumped in. We decided to go straight across the water, the shortest way to camp, confident that our oar would hold together since we had already gone more than half-a-mile with it. The squirmy little dog didn't want me to hold it. I put it down and it put its front paws on the side edge of the canoe and looked at the water. It reminded me of seeing a dog with its head out of a car window taking in the sights and barking at people on foot.

As we neared camp, I realized that Suzy was going to go ape when she saw the puppy. I didn't think Mom would want us to keep it, but maybe Jerry's parents would have a different idea. Of course, Granma or Mrs. Nesbitt might want a happy little dog.

When we were about ten feet from the shore, our new friend jumped into the water and swam ashore. He shook off the water and waited for Jerry and me to pull the canoe on shore. He ran around our legs as we walked toward the fire pit, trying not to step on him. I wondered how long he had been by himself and how hungry he must be. What would we feed him? We didn't have any dog food.

Granma noticed the puppy first. "My goodness, where did you find your little friend?"

Suzy came running from the tent saying, "Where did you find the puppy, Rocky? Can I have it?"

"It's a *he,* Suzy—not an *it.*"

She dropped to her knees and tried to pet the little dog, but I think she scared him and he ran behind Jerry and me for protection.

"Where did you find him?"

"On the other end of the lake. He was near the water, probably getting a drink and looking for food. Ask Mom if she has anything we can feed the puppy."

Jerry said, "Let's get those slingshots made so we can hunt some of those noisy birds. We can roast them and give the meat to Surprise."

"I like that name, Jerry."

Suzy hadn't taken her eyes off the puppy and said, "Is his name Surprise?"

"I guess so, Suzy, at least for now. What would you call him?"

"Hmm, I'll have to think about it. I'll ask Mom for some food for him. He sure is cute."

Jerry and I took Surprise around to show Mr. and Mrs. Morgan and Mrs. Nesbitt. The Morgans didn't seem to be very interested in the puppy, but Mrs. Nesbitt reached out and picked up Surprise. The puppy seemed to like her right away and licked her face. "So, young man, you like older women." She held Surprise at arm's length and he wiggled, so she put him down.

"I think he's hungry, Mrs. Nesbitt."

"I think you're right, Rocky. I wasn't sure he was licking off my makeup or kissing me, but maybe he just wants something to eat."

I replied, "He hasn't eaten anything since we found him—over an hour ago."

"Well, he hasn't been alone very long, he surely isn't skinny."

Suzy and Mom appeared from the big tent. Suzy had a wiener in her hand. Surprise must have smelled it. He ran to Suzy and put his front paws on her legs, stretching to get at the food. Suzy broke off a piece of meat and Surprise took it from her fingers, hardly chewed, and wanted more. That piece of wiener disappeared faster than it would have if Suzy had eaten it.

Mom said, "That little guy is hungry, isn't he? I wonder if he will drink some milk."

Granma reacted, "I wouldn't do that, Sandra. I think cow's milk will make him poop on everything."

"You know, Mom, I think you're right. I seem to remember young cats and dogs will get diarrhea from cow's milk."

I was looking out over the lake when I thought of fish. I bet the dog would eat fish, but all the while Jerry and I were in the canoe, I hadn't noticed any.

"Hey, Jerry, did you notice any fish in the lake?"

"Sure did. Over there where we found the puppy." Jerry pointed in the direction we had come on the way back. "I saw bubbles and little ripples when the fish came near the surface."

Granma said, "Okay, boys, let's make some fishing poles and I'll go fishing with you. I haven't been fishing in a coon's age." She didn't know that Mr. Morgan had some fishing poles in the pickup, but I didn't say anything. He might not want kids to use them.

I had never heard that term before, so I asked, "How long is a coon's age?"

Granma laughed and replied, "That's a long time, Rocky."

It took almost half-an-hour to get ready. I thought we would fish from the shoreline, but Granma wanted to go out in the canoe. I think maybe she hadn't gone canoeing in a coon's age either. Jerry was in one end of the canoe, I was at the other, with Granma in the middle. Mr. Morgan pushed us off from shore. We drifted out about twenty feet before I began paddling.

With Granma in the canoe, we couldn't move as fast as Jerry and I had earlier. Our canoe was deeper in the water now, but we got to the middle of the small part of the lake in a couple of minutes. It felt like we were moving in slow motion. Rowing was boring and I kept hearing those rotten birds. They seemed to be calling back and forth; one would say something and then laugh, then the other one would do it. It was like they were telling jokes. Wait until we get our slingshots. Those birds will make a good snack for Surprise.

"That's far enough, Rocky. Let's see if we can catch a big one." Granma smiled as she fished a big worm out of a can half-filled with dirt and earthworms. She used her fingernail and cut a worm into three parts so we could bait our hooks. I was kind of surprised by her action, but my pocketknife was still stuck in the pocket of my other pair of pants. I had thought she wouldn't like worm guts on her fingers.

I think it must have been about ten minutes before Jerry said, "I've got a bite!" I could see his line pull tight and he began pulling on his pole, guiding the fish toward the canoe. Granma was giving him instructions so she could reach into the water and grab the fish. I think it was a trout—about eight-inches long, but I had only seen a few trout before, so I wasn't sure.

Granma removed the hook from the fish's mouth, put another piece of worm on Jerry's hook, and told him to do it again.

I wasn't having much luck, but Granma pulled in the next one, a little bit smaller than Jerry's. Then Jerry got another one. I was wondering why the fish weren't biting at my bait. Maybe I had a bad part of the worm. Granma put the three fish into an old Wonder bread wrapper and used a rubber band to seal the bag. I felt a tug on my line just as I heard a bang coming from the shore across the lake. I pulled on my line, but I didn't have a fish.

Granma yelled, "Get in the water! Get in the water! Someone is shooting at us!" Jerry and I looked at each other. Jerry's eyes were as big as golfballs. There was a slight delay before we reacted. I jumped out of the canoe at the same time Jerry did. I heard another shot and then I heard a big splash. The canoe had tipped over and in a couple of seconds, Granma's head appeared next to the canoe. I dog-paddled over to her and saw the water turning red next to her left arm.

"Did you get shot? You're bleeding!" I was really worried.

"I don't think so, Rocky. Let me see." She raised her left arm above the water and we could see her skin was torn open near her elbow and blood was trickling out, mixing with the lake water.

"That's not a bullet wound, Rocky, I think a fishhook got a chunk of my arm when I jumped from the canoe. I felt a tug when I hit the water. I guess I'm a pretty big fish—a fish called Marty." She smiled and I knew she would be all right. We heard a number of gunshots, but there weren't any splashes around us. Granma said, "Those were pistol shots, boys, not rifles like the first shots we heard."

Jerry was holding onto the bread bag with one hand and the canoe with the other. I asked Granma, "What should we do; should we swim for shore?"

Granma was very calm and answered, "We'll stay on this side of the canoe and push it toward camp. It's made of wood, so it won't sink. We can paddle and kick. It will take us a little while, but we'll make it. Are you with me?"

Jerry and I both nodded and started kicking. Granma held onto the canoe with her left hand and swam a backstroke with her right. She was a pretty good swimmer, even with her clothes on. She encouraged us with words, "You boys are doing fine. It won't take long at this rate."

After about ten minutes, I guessed we were half-way back to shore, at least the tents were getting bigger. I could see five adults and a kid standing on shore: Jerry's parents, Mrs. Nesbitt, Mom, Suzy, and someone else. I wondered who the other person was. I asked Jerry who all the people were, but he couldn't see as much as I could, since he was at the rear end of the canoe: Granma and I were in his way. I watched Granma, but I could tell she was getting tired, and I could still see blood coming from the cut on her arm. I was glad there weren't any sharks in the lake. I knew they were attracted by blood.

As we got closer to shore, Mr. Morgan took off his shoes and waded out to us, the water only going a little past his waist. When we saw that, Granma, Jerry, and I realized we could touch bottom, so we quit trying to swim and just pushed the canoe as we walked slow motion through the water. When Mr. Morgan grabbed the canoe and began pulling, we hung onto the canoe and let him pull us ashore. The person I didn't recognize from out in the lake was Elena. She had returned from her hike with the lieutenant. I didn't see Lieutenant Nesbitt.

Mom got all excited when she noticed Granma's arm was bleeding. "Mother! Did you get shot?"

"No, dear, I tangled with a fishing hook when I jumped from the canoe."

Mom asked Granma, "Where is your First-Aid kit, mother? I'll clean that and bandage it for you." Mom looked at me and said, "Are you or Jerry hurt, Rocky?"

Jerry looked at me and shook his head. I told Mom, "Nope, just wet."

Mrs. Nesbitt and Elena had gotten some towels for us and we began drying off. Jerry gave Mrs. Nesbitt the bag of fish. Suzy was holding Surprise and watching Mom fix Granma's arm. Mom had gotten the medical supplies from the Desoto's trunk. Suzy was making faces and clenching her teeth together as if she was feeling Granma's pain as Mom cleaned the deep cut.

As I dried off, I talked with Elena, "You came back early."

"Yes, I'm not as strong as I thought. We went about three miles, rested, had something to eat and then started back. When we heard the rifle fire, we ran toward the sounds and saw a man shooting at the canoe."

"Where's the lieutenant?"

"He's on his way, Rocky. He's bringing in the prisoner."

"Prisoner! You have a prisoner?"

"There were two men shooting at the canoe. We got one and the other man got away."

"Did he drive a brown pickup?"

"I don't know—we heard a motor, but couldn't see a vehicle. The trees are too dense over there." Elena pointed west across the lake.

"Jerry and I can tell if your prisoner is the guy that shot you."

"Well, I'm not sure your mom will want you to look at him."

"Why not?"

"He's deceased."

"That won't bother me, Elena. I saw a dead man once—the man that was hit by the truck. I didn't have bad dreams or anything."

Chapter 23

Moving Camp

While we waited for the lieutenant, Jerry and I talked about asking him if we could have the inner tube from his flat tire for our slingshots. It was an hour before the lieutenant showed up with Ensign Thorndike and the body of the shooter. Last year in school we had learned about the Plains Indians, so when I saw the travois carrying the body I recognized it right away. The lieutenant and the ensign had used a large Navy utility knife to cut up the dead man's shirt and belt to tie poles together to make the carrier.

The Morgans and Mom were worried about Jerry and me looking at the dead man, but after some discussion, we had convinced them that we could take it. Mom and Elena took Suzy into the main tent and played with Surprise. Lieutenant Nesbitt and Thorny showed Jerry and me the body. The ensign's jacket was covering the dead man's head; his chest and neck were very bloody. We had seen the man before on the boat, but he wasn't Elena's shooter. We didn't know his name. Thorny put the body in the lieutenant's tent and closed it so Suzy wouldn't see the dead man all covered with blood. Then he left with Lt. Nesbitt to get the Navy pickup that Thorny had left about a mile away on the gravel road. He had heard the rifle shots and parked his truck, ran through the woods, and found Elena and the lieutenant standing over the dead man.

About fifteen minutes later, the two men returned. Thorny and Lt. Nesbitt loaded the body in the Navy truck and Thorny drove off to find the nearest funeral home. Lt. Nesbitt told us the ensign thought there would be at least an undertaker in Stratton, but if not, he would check in four other towns as he drove toward Philips. He would report the death to the sheriff in the town where he left the body and return by way of Rangeley.

Suzy came out of the big tent, squinting in the bright sunlight, looking around the camp, and said, "Where's Thorny, Rocky? I wanted to say hi to him."

"He had to get his Navy truck. He'll be back later tonight or tomorrow morning.

I didn't think she should know about the dead man; she's too young to think about that stuff. She would probably have bad dreams if she saw that bloody body. I asked her, "Where's Surprise?"

"He fell asleep. He got pooped from us playing with him. Have you found any good rocks?"

"Nope. All I've seen are pieces of gravel and gray pebbles." I pulled a handful of small stones from my pocket so she could see what I was talking about.

"Why do you have a bunch of rocks in your pocket?"

"That's ammunition for my slingshot."

"You don't have a slingshot, do you?"

"Not yet, but Jerry and I are going to make two of them; one for each of us."

"Can I have one, too?"

"I don't think so, Suz. You're not strong enough."

"Oh. Well, I don't care. Besides, I've got Surprise. He's more fun than an old slingshot."

Suzy didn't realize we were going to hunt those noisy birds so Surprise would have a dinner of grackle meat. I didn't think wieners would be a good diet for a puppy.

Mr. Morgan came over to Jerry and me and asked us to help him take down the tent.

"Are we going home?" Jerry asked.

"The ladies want us to leave because they are afraid someone might get badly hurt, but Lt. Nesbitt and Elena want us to stick together. The lieutenant is almost through with his job and then we'll all go home. So, we're moving to a different location—one that other shooter doesn't know about. Elena and the lieutenant found a good location for camping."

We all got busy and in half-an-hour, everything was loaded into our cars and pickup. Lt. Nesbitt led the way and we followed as before.

We drove about two miles east and then turned southeast, still on a dirt road, but winding around in the woods towards a good sized mountain. We drove through some dry stream beds that cut across the road. The last one we drove through was very bumpy and the Desoto hit bottom once. We stopped before we got to the mountain because we had reached the end of the road. Everyone got out of the cars and pickup and met with the lieutenant. He looked at the map, pointed, and said, "That is Crocker Mountain, elevation 4,168 feet. We're almost a mile from the center of the mountain."

Lt. Nesbitt was using a 1952 Maine highway map to show us where we were. This place was more deserted than the last camp site. None of us could see any signs of previous campers, maybe because the road stopped and we weren't close to a lake.

The lieutenant said, "Let's look around and find a level spot to set up camp. Come back in thirty minutes, we'll have something to eat, and discuss our findings."

Mom stayed in the Desoto with Suzy and Surprise while the rest of us hiked in different compass directions. Elena and the lieutenant went toward the mountain to the southeast, Granma and Mrs. Nesbitt went directly east, and I joined the Morgan family and went directly west. We had already driven from the northwest, so we skipped that direction.

As soon as we started walking through the countryside, those noisy birds began telling their stupid jokes again. Jerry made up a song of crazy sounds and then laughed, then I would repeat the song, the best I could, and laugh. We repeated our song several times when we heard the grackles.

Mrs. Morgan started laughing and said, "You boys sound like human birds, and just like those birds, I don't understand what you're saying."

Jerry and I started laughing and said, "Neither do we."

I said, "Mrs. Morgan, that's our grackle camping song."

As we made our way through shrubs, tall grass, and trees, Mrs. Morgan hummed what she said was an old folk song she remembered from when she was a kid. She couldn't recall the words. I think she did that so she wouldn't have to listen to the grackles and Jerry's and my crazy song and laugh. We hiked for about fifteen minutes before turning around and going back to the cars. All we had found was a small dry stream bed, not much use for camping.

The first thing I wanted to do when we met with the others was to ask Lt. Nesbitt if we could use the inner tube from his flat tire for our slingshots, but when we got back, Mr. Morgan had us check our clothes for ticks. We didn't find any. Granma said that it had been very dry here and the ticks needed moisture to live, so there probably weren't many around this area, or we were just lucky that none had hitched a ride on us.

A couple of minutes after we checked for ticks, Jerry and I asked about the flat tire. Lt. Nesbitt got the tube from his trunk and gave it to us. Mrs. Morgan helped us cut the rubber into strips with a pair of scissors and Mr. Morgan cut the tongues out of an old pair of hiking shoes he said he should have thrown away long ago. He said he hadn't worn them in years. We used the leather for a pouch to hold a rock when we let one fly.

The lieutenant and Elena told us they had found an ideal place to camp, close to the base of Crocker Mountain. The only problem was that we would have to carry all our camping stuff almost half-a-mile. The lieutenant had an idea, but we would have to unload the pickup first. Everybody helped and it only took a couple of minutes to stack all the bags and boxes in piles next to the cars.

While we unloaded, I figured out what the lieutenant was going to do: he was going to get the travois that had been used to carry that body from the woods to our old camp. It only had a few blood stains on it. I imagined Lt. Nesbitt would wash it off before he brought it back. Mr. Morgan and the lieutenant drove off in the pickup bouncing up and down on the bumpy dirt road. Meanwhile, the women fixed sandwiches and made coffee on a Coleman military burner that was in the trunk of the Navy car. Elena said she had never seen the miniature stove before.

Suzy wanted a cheese sandwich, so after the coffee was made, and the rest of us had lunch meat or peanut butter sandwiches, Granma made Suzy a special order. Granma knew all about the Coleman stove. She had camped out with Granpa many times over the years and seemed to know just about everything there was to know about roughing it, at least the important stuff. Suzy wanted jelly on her sandwich, so Mom smeared grape jelly on it. Suzy sat on the back seat of the Desoto with the door open. Her legs were hanging out the side, swinging back and forth, and her mouth looked like it was getting bigger and bigger as she ate. The grape jelly was all over her face, even on her nose.

Jerry gave me a warm Coke and as we drank, we had a burping contest: Jerry had the loudest, but I had the longest belch. As we watched Suzy eating. He laughed and said, "I'm glad I don't have a little sister. I don't think I could stand it."

"It's not so bad, Jerry, Most of the time I just laugh. Sometimes she says some funny stuff, and I really don't mind watching out for her."

We both started laughing when Suzy got the hiccups. Mom got her some water and that cured the problem. Mom used some of the water to wipe Suzy's face so she wouldn't look like a clown. I asked Suz how the cheese sandwich tasted and she said, "Yum," and smiled. She swung her legs into the car and scooted over to Surprise, who I guess was sleeping since he hadn't been out running around. Mr. Morgan had checked him for ticks, but hadn't found any.

"Let's finish our slingshots, Rocky." Jerry gave his last burp and put his coke bottle in the bed of the pickup. I was thinking that we had gotten lots of burps for only a nickel.

"Yeah, just a second." I tipped my Coke up to get the last drop, burped, and we went to the Desoto's trunk to finish putting the rubber strips on the Y-shaped tree limb pieces. We cut the shoe tongues into ovals, punched two holes for the rubber to attach to the pouches and tied off the rubber with fishing line. Now we were ready to test our weapons.

We started by shooting at tree trunks, but as our aim improved, we tried to call our targets, but without much success. Granma was watching us and said, "If you want to hunt game, you're going to have to be better shots, but after a couple more days of practice, those grackles won't have a chance. You're pretty good shots for the first time using your weapons."

I hadn't thought of the slingshots being weapons, I had thought they were just toys, but Granma was right; they were weapons. We were going to hunt grackles to get food for Surprise.

Jerry told me we might also get a rabbit, but I don't think I would like to kill a rabbit, they don't make any stupid noises, and we don't have a garden for them to raid.

We heard the pickup coming down the dirt road so we put our slingshots away and got ready to load the travois. Mr. Morgan took the travois out of the pickup by himself with Lt. Nesbitt getting the heavy stuff next to it. The men loaded the carrier and we started moving our camping stuff to the place the lieutenant and Elena had found. I hoped it was as nice as the area we had left. What I really hoped for was lots of grackles. Jerry and I were looking forward to shooting them out of the trees.

Everyone carried stuff in backpacks. Elena motioned for Jerry and me to come with her and we led the caravan. Elena's backpack, blanket, and sleeping bag looked bigger than she was, but they weren't very heavy. She looked kind of like an African native woman with a big package balanced on her head. I imagined we were Indians moving our village to follow the game as the seasons changed. Jerry told me he was pretending to be part of a nomadic tribe moving across the continent of Africa looking for a new source of water. Unfortunately, we didn't have any horses or camels. Mr. Morgan and Lt. Nesbitt were our animals doing the hard work. Elena, Jerry, and I moved rocks, limbs, and some shrubbery, clearing the path for the travois. Jerry and I alternated carrying the hatchet and cutting down shrubs and dinky trees.

It took us nearly an hour to get to the new camp location. Everyone was tired when we arrived, especially Mrs. Nesbitt. She hadn't been hiking in a coon's age, so her muscles weren't used to the exercise. We sat down on big rocks and a fallen tree and looked around. There was a little stream, mostly hidden by trees, about thirty-to-forty yards away from the place Lt. Nesbitt thought we should build our fire pit. We knew we were at the foot of the mountain, but we couldn't even see it because of the trees.

I sat on a good sized rock and Jerry came over and sat beside me on the ground.

"Hey, Rocky, I heard your mom and grandmother talking. Your grandmother was shot in the arm; she wasn't cut by a fishing hook. I guess she didn't want us to think someone had shot at us."

"Why would those guys want to shoot my granma? She hasn't done anything to hurt them."

"Maybe they found out she helped take those pictures."

I thought about that, but why would they risk getting caught because of some pictures? Maybe it was because Elena killed that guy in Granma's house, so I bet that was the reason. I kept thinking about it and came up with another idea. Maybe they were shooting at Jerry but he got in the water so fast, the only target left in the boat was Granma, and she was a bigger target, being an adult. She isn't fat or anything, just bigger.

"Did you hear that?" Jerry said excitedly.

"Sure did. We can go grackle hunting tomorrow. There it is again." I heard another grackle song: a joke and a laugh. "That is the dumbest bird song I've ever heard. I'm going to stuff a rock right down its throat!"

"Not if I beat you to it!" Jerry pulled his slingshot out and let a rock fly into the trees nearby, but the grackle sound was too far away for him to have even come close to hitting one.

I think he was just showing me he was ready.

"We'll go hunting in the morning—right after breakfast." I took off my backpack, stretched, and went over to Mr. Morgan and Lt. Nesbitt to help put up the tent. As Mr. Morgan began putting together the grill, Jerry walked up to him, said something, and then disappeared into the trees.

I asked, "Where's Jerry going?"

Mr. Morgan replied, "To see a man about a horse," and smiled.

I figured that Coke had gone through him pretty fast, but I would be doing the same thing before long. I thought I might be going to see a man about a donkey and then I laughed.

Chapter 24

Bad Guys

The tents were all up and the ladies were collecting some good-sized rocks to surround the fire pit. Mr. Morgan had scooped out a hole about six inches deep and a yard across after he put the grill together. He put the grill in place and surrounded the pit with the ladies' rocks. Jerry and I went scouting for pebbles for our slingshots; my ammunition pocket was almost empty, and he had shot his last small stone into the trees.

We were down by the creek when we heard a whistle, but we kept looking for pebbles until we heard another two whistles from camp. Jerry whistled back and said, "Come on, that was my dad. He wants us back."

I stuffed a half-dozen or so small stones in my pocket and ran to catch up with Jerry. We had been about fifty yards from camp, so it only took a half-minute to get back. Ensign Thorndike was talking to Lt. Nesbitt and another man in uniform, wearing a gun at his waist. He was about the size of Mr. Morgan, but not in as good shape; his belly was a little bigger than his belt. He wore black boots, kakis, and a dark-green jacket with a badge over his heart. His light-tan cowboy hat was tilted up so we could see his face. He was a little out of breath from the hike.

When Jerry saw the lawman, he commented to me, "I think he's out of breath from hurrying to get a doughnut." I had to laugh. Mr. Morgan, Jerry, and I joined the men in uniforms, and Thorny introduced us to Sheriff Mathew Dodgen, sheriff of Kingfield, where Thorny had left the body. The sheriff had followed the ensign from our old camp, parked his police car, and hiked with Thorny to our new camp.

"I'd like to meet the agent that was with you when you shot the assailant, Lieutenant."

Sheriff Dodgen had a small notebook with him. I think he was going to ask Elena some questions and take notes.

Lt. Nesbitt asked me, "Rocky; would you please ask Elena to join us? Your grandmother, too."

The ladies were in the big tent talking about making dinner when I stuck my head in the opening. I asked the ladies to come meet the sheriff to get all the introductions finished. Elena and Granma could talk to the sheriff afterwards.

I watched as the sheriff asked Elena questions and looked at Granma's arm, then he said, "You boys were with Mrs. Makler out in a canoe on Pork Chop Lake when the gunfire started?"

Jerry and I both said, "Yes, Sir." Then I said, "Granma told us a fish hook cut her arm. I think she just didn't want us to get scared, but we've been scared before—really scared."

That's when Mom and Mrs. Morgan told the sheriff about our boat ride back in Crafton.

The sheriff kept watching mom. Every time I looked at him, I could see him taking glances at mom. I wondered if he had seen her before. I started looking at Mom to see if she was checking out the sheriff, but I didn't notice anything unusual; she just looked at him when she talked to him. I saw the sheriff smile and say, "If it's all right with you, Sandra, next time I'm in Boston, I'll come by and see how you and your kids are doing."

Mom replied, "That would be nice of you—if we live through the summer."

I was a little surprised when I heard Mom say that a visit would be nice. What if Dad comes home from Korea and finds Mom visiting with the sheriff? But that would be a really big coincidence. The sheriff might be eating dinner with us, that's all. Then I thought about the sheriff kissing mom. I don't really think that would happen. But, if that did happen, I would let the air out of his tires and scratch the side of his car with a sharp rock. He would never know who did it.

Granma asked the sheriff if he would like to stay for dinner, but he said, "I'd better not, but thank you. I've been watching the western sky, we might get some rain tonight. I have to get back to my car and return to Kingfield. It will take me at least two hours to get home. The

Mrs. will be waiting dinner for me." He tucked his notebook in his back pocket, sucked in his belly, pulled up his pants, and said, "It was nice meeting you folks. Be on the watch for that other man, but I don't think he'll be back. You took care of his partner. If you come through Kingfield on your way home, stop and say hello. If I'm out writing parking or speeding tickets, just leave a note in my office. Bye, now."

Everyone said goodbye and we watched Sheriff Dodgen walk away. I kind of wanted to shoot a rock at his big butt. The way he was watching Mom and then saying he was married meant to me that he was nothing like Dad. Mom wouldn't let him get close to her.

Suzy hadn't paid much attention to the sheriff, but when he was gone, she came over to Thorny and asked, "Where is your boss going?"

The ensign answered, "He's not my boss, Susan. He's a policeman; he's the sheriff of a town called Kingfield."

She wrinkled her nose. "He's not in the Navy?"

"Nope. Lt. Nesbitt and I are in the Navy."

"So who is your boss?"

"Well, right now the lieutenant is my boss."

"What about Elena? Who's her boss?"

"I don't know, Susan. You will have to ask her."

"Oh. Can you help me find some pretty rocks?"

Mom was listening to Suzy's talk with Thorny and said, "Suzy, I think the ensign has other things to do. I'll help you look for rocks."

Thorny replied, "That's all right, Mrs. Linfield, I can help her, but I need to give you this backpack of dogfood first." Thorny slipped the pack off his shoulders and handed it to Jerry and me. It was pretty heavy. We carried it over to the cook tent and gave it to Granma, who was talking to Mrs. Morgan. I said, "Thorny brought this from Kingfield. It's for Surprise."

Granma looked into the pack and said, "Thank you Ensign! It's just what we needed." Granma smiled, looked at Jerry and me, and said, "Now you don't need to hunt grackles, boys."

Suzy ran over next to Thorny and grabbed his right hand. "Come on, Thorny, let's go down to the creek and find some pretty rocks for my collection. It won't take long."

Thorny looked at Lt. Nesbitt and he nodded, so Thorny and Suzy started toward the creek hand in hand. Jerry said, "Let's go with them and get some more pebbles for grackle-ammo." We still wanted to hunt grackles even though we had some regular dog food. That was okay by me, so we started following Suzy and her escort into the trees. Mom had yelled at us as we entered the edge of the forest. "Don't be gone long, kids, we're going to eat in about thirty minutes." I looked back at our camp and yelled, "Okay!" I liked the smell of the forest. We had only taken a few steps into the woods when we heard Suzy's squeaky voice ahead of us in the direction of the stream.

I was a little behind Jerry, only a few feet, but I stepped where he did to be sure I didn't trip or turn an ankle. I think he had more experience in the woods than I did. I couldn't tell, but he might have been following Thorny's footsteps. We could hear thunder, louder than the ripples in the stream, and the wind was getting stronger; the tree branches were starting to move back and forth. Just as we got to the water, Suzy and Thorny were leaving the water's edge and drying their hands.

As they began walking toward us, Suzy said, "We're going back, it's going to rain. I don't want to get all wet."

Jerry and I looked at each other and decided to go back to camp with them. When we got back, Mom and Mrs. Morgan said they were glad we came back. They were going to come and get us before it started raining cats and dogs.

I heard Suzy telling Granma, 'It's not supposed to rain, Granma. You said it would be nice all week long."

She smiled, "I know, dear, but sometimes the weatherman and your grandma are wrong—but not very often. The thunder is getting louder and closer. We'd better get ready for a wet evening. Let's have some dinner before everything gets wet."

By the time we were all eating, raindrops were falling on the campsite and could be heard spattering on the roof of the tent. The sun was completely blocked overhead by gray-black clouds, but there was a strip of yellowish sky to the west. Everyone crowded into the big tent and found a place to sit. Mr. Morgan had placed a lantern in the middle of the tent on a wooden box and began telling a story about a soldier doing a clever thing during the Second World War.

A squad of men had ended up in a bombed out church and had decided to stay there one night. One of the men sat down at a dusty, broken organ and figured out how to play it, but only certain notes worked. He gave up and, after eating, went to sleep. The next day he began collecting spent cartridges from rifles and machine guns, cutting them to different sizes, and putting oil or water into some of them. He tied them together and blew across the open ends to make music. He called it his mouth organ. One of his buddies called it a panpipe.

"What happened to the man," asked Suzy.

Mr. Morgan thought for a moment and answered, "I don't know, Susan. Maybe he came back to the states and taught music." He smiled, but looked at the ground. It was quiet in the tent for a few moments except for the noise of falling rain on the roof. I thought it sounded like many tiny drumsticks hitting the canvas.

Granma was the first to talk. "Well, I'm tired. I'd like to go to bed. What about the rest of you?"

There were lots of sighs and yawns. All of us were tired, even Surprise. He was lying beside Suzy on one of the sleeping bags, his eyes almost closed. Every once in a while he would wag his tail. Suzy and Mom agreed with Granma and began to move toward their sleeping bags. Ensign Thorndike talked to the lieutenant and then Lt. Nesbitt talked with Elena. The two navy men stepped out into the rain and ran toward the lieutenant's tent. Elena was going to sleep with us tonight. A minute or so passed as people got ready for bed and then Thorny came back in the big tent with Elena's sleeping bag. We made room for her next to Mom and Granma. Thorny said, "Good night. See you in the morning." A bunch of "Good nights" came from our group and Thorny disappeared into the rain and the dark.

Granma had gotten up early and started a fire. Jerry and I dressed and went outside to see how wet the morning was going to be. The air smelled fresh and clean, but we didn't hear or see any grackles. I think Mom, Mrs. Morgan, Elena, and Suzy were getting dressed as soon as Mr. Morgan came outside to get a cup of coffee. He sat down on a log with Jerry and me and asked, "You guys going hunting today?"

I replied, "Yes, sir, as soon as we eat and find some more pebbles for ammunition."

"We think we can get what we need from the stream, Dad."

"After all that rain, the stream will be higher than it was yesterday. You might have to wade out a ways to find what you want."

"We won't mind getting our feet wet, huh, Jerry?"

"Wet feet won't stop me," Jerry agreed.

"Well, don't expect the water to be clear. With all the run-off, you probably won't be able to see the bottom. You'll have to feel around for stones you can use." Mr. Morgan finished with "Good luck," and went to get some more coffee.

Suzy popped out of the big tent and ran over to the naval tent calling out, "Thorny, will you take me to look for pretty rocks?"

She stood there, about five seconds, waiting for an answer. Then she yelled, "Thorny! Wake up!" but no sounds came from the tent. Suzy bent over and pushed the tent flap open. "Hey, nobody's here!" She ran over to Granma and said, "Granma, Thorny and Lt. Nesbitt are gone. Did you see them? Where did they go?"

"I don't know, dear. I'd guess they're probably scouting the area to see if all that rain caused any damage." Granma looked back toward where we had left the cars and said, "There they are, Susan." She pointed at the trail we had made coming to our camp and Suzy ran toward the two men. "Thorny, I've been looking for you!"

When Suzy jumped to greet him, Thorny caught her and carried her back to the campfire, talking all the way. They were going to hunt pretty rocks and nothing would change Suzy's mind. Suzy was first to finish eating and sat down next to Thorny, waiting for him to finish a plate of pancakes, some bacon, and a cup of coffee. I watched her grab his hand and start pulling as soon as he put his coffee cup down. They started toward the stream and Thorny looked back at us. I think he wanted someone to save him from Suzy, but no one did.

Jerry and I were planning our hunt and decided to follow Thorny and Suzy's path to the stream. We were both low on ammo. We had walked about half-way to the trees when I heard what sounded like a rifle shot, and then, after a few seconds, the loudest scream from Suzy that I had ever heard.

Suz came running toward us, screaming "Thorny's been shot dead! Thorny's been shot dead!" Jerry ran past her toward the river and I caught her and said, "What happened!"

Tears were running down her cheeks and her eyes were so big it scared me. She hit my hands, twisted, and broke away from me, continuing to run toward camp screaming. "Lt. Nesbitt, come quick! Thorny's been killed!" I don't know if anyone else would understand her screaming, but everyone in camp would know something was wrong.

I didn't know what to do, but I decided to follow Jerry into the woods, even though I didn't know for sure which way he went. I headed toward the water as fast as I could, pulling my slingshot from my pocket as I ran. As I got a rock in the pouch, I saw Jerry pulling Thorny from the middle of the stream toward the opposite bank. Thorny wasn't dead, but he had been shot in the back, in his right shoulder. I could see blood spreading down his shirt from the wound.

Thorny looked confused, but was trying to sit up. Jerry had taken off his own T-shirt and was pressing it against Thorny's shoulder trying to stop the bleeding. There was nothing I could do to help, so I turned back toward camp to help the lieutenant find us.

Mr. Morgan came through the trees first, carrying his rifle in his left hand as he jumped over a downed tree. "Where's the shooter?" he asked.

"I don't know. Thorny and Jerry are over there." I pointed upstream and said, "On the other side of the creek." Mr. Morgan turned and ran in the direction I had pointed,

Lieutenant Nesbitt arrived a couple of seconds later, with his handgun drawn. I didn't need to say a word, I just pointed and he ran after Mr. Morgan. I glanced back toward camp and saw Granma walking toward me with her arms swinging, almost like she was running. I waited for her and she said, "Where are they?"

"Come on, I'll show you."

Lt. Nesbitt was checking Thorny's wound and Mr. Morgan was searching around the nearby trees with Jerry. I figured they were looking for the shooter's tracks so they could follow him. Granma knelt beside Thorny and called out, "Jerry, tell your mom to get the big First-Aid kit from my car—it's under the back seat—and get ready for a patient." Jerry took off running toward camp. "Lieutenant, get the travois. You and Rocky can get Ensign Thorndike back to camp. Give me your sidearm." She held out her hand. Lieutenant Nesbitt hesitated a moment and then gave her his forty-five service pistol.

"Does it have a full clip?"

"Yes, Ma'am."

"Okay. I'm going to follow Mr. Morgan and make sure he follows the shooter's trail."

She stood up and walked into the woods where Mr. Morgan had disappeared from sight.

I stayed with Thorny while the lieutenant went after the travois. "You'll be all right, Thorny, Mrs. Morgan works at the hospital in Crafton—she's just like a nurse." He was kind of leaning over, sagging to the left, so I got behind him on the ground and had him lean back. It seemed a long time before the lieutenant arrived with the travois, but I think it was only about five minutes. As we waited, I listened to the stream's soothing sounds and heard a few grackles making their stupid song before I heard the travois being dragged across the pine needles, rocks, and tall grass.

Lt. Nesbitt and I helped Thorny through the water. We got him onto the travois and started back to camp. We tried to find a smooth path, but there were a few bumps, and Thorny made sounds like he was in a dental chair, the dentist drilling without Novocain. It took us about ten minutes to get him back to the big tent where the ladies would check his wound and bandage him.

Mom, Elena, and Mrs. Morgan cut off Thorny's shirts and started cleaning blood off his skin. I didn't want to watch, so I stood nearby and listened. Mom suggested that Lt. Nesbitt and Elena should take Thorny to a doctor in Rangeley for surgery, so after I heard that, I went to my backpack and got a sweatshirt, gave it to Jerry, and then we ran back to the stream and started after Granma.

Chapter 25

Prisoner

Jerry and I found lots of tracks in the wet grass. The footprints were all going in the same direction, so we carefully followed them, moving slowly and watching closely, listening for unusual sounds as we moved forward. I didn't want Granma or Mr. Morgan shooting at us. After about two minutes, I saw Granma ahead of me. I stood behind a tree about twenty feet away and whispered, "Granma," and listened for her voice.

I waited for a few moments and was surprised when a hand covered my mouth. Then Granma whispered from behind me, "Don't make any noises. Don't even whisper." I nodded and she removed her hand from my mouth. She had the forty-five in her left hand. She motioned for me to sit down. Granma crouched beside me, put her mouth up to my ear, and said, "Mr. Morgan is about thirty yards ahead of us moving up the mountain. We don't want to distract him from behind."

Granma whispered, "Do you have your slingshot? I want Mr. Morgan to know were coming up from behind."

I didn't answer her, trying to keep quiet, but I pulled it out of my back pocket and showed it to her.

"Good. Do you think you can hit that big tree up there?"

I looked where Granma was pointing and whispered, "Sure." I was nearly an expert at hitting trees, sometimes from forty to fifty yards— when there wasn't any wind, but I had to aim pretty high to get the rock to carry that far. I felt for a round pebble and loaded the pouch, got on my knees, stretched the rubber back to my ear to be sure the rock would make it, and let it go.

We heard a whack and I knew I had done what Granma wanted. She patted me on the back. A couple of seconds went by and then Jerry started up the hill, crouching low so he couldn't be seen. He slipped once and slid on his butt a couple of feet, but then crawled forwards, like an army man on the ground, until he got to his dad. We watched Jerry talking to Mr. Morgan and then the green sweatshirt started coming back towards us. When Jerry arrived, Granma asked, "Do you know where the man is?"

"Yes, Ma'am. Dad said the man is behind a big rock between two trees. He's about forty yards up the mountain, a little to the right from Dad. I didn't see him."

Granma was quiet for about a minute, then she said, "I have a plan. Tell your dad Rocky and I are going up the hill to the right. When we can see the man, Rocky is going to shoot rocks into the trees above him and I will shoot at him. He will think we are your dad and will move away from us. When he moves away from the rock and trees, have your dad get the jump on him. Can you remember that?"

Jerry smiled and said, "Sure. That's easy. Shall I go back to Dad now?"

"Yes. Stay low so the shooter won't see you. We'll start moving as soon as you do. Is everybody ready?"

Jerry and I both nodded. Granma whispered, "Let's go!" Sheriff Makler set the safety on her gun, stuffed it in her waistband, and began moving from tree to tree, and I, Deputy Linfield, followed close behind, making good use of shrubs and trees to keep out of sight of the Russian gunslinger. We both slipped a little on pine needles, but made good progress as we clawed and crawled up the slope, circling to the shooter's left. The sheriff placed her finger to her lips to be sure I didn't talk. We had to keep our position a secret from the gun-happy cowboy.

After five minutes of sneaking uphill through the forest, we stopped and checked our position, looking for an open shot at the crazy cowpoke. The sheriff motioned for me to look in the direction she was pointing. I could see a portion of a plaid shirt between a large fir and a big boulder. I couldn't tell if he had on a hat. She motioned for me to take a shot and then hit the ground.

I fished a rough fifty-caliber stone from my pocket, hoping it would do more damage than a rounded one, loaded it into my slingshooter, took aim and set it on its way. In less than a second, the plaid shirt turned in my direction, but too late to fire back. Sheriff Makler had already gotten a shot off. Her forty-five bullet hit the rock and wined off into the far woods. She hadn't hit him, but he moved away from us, only to get shot at by Marshall Morgan. When I heard the Marshall's rifle fire, I knew we had him. Either he would give up, or he was a dead man, ready for planting on boot hill.

I hoped he was dead. It would serve him right for shooting Elena, the pretty dancehall girl I had spent the evening with the night before. But then I changed my mind; he should go to jail and serve time. That would give him a chance to think about the bad things he had done. Maybe he would come out of jail with a new look on life; a reformed man.

We heard the grackle sound from Jerry and knew we could come out from our protected position in the trees. The man had been disarmed. Everyone was safe.

Granma and I worked our way to the big boulder and found the man with the plaid-shirt lying on the ground spread-eagled with his face in the dirt. Mr. Morgan had his rifle pointing at his bearded head and Jerry held the man's weapon. I had never seen a rifle like it before, maybe foreign surplus from World War II.

Granma asked, "Have you searched him?"

"No. I thought I'd better wait for you. Hold your gun on him."

Granma pulled her forty-five and told Jerry and me to step away, about twenty-feet or so. She took off the safety and watched Mr. Morgan search the prisoner. There was a wallet in his left-back pocket, and a switch-blade in his right-front pocket. When Mr. Morgan turned him over during the search, the captured man asked, "I know the boys, but who are you and the woman?"

Jerry was quick to answer. "He's my dad and she's Rocky's grandmother, and you're the guy that shot the FBI agent. I recognize your voice.

The prisoner hung his head and uttered, "FBI? How embarrassing— caught by two kids, a father, and a grandmother. My comrades will laugh at me."

Granma laughed, almost as if she were still whispering. "I don't think you'll ever see them again. You're going to be in a federal prison for a long time. But you'll probably see some of your friends there. You can discuss the failures of communism."

Mr. Morgan smiled, but then he became serious. "Boys, I'd like you to go back to camp and get some rope. Mrs. Makler and I will stay here and guard the prisoner. Take his rifle with you, he won't need it anymore. I unloaded it. Jerry, you take his knife—give it to your mother. Hurry, so we can all get back to camp for lunch."

Jerry and I slid and ran in spurts down the slope and picked up speed when we hit level ground. We almost fell a couple of times, but were able to stay on our feet, jumping over fallen trees and bushes growing up through pine needles which almost covered the dirt between the evergreens. I led for a few minutes, watching the tracks closely so we didn't waste time trying to find the trail. We stopped for a moment to get our breath, and then Jerry took the lead.

I could hear some grackles and wanted to go after them, but knew we had a job to do, so we didn't stop again until we came to the stream close to camp. We waded through the water wiggling our toes in our sneakers to help cool our warm feet. Then we squished our way to camp where Mrs. Morgan, Mom, and Suzy were waiting for someone to return from chasing the bad guy.

Mom took the gun from me and Mrs. Morgan hugged Jerry. Mom dropped the gun on the ground and threw her arms around me. "Where are Granma and Mr. Morgan?" Mom asked. She was really squeezing me.

"They're with the guy that shot Thorny. We caught him. Mr. Morgan needs some rope so they can tie him up and come back for lunch. Jerry brought back his knife. Mr. Morgan said to give the gun and knife to Mrs. Morgan. I guess she'll put them in a safe place."

Jerry carried the gun and knife to the truck where Mrs. Morgan used the switchblade to cut two pieces of rope from a large roll stored in back of the pickup. She gave me the smaller rope and coiled up the longer one for Jerry then gave him the knife. "You might need this to cut the rope into smaller pieces. I don't know if your father has his knife."

"Okay. Rocky and I will be back with Dad, Mrs. Makler, and the prisoner in about an hour. I'm not sure how long it will take to get back here with him tied up. An hour is just a guess."

"Can I go with them to get Granma?"

I told Suzy, "We have to run, Suz. You wouldn't be able to keep up."

Suzy looked at Mom for permission, but I knew Mom understood. "We need you here, Susan. You have to help us fix lunch. They'll be hungry when they get back."

Mrs. Morgan told Jerry he should change out of his wet socks, but he replied, "We have to go through the water two more times, mom. Can we go now? Dad and Mrs. Makler are expecting us go get back with the ropes. They said to hurry."

"Well, all right. Just be careful."

Jerry looked at me and I said, "Let's hit the trail, Rock."

We took off running, until we came to the water. We were careful where we stepped so we didn't slip on any slick rocks that were slimy or stuck above water, covered with moss. We didn't try to find where we had crossed the stream before. The trail was easy to follow now, seven pairs of feet had knocked down the grass and weeds. In ten minutes we saw Granma and Jerry's dad sitting on a log talking to the prisoner, who was on the ground sitting on his butt with his hands behind his back.

His hands were tied with a shoestring taken from Mr. Morgan's left shoe. Mr. Morgan thanked us for getting the ropes and made a loop in one end of the longer rope. I could see hitting his horse so he would hang as the horse bolted away. "Granma, what's his name?"

"He wouldn't tell us, Rocky; We'll let the FBI figure that out."

Jerry and I watched as Mr. Morgan tied his hands behind his back and then to his waist. The loop was placed around his neck to lead him on the return to camp. Granma held the rope while Mr. Morgan untied and removed the shoestring, and laced his shoe.

"Okay, boys, let's go home." Granma started, followed by Jerry's dad giving a little jerk on the rope forcing the prisoner to come along. Jerry and I trailed behind, watching and listening for grackles, our slingshots ready to shoot them out of the trees. Our posse was about twenty-to-thirty feet long, moving slowly at first until we reached level ground. Granma picked up the pace, but our movement through the forest was making too much noise. Any nearby grackles were scared and flew away. Jerry and I didn't get even one shot, and we weren't trying to conserve ammunition. We did hear some wings flapping, though. Those grackles that escaped were lucky.

When we got to the stream, Granma started across, but slipped and fell into the water that was more than a foot deep. I saw her fall, almost like a cartoon character slipping on a banana peel; her legs suddenly went into the air and her rear went clear to the bottom, causing a big splash. Jerry and I helped her up while Mr. Morgan and the prisoner waited for us to clear the way. Granma wasn't hurt. She said, "I did need a bath," and laughed. I was afraid to laugh out loud, but I did inside. I smiled at Jerry and he smiled back.

Mom was waiting for us as we came out of the stream. She walked with Granma to the big tent. During the ten minutes it took for Granma to change to dry clothes, Jerry and I took off our wet shoes and socks and put them next to the fire on a rack of sticks. I was wondering who had started the fire; the logs were arranged differently than other times.

The lieutenant and Elena had taken the pickup to check out the road. They told Granma the river bed we had crossed might be impassable by car. Granma told me they wanted to take Thorny to a hospital and when they returned, we would pack up and return to Crafton with the prisoner. The women had stopped Thorny's bleeding and he was asleep in the big tent. Every time Suzy heard Thorny's name mentioned, she cried, so she took Surprise and went into the lieutenant's tent.

Lt. Nesbitt and Elena backed the pickup up to the big tent, and with Mr. Morgan's help, they loaded Thorny into the back on top of three sleeping bags to cushion the ride. The lieutenant was going to do the driving and Elena would ride in back with Thorny. Granma gave them some sandwiches and they drove away slowly. I could see they had driven through some high water; there were mud marks above the running boards on the side of the driver's door and also on the fenders. The cars won't make it through water that deep. We'll have to wait for the water level to drop before we can leave the campsite. It had rained a lot more than I thought.

We ate lunch while our make-shift ambulance was gone. Mom and Mrs. Morgan even fed the prisoner. He asked them if he could talk to Jerry and me and they said he could, as long as someone was nearby with a gun. Granma volunteered.

"How did you get out of the cargo hold, boy?"

Jerry and I laughed and made up a story of how we were able to concentrate and move through metal like it was water. It took both of us to get one of us through the metal, so someone had to stay behind.

"I don't believe. No one can do that."

Then we told him what we had really done.

When Elena and the lieutenant came back two hours later, Jerry and I, bare-footed, tip-toed to the pickup to meet them, trying not to step on rocks and twigs, and asked how Thorny was.

Elena smiled, "We took him to Rangeley where a doctor examined him. Dr. Klein helped us put him on a plane to Boston. He's a real trooper, but he had to have surgery to remove some bone fragments. He'll come see you when he gets out of the hospital. He said you should shoot some grackles; he doesn't like them either."

"We're glad he'll be all right. Come look at the guy that shot you, Elena. Jerry and I helped catch him."

"Where are your shoes, boys?"

"Over beside the fire. They're drying out; we went through the stream three times today. They got pretty squishy." I grabbed Elena's hand and led her toward the pickup. Lt. Nesbitt had his arm around her waist and Jerry was right behind me. As we got within a few feet of the prisoner, Elena slowed down, taking small steps, as if she might be scared to look him in the face. I asked Elena, "Is this the guy that shot you?"

"I really don't know. I didn't see him. There was a bang and then nothing. The next thing I remember is the hospital and the nurses. I remember you came to see me."

The prisoner looked at Elena and said, "I never even see this woman before. On my mother's grave, I, Nikolai Surikov, never shoot such a pretty woman. I only shoot soldiers."

Jerry stepped next to the pickup and said, "But I heard you tell someone in the lighthouse that you shot the girl in the bait store."

"I was just making a story. My shipmates tease me about never doing nothing dangerous. She is FBI? Woman in KGB only secretary— big and fat, answer phone, type reports and letters."

"So you don't know who shot me?"

"I do not know."

I asked, "Could it have been the boat's captain?"

"No. He is paper pusher—does not get hands dirty; Nobody from boat shoot you."

"Why did you shoot my Granma?"

"I not shoot. That was Sergei. He better long distance shot."

"But why?"

"Following orders. Shoot the old lady. So we try shoot the old lady."

Lt. Nesbitt reached into the truck bed and checked the ropes on Nikolai's wrists.

"I've got a pair of handcuffs that would be more secure. We'll tie the handcuffs and both feet to the truck. He'd have to be a magician to get loose. We'll stay here tonight and leave for Crafton in the morning."

Jerry and I looked at each other, realizing we wouldn't have an opportunity to hunt grackles in the wilderness. I thought about it as we walked back to the campfire. I checked my shoes and they were still wet. I was thinking we would have an hour or so after dinner before the sun went down to go after some birds, but I didn't want to hunt wearing wet sneakers.

Jerry said, "Let's get up early tomorrow and see if we can get a couple of grackles, okay?"

"Good idea! The grown-ups will be eating breakfast and cleaning up. We'll go hunting for a bit and then come back and help load stuff. They'll save us some breakfast."

"Yeah! Have you ever gutted a bird?"

Chapter 26

Signals

The next morning was disappointing. It wasn't because of the weather, or the lack of grackles. Jerry's parents and Mom wouldn't let us go hunting for birds. We had to eat with everyone else and then load the camping equipment. It was a quarter after nine when we started back to Crafton. When we were eating, Mr. Morgan and Lt. Nesbitt checked out the depth of the water in the stream crossing the road north of the campsite. The stream was only a trickle so the cars could go across now.

Jerry and I weren't allowed to ride in the pickup with Sergei. Granma and the lieutenant thought it was too dangerous; two boys with a dangerous grown man, so he was tied up in the backseat of Lieutenant Nesbitt's car. Elena sat in the front seat, holding a gun, with her back against the door, ready to act in case Sergei tried to do something. At least that was the arrangement when we left the camping area.

I figured Lt. Nesbitt and Elena would leave Sergei in Kingfield in Sheriff Dodgen's jail.

I was wrong. We went back to Rangeley, the way we had come, but we didn't stop at the lake. Those girls were probably gone anyway. I didn't care, but Jerry said he thought one of them was cute. Then he said she seemed be their leader, probably too old for him—and he had no money and couldn't drive. I smiled inside; he had nothing to drive, even if he could. He said it would be better if he learned more about girls from the ones in his class at school. When he asked his dad about girls, he was told to ask his mom, but Jerry thought since his mom was from Russia, she wouldn't know about American girls. Jerry and I talked about stuff like that on the trip back to Crafton. I liked talking about hunting grackles a lot more than about girls; I was surrounded by women all the time: Granma, Mom, and Suzy.

Our caravan stopped for lunch in Farmington. Mr. Morgan and Lt. Nesbitt took the prisoner into the men's room at a gas station, came back out, and tied him up in the back seat again. After lunch, we drove for about two hours and got to Crafton a little after 3:00 p.m.

Elena made a phone call from Granma's house and while we were unloading the Desoto, we heard an airplane. It was a two motor amphibian that landed in the water near the lighthouse. That's what Elena told us. She was going to take the prisoner to the FBI office in Boston.

Lt. Nesbitt and Elena drove away with Sergei still tied up in the back seat. Jerry and I went with Mr. and Mrs. Morgan to unload the pickup and get our bicycles out of Morgan's garage. Knowing what was in the containers in the pickup made unloading much easier than loading had been before we left on our trip. Jerry and I pushed some of the containers out onto the ground, but were careful with other stuff. As soon as Mr. Morgan said we were done, Jerry and I rode off on our bikes to the lighthouse.

We expected to see Mr. W when we got to the library, but the buildings were all locked and Mr. W wasn't there. We pounded on his door, but no one answered. There was a handwritten sign on the lighthouse door saying the library was closed until tomorrow.

"I guess we won't be looking up anything about grackles until tomorrow, Rock."

"Let's come over after breakfast. The library should be open in the morning. Granma said Mr. W gets up early."

As we were getting on our bikes, we heard a noise, a kind of thump, from the top of the lighthouse, but when we looked up, we couldn't see anything or anybody. Jerry laughed and said, "I think a grackle flew into the glass and killed itself." But it wasn't that kind of noise. We decided it must have been an electric switch or something that worked automatically, there wasn't any wind to blow anything open or closed.

We rode to Granma's and went in the house to watch TV until time for dinner. Mom, with her back to us, was on the phone talking quietly. I didn't know if she didn't want us to hear what she was saying, but it wouldn't have made any difference, the TV was louder than her voice. She didn't tell us to turn the sound down; it really wasn't very loud, just normal for watching TV

Granma came into the living room and asked, "Jerry, do you want to stay for dinner? We've got lots of leftovers from the camping trip."

"No thanks, Mrs. Makler. Mom and Dad want me home for dinner. Mom said I should be home by slx o'clock."

I watched Jerry take a look at the grandfather clock. It was five-twenty-five. The news was coming on in five minutes. I didn't pay much attention to the news unless there was talk about an accident or an actor that had died. The political and stock market talk made no sense to me. I usually watched the sports reports, especially if it was about the upcoming football season or baseball in the spring. I used to like to play catch with Dad. I had a first-baseman's glove and a hardball. Dad had a catcher's mitt. I didn't pay much attention to basketball.

When the newscast started, Walter somebody was talking when Jerry said he had to go home. I went outside with him and we made plans to meet in the morning and go to the library. We needed to find out more about grackles to improve our chances of knocking them out of the trees. Jerry thought there might be some bait that we could use to attract them. Then we'd get a clear shot.

"See ya, Jerry."

He waved and said, "In the a.m." He rode off and I went back in the living room.

After dinner, before the sun went down, Mom wanted to take a look at the lighthouse, so we piled into the Desoto with Surprise and drove to the library. Granma, Suzy, and Surprise took a sandy pathway outlined with rocks, between two massive boulders, and went down to the water. Suzy wanted to look for some pretty rocks for her collection. I wonder if I want to hunt a grackle more than she wants to hunt for pretty rocks.

I think Surprise will be interested in the water slapping against the rocks. I'll bet it will remind him of the water where Jerry and I found him, but if he takes a drink, he'll be surprised that the water is salty, not like the water in the lake. Granma went to make sure no one fell in the ocean. I wish I had known of the path when I swam in from the boat; climbing the rocks wasn't easy, since I was tired and wet.

I showed Mom around the buildings, telling her what I could about what was inside from things I had heard from other people, including

Mr. W. Since the door was still locked, I described the inside of the lighthouse. She tried to look through the door window, but it was completely dark inside. She said she couldn't see anything. When the lighthouse light comes on, she might be able to see inside. By the time Mom and I had looked at all the buildings, Granma, Suzy, and Surprise had returned from the water and were standing next to the car.

"Well, I'm ready to go. I'll have to come back when someone is here. I wanted to see inside the lighthouse. Rocky has given me a good idea of what it looks like, though."

Granma said, "You'll have to meet Mr. Waicukauski; he's quite a character. He's been real nice to the children."

As we got into the car, the beacon light came on. The noise was the same as the sound Jerry and I had heard earlier. We looked up at the light for a second. It was so bright shining out to sea, ships from miles away would be able to see it. I remembered how it was when I swam in from the boat. But something was different, the light started blinking.

"I wonder why the light is blinking, mom. I've never noticed that before. Maybe it's about to burn out."

Mom said, "Get in the car, Rocky. Mother, you'll have to drive Rocky and Susan home. I have to stay here."

Granma got out of the back seat and slid into the driver's seat. Mom had the keys and went around to the trunk and got something. I couldn't see what it was until she came to the front to give the keys to Granma. Mom had a rifle.

I had never seen Mom with a gun before. She was holding it like Mr. Morgan did when he walked toward the brown pickup several days ago, like it was light, and she knew how to use it. Granma started the car and backed up, turned, and started down the gravel lighthouse lane to the main road. I got on my knees and watched Mom from the rear window. She shot at Mr. W's front door and then broke into his house. We started toward Granma's on the main road as I watched light appear in the lighthouse windows. Mom must have gotten the keys to the lighthouse door.

When we pulled into Granma's driveway and stopped in front of the garage, a police car pulled up behind us and two police officers got out. I was wondering what law Granma had broken while driving home. I knew she hadn't been speeding, I had watched the dial on the speedometer and it was almost always at the speed limit, only a little over once in a while. One of the officers spoke with Granma, her window was rolled down for air to flow through the car on humid nights like tonight.

"Hello, Mrs. Makler. We'd like you to follow us over to the Morgan's home." He looked in the back seat at me and at Suzy in the front seat. "It's for the safety of you and the children."

"What's going on, Ronny?" Granma's face looked very serious. "Is Sandra all right?"

"She's fine. Your daughter called us and said to get you and the kids away from the lighthouse area. She said the Morgan's would be a good place. Do you want to follow us, or do you want to ride with us?"

"We'll follow you."

"Okay, let's go."

The officers pulled out onto the street and waited for us to get behind them, then they drove slowly over to the Morgan's with us following. When we got there, Jerry was waiting on the front porch, waving as we pulled into the driveway. The police car drove off pretty fast.

"Hey, Rocky, what's goin' on?"

"When we got home, the police told us to come over here, so we followed 'em. They didn't tell us much. Mom told 'em to bring us here. I don't know why."

We heard the phone ring. Jerry looked into the house and then said, "Where's your mom?"

"She's at the library. We went over there to show her around. When the light came on, it started blinking and then Mom told Granma to take Suzy and me home. I was really surprised when she got a gun out of the trunk. I've never seen her with a gun."

Jerry's eyes got big and he said, "Do you think she works for the police?"

"My Mom?" I frowned at Jerry and said, "Nah, I'd know that."

Mrs. Morgan came out on the porch and asked Granma if we had eaten yet. Before Granma could answer, Suzy said, "Granma, we didn't have any dessert."

"I guess that answers your question, Natalie. Could we impose on you for dessert?"

"No problem. Come in. We were just going to have dessert. We had spaghetti and meatballs. I made enough for a squad of marines. I'll warm some for you and the children if you want more dinner."

Mrs. Morgan held the screen door open and we went into the living room. I could see Mr. Morgan digging ice cream out of a half-gallon container: it was chocolate, my favorite. The table had already been cleared, so we all sat down. Mr. Morgan got us each a big helping of ice cream. As the chocolate ice cream was melting in my mouth, I began to think of Mom being all alone at the lighthouse, but she must have expected trouble; she had gotten that gun from the trunk. I thought of what Dad would have done and decided I'd better go help her. I excused myself from the table, even though I hadn't finished dessert, and went outside. Jerry followed me; he was finished with his ice cream.

"Jerry, do you have any fireworks?"

"Why?"

"I need to help my mom. Do you have any?"

"Sure, I've got half-a-dozen cherry bombs and some sparklers."

"Can I have the cherry bombs and your bicycle?"

"Ah, yeah, but I'm going with you. We'll ride double—I'll peddle."

"We'll need a lighter and our slingshots. I've got mine. Do you have a lighter?"

"I'll get a package of stick matches from the camping gear. My slingshot's in the garage."

"Okay, get that stuff, I'll get the bike. We've got to hurry, Mom might be in trouble."

Jerry went back in the house to get the fireworks from his bedroom. I heard Mr. Morgan ask Jerry, "What are you guys up to?"

"We're just talking about shootin' grackles, Dad." Then I heard Jerry climbing the stairs to his bedroom. I got his bike out of the garage and he met me outside the backdoor. I stuffed three cherry bombs in my pocket and we climbed on the bike. I rode sitting on the handlebars. We started slowly, a little wobbly, but as we went faster, the wobbles disappeared.

As we neared the lighthouse, the sun was almost hidden below the horizon. We were at the turn from the main road. I signaled Jerry to put on the brakes and I jumped to the ground and rubbed my butt. Riding that far on the handlebars wasn't much fun. Jerry laid the bike in the ditch and we began walking in the grass and weeds next to the gravel road leading to the library parking lot.

We crouched down as we moved, stopping at Mr. W's house. We loaded our slingshots and sneaked into his house looking for guns. I went first because I had looked through the screen door before and knew where the furniture was. No lights were on at the lighthouse, except the big beacon. Mom must have turned off the inside library lights. We could make out the furniture from the beacon light reflecting off the buildings giving just enough light so we didn't trip on anything. We looked around the living room, but didn't find any guns.

I touched Jerry's shoulder and said, "Let's go to the lighthouse." We ran to the library door where I told Jerry to wait while I climbed up to let Mom know we were there. As I went up the steps, I was thinking Mom was going to be real mad at me for coming back to the library.

When I reached the top step, I looked up at the sky through the opening to the gallery and whispered, "Mom, Jerry and I are here to help. Can we come up?"

"Rocky! Why are you here? I told Granma to take you kids home. Didn't you go to the Morgan's?"

"Yes, but Jerry and I left while the others were eating dessert. I wanted to help you. We brought six cherry bombs with us."

There was a pause and then Mom answered back, "Okay, you can come up. Be careful on the ladder."

I was going to yell at Jerry, but instead I made our grackle sound. I could hear him coming up the steps. I hoped he didn't trip on any of the books. He was breathing hard when he got to me, so I let him get his breath before I told him we were going up the ladder. When we got on top, Mom said, "Don't look at the light, you'll be blind and of no help to me."

"What can we do, Mom?"

"I want you to lie down and watch the water for boats or any activity of any kind. When we see something, I'll tell you what to do. Do you have your slingshots?"

Jerry said, "Uh-huh," and I said, "Yes, and we have a box of stick matches."

"Good. Now I know what we will do."

"Where are the cops, Mrs. Linfield?"

"They'll be here as soon as they can. I think someone created a diversion so the lighthouse would be unprotected. I heard some sirens about ten minutes ago. I think the sounds were from the harbor."

I was scanning the water for a boat but it was hard to see very far out on the water. Just when I thought I saw something, it would disappear, probably a reflection of the beacon from the tops of small waves. The water was pretty quiet tonight.

We watched the ocean for about ten minutes before Jerry said, "I think I see something—over there." He pointed a little to our left, about fifty yards out from shore. Mom and I squinted and looked where he was pointing.

"Good eyes, Jerry. It's a small rubber boat with three or four men. When they get about twenty yards out, I want you both to start shooting your cherry bombs at them. I'll shoot holes in their boat. If they shoot back, get behind the beacon, okay?"

We both said "Okay" and loaded our pouches with cherry bombs.

The Marshall said, "Give me the matches and I'll light the bombs. Aim straight at the wagon, we're way above it so you don't need to make any correction on your first shots. Get ready, they're almost where we want them."

Jerry and I were side-by-side on our knees and Marshall Linfield got behind us with the matches. She struck a match on the bricks below the beacon and lit my bomb, then quickly lit Jerry's. The fuses burned a couple of seconds before the Marshall said, "Shoot!"

Chapter 27

Arrests

My cherry bomb went off first, right in front of the wagon. I was able to see the burning fuse, tumbling, as the bomb went towards the four men. I'll bet those guys were surprised, the sound must have broken their eardrums. Jerry's bomb went into the wagon and went off about a second after mine had exploded. The four men started yelling and jumping into the sagebrush. Then Marshall Linfield moved to the edge of the canyon wall and shot two bullets into the wagon. We could hear the cussing and yelling of the men as they looked for cover from our bullets and bombs.

We reloaded our guns, the Marshall lit another match, and we did the same thing a second time, but shot directly at the men closest to the walls of the canyon. The bombs went off within a couple of feet of each man and they started yelling something I couldn't understand; it didn't sound like English or Spanish. The Marshall lit another match and we shot our last two bombs at the other two men with the same result.

I turned toward Jerry and asked, "What are they yelling?"

"It's Russian." They're saying, "Quit shooting, we give up!"

I blinked my eyes and stared down at the water. The four men were treading water, had their hands over their ears, and moving toward the shore rocks.

Mom said, "Tell them to stay in the water. If they come out of the water, they'll be shot."

I almost laughed when Jerry tried to lower his voice. Jerry yelled down to the men, and when he finished giving them orders, we heard police sirens coming from Crafton on the lighthouse road. Two different sirens were getting louder and louder. If anyone living near the road had gone to bed early, they must be awake now. We could see the headlights and red lights flashing from about a mile away. I didn't know what was more exciting; shooting cherry bombs at the Russians, or listening to the screaming sirens.

When we saw the cars turning off the highway, Mom told us to stay on the gallery. She started down the ladder to meet the cops at the library entrance. The two police cars skidded into the parking lot and four policemen came running toward the lighthouse. We could see them clearly when they crossed in front of their cars' headlights. Then we heard another siren, much louder than the sounds from the police cars. Jerry and I smiled when the Crafton Fire Department truck pulled into the parking lot.

Jerry said, "The police and the fire department are here, but where are the FBI agents?"

That question got me thinking. How did Mom know to get the rifle from the trunk of our car and send us away? Why did she tell the police to take us to Morgan's?

Below us, we heard policemen yelling, and saw flashlight beams pointing at the men in the water. Then I saw Mom, the policemen, and eight firemen start pulling the Russians, wearing black wetsuits, out of the water one by one and placing them in handcuffs. It only took about ten minutes to search the four men and put them in police cars. The only weapons they had were knives. They had no chance against our exploding cherry bombs and Mom's rifle. The enemy had to give up or die; they were out-gunned.

When we climbed down from the gallery, Mom was talking to the Fire Chief and the Chief of Police. She called Jerry and me over and introduced us, telling how we had helped capture the invaders. The Fire Chief was pretty funny, after he shook our hands he told us, "You shouldn't be shooting off fireworks unless it's the Fourth of July. It's illegal." He turned to the Chief of Police and said, "Chief, I want you to arrest these young men for disturbing the peace."

I wasn't sure if he was really serious then because he wasn't grinning or smiling, but Mom was smiling, so I knew he was kidding. Then the Fire Chief said, "Climb on the fire engine and we'll give you young men a ride to the Morgan's. We saw a bike over by the road, is that yours?"

"Yes, Sir. We rode double to get here," Jerry replied.

The Police Chief said, "That's another infraction—riding double at night without a light. There's a fine for doing that. If you can't pay the fine, I'll have to confiscate the bike and sell it at auction."

Jerry said, "You're pulling my leg, aren't you, Sir?"

"No, but this time we'll let it go, since you did such a good job of police work."

Mom put her hands on our shoulders and said, "He's right about that, boys, you did a super job."

Then the Police Chief said something that really surprised me, "Agent Linfield, do you want to ride with the boys?"

"I'd appreciate that, Sir."

I turned and looked at mom. I think my mouth was open. She just smiled at me and said, "Rocky, I'm a special agent of the FBI."

"Holy cow, mom. I was just beginning to think granma was a secret agent, but it's not her, it's you!" I was never so proud of mom. She was a secret agent!

The fire engine pulled up beside us, the engine throbbing, and the firemen helped us climb on board. The first step was a big one. One of the firemen grabbed my hand and hauled me up on top. Jerry's bike was already there, on top of the ladders. As we left the parking lot and drove onto the main road, I could feel the power of the engine. I imagined it was like a bull at a rodeo, ready to charge out from a stall, bucking into an arena with a rider on its back, all its muscles working together to throw off the rider.

The firemen helped us down from the truck when we arrived at the Morgan's. They tooted their horn when they drove away. We went into the house where Mom told the Morgans, granma, and Suzy what had happened. Mrs. Morgan was a little mad at Jerry, but Mr. Morgan congratulated us on doing a good job. He thought it was neat that we used the cherry bombs like hand grenades.

Suzy asked me, "How many bad guys did you catch?"

"Four."

"Only four? That's not very many."

"They had big knives, Suz. We didn't know what they were going to do to Crafton or any of the people."

"So, Mommy, you, and Jerry are heroes."

"I guess so, but we had help from the police and the firemen."

"Oh. How many of them helped?"

"Twelve."

Suzy started laughing, "Those bad men didn't have a chance. Are we going home to Boston, Mommy?"

"We're going to spend the night with grandma and go back to Boston tomorrow. I think we've had about enough excitement for a year, and we've got four more months to go. You and Rocky have to go to school on Monday."

We thanked the Morgan's for dessert and said good night. Jerry said he would come over in the morning before we left for Boston. On the way to granma's, I told Mom how surprised I was that she was a secret agent and we didn't even suspect her.

"Well, Rocky, you were almost correct, thinking your granma was a secret agent. You know, your grandmother was an FBI agent. She retired two years ago."

"How long have you worked for the FBI, Mom?"

"Just over twelve years, but I'm going to quit and get a regular job so I can be home with you and Suzy while you're going to school."

"But don't you work at the parachute factory? Isn't that a regular job?"

"No, Rocky. The parachute factory is the Boston FBI unit."

"Did Dad know you were an FBI agent?

"Not at first. He was in the Navy at Groton and I was working for the FBI as a waitress. He and some pals came in to the restaurant and I waited on them. As they were leaving, he asked me out, and I said yes. He was handsome and nice. He also had a very gentle way of speaking."

"Where'd you go on your first date?"

"He took me to a movie. It was a long one and I fell asleep with my head on his shoulder. He thought about waking me up at the end, but he said I smelled so good, he didn't want it to be over. The usher had to ask us to leave."

"What was the movie about?"

"It was called *Gone with the Wind;* a romance story."

"Oh. And then you got married?"

"Not right away, about a year later. He was training to be a Navy pilot."

I thought for a moment and said, "That was during World War II; did he ever fight the Nazis or the Japs?" I had never asked about the war before, I don't know why.

"Luckily, he didn't have to. We never could figure it out, but his orders changed each time he was going to go overseas. He was on an aircraft carrier at the end of the war—out in the Pacific Ocean. Then he was trained to fly Sabre jets."

I said, "And then he was shot down over Korea by a MiG." I waited to see what Mom would say. She didn't look at me, but said, "That's right. I just hope he's still alive."

I remember when Dad would come home, he would always say, "Hi, Beautiful," to Mom, and then they would hug and kiss. I can't remember one time Dad didn't say "Hi, Beautiful."

When I got up in the morning, everything that had happened at the lighthouse seemed like it had been a dream, but that feeling changed quickly as we were eating breakfast. Mom got a telephone call and she motioned for granma to come close and listen. When Mom hung up the phone, she sat down at the table and told us, "Mr. Sherner was arrested last night. He's the one that shot Elena. He found out she was an FBI agent and had to get her out of the way so he could work with the men from the boat without anyone knowing what they were up to."

"What about the men on the boat? Did they get arrested, too?" I hoped she would say yes, but I was disappointed by what she told me.

"No, Rocky. The boat was in international waters and the authorities couldn't do anything about it, but your report of what you and Jerry saw was very important."

"What about Mr. Waicukauski? Why wasn't he at the lighthouse yesterday?"

"He was in Boston interviewing for another job. He'll be back today—just like his note said. The FBI is going to pay to have his door fixed. An electrician is going to fix the beacon so it won't blink."

There was a loud knock at the front door, kind of like a grackles song; several hard knocks followed by a bunch of quick taps, "Hey, Rocky! Can you come out?"

It was Jerry. I looked at Mom for permission and she nodded, "Don't go too far, Rocky. We have to get things packed so we can leave for home; right after lunch."

I went out on the porch with Jerry and we sat quietly for a minute. "I'm going back to Boston—right after lunch. I guess we're not going to hunt grackles together. Maybe next summer when we come back to visit granma. Mom will have a different job then, so I don't know when that will be."

"I'll be spending some time at the lighthouse. I'm gunna find out all I can about grackles. I'll see if the school library has a book about them, too."

"I'll do the same in Boston. We'll be prepared. I'm going to try to get a BB gun, maybe for Christmas."

"Good idea. I'll ask Dad. I don't think Mom will want me to get one, though. She's afraid I'll shoot somebody's eye out. That's what she said when I showed her an ad for a Red Ryder model."

"I bet we won't get BB guns. We'll have to hunt with slingshots."

Jerry nodded, "Those grackles are pretty big birds, a rock might be better than a BB anyway."

I stood up and said, "I have to pack my suitcase and then help Mom load the car. Let's shake hands. I'll see you next summer."

Jerry stood up and shook hands and then, as he gave me a big Russian bear hug, he said, "Best friends."

I said, "Best friends," and waved goodbye. As he rode away on his bike, he looked back and waved.

Suzy started crying when Mom told her we couldn't take Surprise home with us. I was sad, too. That little dog had become one of the family, but I knew granma would take good care of him. She liked having someone around the house besides Mrs. Nesbitt. Granma could take Surprise out for walks to the lighthouse to see Mr. Waicukauski. Surprise was too small to be a guard dog, but he would get bigger, he's just a puppy.

Granma and Mom explained why we couldn't take Surprise to live in Boston. It wouldn't be fair to him to be cooped up in a house all day while we were all at work or school. Dogs need to be able to run and play outside where they can pee and poop without stinking up the house.

"Will you send me pictures of him, granma? I want to see him as he grows up."

"Certainly, Susan. I'll send you a picture every month so you can see how he's doing."

Suzy seemed to be happy with the arrangement for Surprise. She got his leash, clipped it on his collar, and took him out for a walk to Nesbitts' house to tell Mrs. Nesbitt that Surprise would be staying with granma.

Chapter 28

Mom's New Job

We didn't get back to Boston until seven o'clock in the evening. I had read my Lone Ranger comic twice on the trip, but all I could think about was getting the school year over so we could go back to Crafton. Suz inspected her rocks several times, holding them so sunlight would show different colors as it went through them. She was disappointed that sunlight wouldn't go through the black ones. I thought that was kind of funny, but I didn't want to make trouble, so I kept my mouth shut.

When we got home, a small white house with shrubs and a couple of maple trees in front, Mom was tired of driving, and just wanted to relax. We didn't unload the car, except for our suitcases, so we'd have our toothbrushes and clean underwear to put on in the morning. We had a lettuce and carrot salad, beans, and wieners for dinner, watched TV for about a half-hour, and started getting ready for bed. I had to wait for Suzy to finish using the bathroom, so I put on my pajamas, sat on the floor next to the door, holding my toothbrush. I heard Mom making a phone call, telling the operator the long-distance number in Maine. She was calling granma to tell her we had made it home safely.

"Hurry up, Suz, I have to go."

"Just a minute, I'm almost done brushing my teeth."

Sunday was spent getting ready for school. Suzy was worried about what she was supposed to do, but Mom had a letter from the school saying what room Suzy was going to be in, her teachers name, and what supplies were needed. Mom said she would go with Suzy, help find her room on the first floor, and meet her teacher. I remember when Mom went with me the first day when I started the first grade.

I was in the same three-story building, but on the third floor. My room number was 302 and my teacher's name was Miss Hill. I didn't need any help, I knew that school as well as I knew my slingshot. Mom picked us up at two-thirty every day that week. On Friday, when Mom got us in the car, she said, "I have a surprise for you."

Suzy was excited, she squealed, "Oh, goody. Did you bring Surprise home from granma's?"

Mom smiled, "Nope. That's not it."

I didn't know what to think. I know she didn't buy me a BB gun; she didn't even know I wanted one for Christmas. The only person I had told was Jerry, but maybe she heard us talking on granma's porch. Then I asked, "Is the surprise for both of us?"

Mom nodded and said, "Yes, it is."

I thought to myself, "Hmm. Something we'd have to share."

Suzy was about to bubble over. "Tell us—*please, Mommy, please!*"

"As soon as we get home. If you get too excited now, you might cause me to wreck the car."

I gave up trying to figure it out, but it must be something big for her to say that. When we got home, Mom said we should go in and sit on the sofa. After Mom unlocked and opened the front door, Suzy and I both dropped our school stuff beside the sofa and sat down as she had told us. Suzy and I watched Mom come over and sat on the floor in front of us.

"I have a new job—as a librarian."

I asked, "At our school?"

Mom had the biggest smile I had ever seen. "No, in Crafton."

I couldn't believe what she had said. I could hardly speak, but I squeaked out, "The lighthouse library?"

"Yes! Mr. Waicukauski has moved to Portland so the job is open."

I said, "Portland isn't that far away. We can still see him once in a while, can't we?"

"He's in the FBI, Rocky, and he's going to Portland, Oregon, not Portland, Maine."

"Oh. That's really far from here—near the Pacific Ocean."

"Your grandmother called me on Wednesday and asked if I wanted to apply for the lighthouse job. I said yes and she told the Crafton mayor, Mayor Griswold, that I wanted the position. Granma called me at noon today and told me I got the job. I can run the lighthouse and the library."

"Oh, good! Surprise will be with us. I can see him every day. We'll grow up together!"

Mom had a serious look. "What about school here in Boston? You just started and now you'll be going to another school."

"That's all right, I don't like Carolyn anyway."

I had never heard of Carolyn. "Who's Carolyn, Suzy?"

"She's a rich girl. Her dad is a banker or something. Nobody likes her. She thinks she's pretty—but I don't."

"What about you, Rocky? Do you mind going to another school?"

"Nope! I'll be in the same school with Jerry. We can go hunting grackles all year long, not just during the summer."

"Okay, then, we'll move to Crafton on Monday. I'll arrange for our furniture to be shipped. We'll use the lighthouse furniture until ours arrives.

I was thinking about Mom quitting the FBI. I think it was the only job she ever had, and she was really good at it. "What about you, Mom? Do you know how to run a lighthouse?"

"No, but I can always get help from Lt. Nesbitt and Mr. Morgan. The lieutenant can tell me all about the beacon and the rules of the sea. And, if anything goes wrong, Mr. Morgan can fix it—until I learn how. The library job should be easy. I imagine it's kind of like checking out groceries at a market, except the customers bring back the books."

Suzy said, "It would be bad if customers brought back food after using it." She arched her eyebrows and smiled. Mom and I started laughing.

We arrived in Crafton at noon on Monday. The moving company had promised our furniture and things would arrive on Friday. We went to granma's for lunch and then all four of us went to the lighthouse to clean the rooms where Mr. W had been living. Surprise was happy to see us back; he ran around in circles and licked our faces. I thought his tail might fall off it was wiggling so much. When he calmed down, we tied his leash to one of the fence posts so he could be outside as we cleaned. I don't think ammonia vapors are good for dogs.

It was a school day for Jerry, but I figured he would be home after four o'clock, so I asked Mom if I could ride granma's bike to Morgan's. Granma said that the garage was unlocked. I ran most of the way to granma's house, gulped some air as I wheeled the bike out of the garage, and rode like a maniac to Jerry's place.

I dropped the bike on the lawn, ran to the front door, and knocked like a grackle. I waited, but no one came to the door. I thought Jerry must be at the hospital or down at his dad's shop. I would have to come back after his parents got home from work. Mom would let me come back after dinner.

I jumped down from the porch and walked to the bike. As I bent down to pick it up, I heard a voice from behind me. "Rocky! Is that you?"

I stood up and walked over to him. "I'm back. Mom's going to run the lighthouse and the library. We just got here today. I'll be in school tomorrow."

"That's really neat. My class is mostly girls, and I haven't made friends with any of the boys—there's only five. There's twelve girls. I think my class heard that I speak Russian and they're suspicious." Jerry raised his eyebrows and smiled. "I wonder what they would think if I spoke German." We both laughed.

"You'd better be careful. Don't say anything about Nazis or Hitler. When they get to know you, they'll see that you're all right. Have you gone after any grackles?"

"Nope. I haven't even gone to the library yet. Every time I thought about it, I wished that you were here. I thought I would wait until next summer to read about those birds. Boy, I'm sure glad you're back."

"Me, too. Can you come over to the lighthouse? I have to go back and help clean the place. I just wanted to tell you I'm back."

"No, I can't leave the house until Mom or Dad is here. When I heard the knock, I didn't want to answer the door. They told me not to, but I looked out and saw who it was and opened the door. I'll see you tomorrow at school. Thanks for coming by."

"Okay. See you at school."

The rest of the week was kind of fun. All the new faces might become friends, but I already had one friend, even though he was in the fifth grade. During recesses when we played kick-ball, baseball, or flag football, Jerry and I tried to get on the same team. I could see he was a better athlete than I was, so I just tried harder than I normally would have.

Suzy liked her new classmates. There wasn't a Carolyn in her class. Many of the other kids had dogs or cats and they shared stories about their pets. She told the kids about the summer, but they didn't believe her, especially about capturing a prisoner in the woods. First-graders asked Jerry and me if what she said was true. She was the center of attention until after her birthday, when the summer activities were almost forgotten, and things returned to normal, especially school activities. Mom helped Suzy's teacher with a party at the lighthouse where the first-graders learned about the library. That was on the first Wednesday we were back in Crafton. There were several days when balloons were drifting down from the bottom of the gallery floor, after most of the helium had leaked through the thin rubber bag.

Granma came over Thursday night and helped us move furniture out of the house and into the storage buildings. I had been wondering what had happened to the four men we had captured at the lighthouse. As I helped her carry a chair out of the house, granma said, "Two of those men were going to Groton to spy on the nuclear submarine, and the other two were replacement crewmen for the Elena. They were all sent back to Russia."

We moved stuff out of the house 'til Suzy's bedtime. The living room was almost empty; except for Mr. W's old sofa and the TV. The rug was gone, too, and we could hear the clicking of Surprise's paws as he walked across the bare floor.

Jerry and I could hardly wait for school to be out on Friday. He had gotten permission to come to the lighthouse after school. From there, we would begin the search for grackles in the trees outside the northern city limits. Neither of us had been on the road before: State Road 117A.

When we got to the lighthouse caretaker's home after school, there was a large truck parked on the gravel road from the highway to the lighthouse. No cars could get around the New England Moving Company's truck without going off the road into the ditch. Jerry and I watched two men unloading our Boston furniture for a few minutes before I went in the house to talk to mom. I asked her if I could go with Jerry to look for grackles and she told me okay, but not to go down to the harbor. I think Mom was afraid we might end up in Shanghai. Granma had told me about sailors being shanghaied in the olden days.

With our slingshots and pebbles in our pockets, we road about a mile before we came to a clump of trees fenced off from the road. We parked our bikes about fifty yards away and began sneaking towards the trees. We heard a grackle, but we couldn't see it. I motioned for Jerry to circle around to the other side of the trees. He climbed through the barbed-wire fence and moved straight under the trees. As he walked, looking upward into the limbs above him, he tripped and fell. He said, "Goddarnit!" and the grackle flew away. I started laughing and couldn't stop. I had never heard him cuss before. He came back through the fence and stood in front of me.

"What's so funny, Rocky, haven't you ever seen anybody fall down before?"

"I didn't know you could speak French."

"What does that mean? That wasn't French."

"I know. One time when my Dad said Goddamn, he said, 'excuse my French.' It's kind of a joke. I'm sorry I laughed, but when you fell down the bird flew away. I just thought it was funny."

"Well, let's go back home. The next bunch of trees is way out there." Jerry pointed down the road. It looked like we would have to ride another half-mile.

As we rode back home, Jerry said, "Next time, you go under the trees. Maybe a bird will crap in your hair and then I'll laugh." We joked like that all the way home.

The moving van was gone when we got back to the lighthouse. There was a car in the parking lot. Jerry said he would see me tomorrow and he rode off. When he got to the road, we waved to each other. I went in the house and was surprised, the whole living room was full of furniture, but it wasn't arranged like a real room, it was just piled up. The only thing that was right was the rug.

Suzy was watching TV. I asked, "Is Mom in the library?"

"Uh-huh."

"Someone wanted a book?"

"Uh-huh. She said she'd be right back—don't go anywhere. So I didn't go anywhere. I just turned on the TV."

"What's on?"

"I don't know. A man is talking. I think it's the news."

Mom came in the living room and sat down on the sofa. It was our gray-blue one, not the one Mr. W had. His was brown and smelled funny. The only other furniture was the table near the kitchen. There were four chairs around it.

"Who was it, Mom?"

"Mr. and Mrs. Griffith. She wanted a book on pruning roses."

"Oh. I remember them. He helped us with our books one day."

Mom stood up and said, "Well, I'm going to get dinner. Are you hungry? I am."

Suzy said, "Uh-huh."

I said, "Yes. What are we having?"

Mom started into the kitchen and said, "If you don't help me, you might get dog food."

Suzy reacted, "You mean the same as Surprise eats? Mommy, that smells bad."

"I'm just kidding, Susan. You can set the table. The silverware is in that small box over there. It's kind of heavy." Mom was cutting up some carrots and she pointed with a paring knife. "Rocky, could you help Susan. The box is taped shut."

I tried to take off the lid, but it was taped on, just as Mom had said. It was on top of the breadbox, so I moved it to the table and ripped off the tape. That's when the doorbell rang.

"Susan. Would you go to the door? See who it is."

"Okay. Rocky, but leave the silverware in the box. I want to set the table."

Suzy went to the door, opened it and said, "May I help you?"

"Who is it Susan?" Mom turned her head and listened.

"It's a man with a beard. He has on a uniform. He wants to talk to you.

"Does he have a Bible?"

Suzy came to the kitchen and said, "He has a book, but I don't know if it's a Bible. I can't read what it says."

"All right. Ask him to please wait. I'll be right there." Mom moved slowly, she looked worried. I could tell she was thinking about something bad.

Mom dumped a handful of sliced carrots into a pan of water on the stove, dried her hands, and walked to the front door.

I was listening closely now. All I heard was, "Hi, Beautiful."

www.ingramcontent.com/pod-product-compliance
Lightning Source LLC
Chambersburg PA
CBHW070940190726
48292CB00004B/1270